SHOWDOWN CITY

TODD BERGER

DIVERSIONBOOKS

Berger

Diversion Books
A Division of Diversion Publishing Corp.
443 Park Avenue South, Suite 1008
New York, New York 10016
www.DiversionBooks.com

For more information, email info@diversionbooks.com

First Diversion Books edition June 2016.
Print ISBN: 978-1-68230-066-4
eBook ISBN: 978-1-68230-065-7

"Why should I obtain by force
that which I can obtain by cheating?"

—Doc Holliday

CHAPTER 1

Huey Palmer sat at the bar inside Lucky Pete's Gamblin' Hall and
stared up at a stuffed buffalo head on the wall that seemed to be
staring right back at him. He wondered how much a head like that
was worth, and it occurred to him that he knew absolutely nothing
about the financial realities of taxidermy. The head could be worth
five dollars or five thousand dollars and he would honestly believe
either, a thought he also once had about women's bras.

"Another bourbon?" Huey snapped out of his trance and
looked over to see the old tattooed bartender gesturing to an empty
shot glass before him. When Huey had first sat down hours before,
he had ordered the good stuff, or at least what he understood to be
the good stuff since it came in a classy-looking bottle with a picture
of a mustachioed man on it. But as the night progressed and his
luck dwindled, Huey had switched over to the well, which came in a
plastic brown bottle and had a childproof cap.

"Another bourbon?" the bartender said again, seeming to grow
impatient. Huey noticed a particular tattoo on the old man's forearm
of two snakes wrapped around a pole like you see on the sides of
ambulances. He wondered if the old man had gone to medical
school before deciding serving deviants like Huey terrible whiskey
in a gambling hall was his true calling.

"Just a soda," Huey said. Huey grabbed the shot glass and
turned it upside down. He of course did want another, but knew if
he partook he'd be in no condition to make it to work later. He had
mastered the art of sobering up before arriving to work, or at least
seeming to be sobered up, years ago.

"Like a Coca-Cola?"

"No, like soda water. Like seltzer."

"Well, which one? Soda water or seltzer? There's a difference." Huey was fairly sure this was untrue, and his look to the bartender conveyed as much.

"Soda water contains a different chemical makeup from ordinary sparkling water," the bartender said. "It often has added salt, sodium bicarbonate, or potassium citrate to give it a slightly salty, slightly acidic taste."

Huey now had a million questions about the snake tattoo, but he'd save it for another time. "Just water is fine," he said. A moment later a glass was placed in front of him and he immediately regretted the decision. He glanced back up at the giant buffalo head above the bar, convinced the animal's expression had slightly changed to "Water? Really? What are you, a pussy?"

He took a sip of the water and glanced around the place, noticing that it had gotten pretty full. Most certainly everyone was here to watch the fight, since normally Lucky Pete's stayed empty save for a couple of drunks until at least 11:00 on a Saturday night. But now, at only 9:22, it was nearly standing room only because the price of watching a UFC match at home on Pay-Per-View had gotten outrageous. Five fights for $59.99, most of which could last fifteen minutes tops. Why anyone on earth would shell out that much money seemed insane to Huey when they could head down to just about any bar here in Las Vegas and watch it for free.

Huey didn't come to Lucky Pete's just to watch the fight, however. Nor did he come for the energy of the crowd or kinship of his fellow fight fans. No, he drove halfway across town just about every single weekend for Las Vegas's best kept secret: the Lucky Pete's sports book. It had what he considered the best odds of any casino, and he had been to them all. Bellagio's was, of course, the classiest, but you couldn't even sit at a table unless you were planning to order bottle service, and the cheapest bottle, some vodka from Finland, was about $800. Caesar's Palace was the most fun since the waitresses wore togas and there were free roast beef sandwiches during college football games, but because of those two facts you had to show up literally before sunrise just to get a good seat. Lucky Pete's, though, was the only choice for a gambling degenerate such as Huey and solely because of the odds. The place was a couple blocks off the strip, between a gas station and an all-you-can-eat Mexican buffet, and the clientele was pretty much limited to locals because any tourist with a lick of common sense took one look at the faded sign (a Jack of Hearts holding two pistols) and knew better than to set foot inside. The whole thing had been built in 1974 by "Lucky" Pete Kowalski, a Polish immigrant obsessed with the Wild West, and it had been decorated to resemble a saloon in the way that only a Polish immigrant in 1974 could have imagined. Taxidermied animal heads, mounted rifles, and wooden Indians that even forty years ago would have been considered bad taste.

The bar overlooked the casino floor, a collection of a dozen or so table games surrounded by slot machines as far the eye could see. Huey had never been one for slots since he liked to be in control of his own fate, a fact that probably said something about his thoughts on predestination. Also, as his father used to say, "Slot machines are for little girls and housewives."

The crowd at the bar began to quiet down and Huey knew that meant that the main event was about to begin. He had already sat through four undercards and was 1-3 with bets, but he knew deep down that it didn't really matter since the bulk of his cash was all on the final fight, Johnny "Destruction" Messonnier vs. Han "Japanese Tornado" Jin. He often wondered why every UFC fighter had a nickname, and if they were mostly self-imposed like rappers or given out by others like in the military.

He had no real interest in the "sport" of the Ultimate Fighting Championship, nor did he even really think of it as a sport at all and honestly found it a bit boring. He sort of agreed with whichever US Senator had once called mixed martial arts "human cockfighting." He supposed the difference being these cocks willingly stepped into the ring. Huey had become fascinated with UFC only upon realizing that Las Vegas oddsmakers often had no idea where to set the lines, and therefore it was quite possible to make out like a bandit. More than any other sport Huey had ever seen, the underdog often won, and he realized years ago that a fighter's personal win/loss record was irrelevant because in UFC you could fight in any style you wanted, be it boxing, jiu jitsu, wrestling, judo, or whatever, so what you had to pay attention to was a fighter's record in his style versus the other fighter's style.

Huey was no genius for figuring this out, anyone who knew anything about UFC understood it, but the average Las Vegas tourist visiting a sports book was totally in the dark and liked to bet on record and more often cool nicknames alone. After all, casinos aren't about setting accurate odds, they're about getting people to bet. This is why the Japanese Tornado was a 5-to-1 underdog even though Huey knew the fighter was going to win. So confident was Huey in this fact, that he had borrowed the largest amount in his own personal history from his friend Mark. The term "friend" was used loosely and deep down Huey knew that the more common vernacular for a man in Mark's position would be "loan shark," but he didn't like to think about such things. Mark had lent Huey $25,000, with 8% interest. Huey knew he was about to quintuple that amount and finally be able to cover his daughter's college tuition in full.

Jenny Palmer had recently been accepted to Northwestern University in Chicago where she planned to study pre-law. She would be the first Palmer to ever attend college, an accomplishment that excited Huey to no end. The only hurdle was the fact that even after the grants and scholarships that Jenny was eligible for, out-of-state tuition to Northwestern would cost $112,100 for four years. Huey's ex-wife Terry, whom he was not currently on what one would call "speaking terms," had been pushing for their daughter to just attend the University of Nevada Las Vegas for the low price of $39,400. Huey, however, wanted to get the girl as far away from this city as possible. Too many times had he drunkenly ended up at a dingy strip club on Industrial Road and chatted up a dancer only to learn she was a UNLV student just trying to earn some extra cash.

The crowd at Lucky Pete's turned whisper quiet as the bell rang and the fight began. Huey took a deep breath and turned his attention to the large HDTV above the bar, which was nestled between the buffalo head and a pro-Custer painting of Custer's Last Stand. UFC main events last five rounds of five minutes each. In twenty-five minutes, Huey's fate would be decided. In twenty-five minutes, Huey would know if his daughter would get the education she deserved.

But the fight didn't last twenty-five minutes. It didn't even last twenty-five seconds. Johnny "Destruction" Messonnier broke Han "Japanese Tornado" Jin's jaw within seven seconds and the fight was declared over.

CHAPTER 2

Ernie Swords had never heard of dim sum, let alone tried it. He had been to Asia on countless occasions for business, but was admittedly a picky eater and mostly went for whatever variation of fried chicken he could find. Over the years he had been to Japan, South Korea, Thailand, Laos, The Philippines, Vietnam, China, and Taiwan, but dim sum had never entered into his life until he visited Empress Chow's in downtown San Francisco at the age of sixty-two.

Ernie found the process fascinating. Instead of ordering off of a menu, women pushed carts containing precooked dishes around the room that you pointed at and they then handed to you. Ernie didn't speak a word of Cantonese and they didn't speak a word of English, so what exactly he was ordering was anybody's guess and he had to go off of pure aesthetics. As he took a big bite out of what looked like a neon orange petit four made of pork, he wondered if he could make the same concept work with sliders and wings back in San Antonio. Maybe at a sports bar. The women pushing the carts could wear miniskirts and low-cut referee shirts. His last few bar/restaurant endeavors had been failures, but that was a combination of bad marketplace and poor concepts. The dim sum sliders and wings idea, though? That could be gold.

He glanced down at the briefcase between his feet, nudging it a bit more underneath the tablecloth to hide it from view. He had picked it up at Quincy's Spy Shop in San Marcos, a surveillance equipment store that he suspected an actual spy had probably never set foot in, but hundreds of suspicious spouses had in order to buy tiny cameras and GPS tracking equipment. The briefcase had a false bottom only accessible if the right three-digit combination was entered, and the hidden compartment within was currently holding $100,000 in unmarked, non-sequential US currency. Ernie assumed that the Crimson Mantis, his contact, would be impressed by the case.

He checked his watch, a 24-carat Movada Series 800 that his wife had picked up for him in Switzerland on a ski trip, and noticed it was almost 2:15. The Crimson Mantis was late. A thought occurred to Ernie and he glanced around the restaurant, taking note of the other patrons. Had the Crimson Mantis actually been sitting in plain view this whole time, sizing him up and waiting to reveal him or herself? One of the dim sum cart ladies caught Ernie's attention. She was an attractive young woman who seemed a good twenty years younger and 60% more attractive than the others. She flashed Ernie a smile and he wondered if this was indeed the person he'd been in contact with over e-mail. Perhaps this secret rendezvous would end up back at his hotel room later.

"Excuse me? Mr. Swords?"

Ernie looked up to see a young bearded man, no older than twenty-five, standing across the table from him. The man wore a t-shirt, plaid shorts, and retro black eyeglasses.

"Yes?" Ernie said.

"Oh hey, I'm Kirk." The man sat down and reached over to shake Ernie's hand. "Oh, my bad," Kirk said. "I mean I'm the 'Crimson Mantis.'" He made air quotes and laughed. His gaze quickly shot to a metal dish on the table containing some half-eaten Shrimp Shu Mai. "You gonna finish that?"

Ernie shook his head. This is not what he was expecting from his secret intelligence contact. This did not look like the slick James Bond villain he was hoping for.

"So I looked into you," Kirk said as he stuffed one of the dumplings into his mouth. "You're a pretty weird dude."

"Now come on," Ernie said. "Don't you know the old expression? Poor people are weird. Rich people are eccentric."

Kirk laughed. "Ain't that the truth? You'll have to hook me up with some tickets to a Swordsmen's game." Kirk was referring to

The San Antonio Swordsmen, an arena football team that Ernie had acquired a few years before. At the time of the purchase the team was called the Armadillos, but Ernie changed the mascot to his own namesake and the team's logo to himself as a dashing swashbuckler. Some within the sports community had been critical of the decision, but Ernie thought it was hilarious.

"I'll see what I can do," Ernie said. "Now, shall we get down to business?

"Sure," Kirk said. He then took out a small USB thumb drive and placed it on the table. "So what exactly do you want this for?"

Ernie eyed it and felt his pulse quicken. This was really happening. He glanced down at the briefcase between his feet, just to make sure it was still there. "Does it matter?" Ernie said.

"Um, yeah it matters. I need to make sure you're not gonna go blow up a federal building or something."

"I'm not."

"You know what I'd get charged with if you blew up a federal building? Treason. You know what happens to people convicted of treason? No, you don't. No one does. Because you just get renditioned off to some secret torture facility in Estonia. And on top of that, I would feel really shitty about it because I personally have nothing against federal buildings."

"I'm not going to blow up a federal building."

"Then what do you want this for?" Kirk tapped the USB drive, edging it a little away from Ernie's side of the table and closer to his own.

"Smitty told me I wouldn't have to explain," Ernie said. Paul "Smitty" Smith was Ernie's college friend and fraternity brother from Texas Christian University. Smitty had become a venture capitalist in Silicon Valley a few years before, and he was the first person Ernie had thought to contact in his quest to acquire what was on that USB drive. Smitty had subsequently put Ernie in touch with the Crimson Mantis.

"Smitty's not here," Kirk said.

"I'm just looking for something."

Kirk's eyes widened, as if he had finally put it all together. He let out a huge laugh and popped another dumpling into his mouth. "Dude," Kirk said. "I hate to break it you, but there's nothing there."

"What do you mean?" Ernie wasn't sure what Kirk was getting at. Did Kirk somehow know what he was after? How was that possible? Ernie had been so careful.

"You think you're the first person to contact me looking for UFOs at Area 51?"

"I'm not looking for UFOs."

"It's just an old Air Force base. Really actually pretty lame. All you can see in the photos are a couple of runways and a cluster of buildings."

"I'm not looking for UFOs."

"Right, okay. Wait, I got it." Kirk leaned in closer and whispered. "You want to buy all the domestic satellite images that the NSA has requested us to classify because you're looking for Bigfoot. Well, the resolution's really not that good. I mean he's big, but not that big." Kirk laughed again.

Ernie's patience was wearing thin. He grabbed the briefcase from under the table and held it up. "Do you want the money or not?" Ernie said.

Kirk stopped laughing. He leaned back in his chair and studied Ernie's face. "Yeah. I want it. Just know that if you blow up a federal building, I'm going to be pissed." Kirk pushed the thumb drive over, then grabbed the briefcase. He opened it ever-so-slightly to see nothing but a collection of papers and pens inside.

"What the fuck is this?" Kirk said. "Where's the money?"

"There's a secret compartment in the bottom. The money is in there."

"Why?"

"Just enter 433 as the combination."

Kirk did as he was told. A moment later he reopened the case and a devilish grin crossed his face as he eyed the rows of $100 bills. "Excellent," Kirk said. He put the briefcase down by his side and then looked around, spotting a passing dim sum server. He waved to the woman, who showed off that her cart contained radish cake. Kirk nodded, and the woman placed a serving of the dish on the table between them.

"What are you doing?" Ernie said.

"I thought we were having lunch. Isn't that why we met at a dim sum place?"

"Well, yes, but I just figured you'd leave when the transaction was over."

"Why would you think that? I'm starving." Kirk popped some radish cake into his mouth and the two men awkwardly sat there for a moment. Ernie didn't really know what to say, so he opted for small talk.

"So," Ernie said. "How long have you worked at Google?"

CHAPTER 3

Dr. Douglas Rainey was convinced that not a single one of the 235 students currently sitting in his lecture hall was paying attention to him. Sure some of them were literally looking at him, but paying attention? Doubtful. It didn't used to be this way. When he was a student here at the University of Texas at Austin in the 1970s, people not only paid attention, they dressed up. The men wore slacks and the women wore dresses, or slacks if they were progressive. Now, though? There was a girl in the front row literally wearing pajamas. Full pajamas. Flannel with little, pink cupcakes on them. She wore no makeup and looked like she just rolled out of bed. Dr. Rainey would love to complain about this to the dean of the History Department, but walking in and stating "I don't think the girls dress classy enough" is something that gets academics brought before ethics committees.

Dr. Rainey knew that there were two main motivating factors for why everyone had stopped paying attention to not only him, but professors in general. The first was that six years ago, the university made it mandatory that all incoming freshman own a laptop computer, and even provided one for low-income students. This meant that all 50,000 students began bringing those laptops to class, and with the ability to hop on the campus's free Wi-Fi this also meant that they had the entire internet and all the social networks therein to occupy their time. The second reason was the rise of note-taking services like Koofers.com, a website that offered, for a price, downloadable PDFs of that day's lecture notes taken by a student in the class secretly under Koofer's employ. This student would take diligent notes on the aforementioned laptop, fix up any spelling or grammatical errors, and upload it to the service for anyone else in the class to download within an hour of the class ending. In theory this would mean that there should be at least one student paying attention to Dr. Rainey at this moment, but he had been teaching the same exact syllabus of History 373: The American West for twelve years now, and Koofers.com figured out long ago there was no point in paying some secret student to diligently take the same exact notes the site already had on file. Of course, Dr. Rainey could challenge this if he wished and change the syllabus up, but he had come to terms years ago with the fact that this was a Sisyphean task. Whether they were paying attention or not, he would lecture today just like he did every day, because that's what the university paid him to do.

He pressed a button on a projector and a moment later the image of a man atop a horse appeared on a large screen above him. The man donned a classic cowboy hat and brandished a steel revolver. "Does anyone know who this is?" He looked to the room, knocking some of the students out of whatever train of thought they were in. He knew he was going to have to ask the question again. "Does anyone know who this is?"

A young woman in the third row sat up in her chair, smiling. "It's Yul Brynner," she said with pride. "A production photo from the 1960 film *The Magnificent Seven* directed by John Sturges, which is a remake of the Akira Kurosawa film *The Seven Samurai*." Dr. Rainey immediately knew that the young woman was a film student. She was probably taking this class to fulfill her history requirement and had watched *The Magnificent Seven* in her RTF 318: Intro to Film History class. He disliked most students because of their lack of information about history, but he disliked film students even more for their abundance of misinformation about it.

"That's correct," he said. "A film that some consider one of the greatest 'Westerns' of all time. Now can anyone tell me what's wrong with the photo?" He pulled out a laser pointer and began to circle Yul Brynner's body with a red dot. The students eyed the photo, confused. No one said a word. "I'll give you a hint. There are two glaring historical inaccuracies."

"The horse?" a student in the back said.

Dr. Rainey looked up to the horse, a brown mare. "The horse? How would the horse be historically inaccurate?"

"Maybe there, like, wasn't that kind of horse in the Old West?"

Dr. Rainey wasn't even sure what that meant. "It's not the horse."

The students continued to stare, clueless. Dr. Rainey knew he was going to have to help, so he pointed the laser at the cowboy hat atop Yul Brynner's head.

"First up is the hat, the classic Stetson. When most people hear the word 'cowboy,' this hat is the first thing that pops into their heads. That's why it's usually just called a 'cowboy hat.' In actuality, though, rough riders in the old west were much more likely to wear this…"

He clicked a button and the image changed to an old black-and-white photograph of a man wearing a black bowler hat, the kind most would associate with Charlie Chaplin or a Magritte painting. "The average cowboy preferred the bowler hat because it didn't blow off all the time." One student laughed, and Dr. Rainey appreciated that. "This photo is of William Bonney, better known to most of you as 'Billy the Kid.' Bonney was photographed a handful of times in his life in a variety of different hats, and not one of them was a Stetson." Dr. Rainey cycled through a series of photographs showing Billy the Kid wearing a center crease, a slouch hat, and a sombrero. "And as for law enforcement, the white ten-gallon 'cowboy hat' was of little use because it made one quite the easy target. Wild Bill Hicock, Wyatt Earp, and Bat Masterson all predominately wore low-crowned black hats as not to be seen from literally a mile away." Dr. Rainey thought some students might laugh at that one. They did not.

He pressed the button and the image returned to Yul Brynner. "So a veteran Cajun gunslinger living in Dodge City in the late 1800s, which Yul Brynner was portraying in *The Magnificent Seven*, would have never worn a Stetson. What else wouldn't he have done?" The class sat quiet again for what seemed like forever. Dr. Rainey was going to have to give them this one too.

"He would have never carried a revolver." Dr. Rainey clicked the button again, and the image changed to show a classic Colt revolver. This actually seemed to perk the interest of a handful of students. The hat, not so much, but the gun? That gets them every time. "Despite the perception that Hollywood movies have given, gun control laws in the Old West were actually stricter in the 19th and 20th century than they are now, especially in the West. In fact, one of the first things that any new frontier town would do is outlaw guns altogether."

Dr. Rainey pressed the button and the image changed to an old black-and-white photograph of a frontier town. He used the laser pointer to highlight a wooden kiosk near the entrance to Main Street. "This is a photograph of the actual Dodge City, Kansas circa 1878. Note the sign greeting any visitor to the town." The students squinted and looked closer. The sign read THE CARRYING OF FIREARMS STRICTLY PROHIBITED.

"It's true that lawmen carried guns, much like they do today, but not every random citizen was packing heat." Dr. Rainey was not sure if people still used that expression. "And the image of bandits constantly sticking up banks is also a major falsehood. In fact, before 1900 there wasn't a single successful bank robbery reported in Colorado, Wyoming, Montana, the Dakotas, Kansas, Oregon, Washington, Idaho, Nevada, Utah, or New Mexico. There are more bank robberies in a year in modern-day Detroit than there were in a century of the Old West. In addition…"

He pressed the button again. A still photo from the 1952 Gary Cooper film *High Noon* appeared on screen. It showed two men, one of them Cooper's Marshal Will Kane, facing off in a duel on Main Street. "There is no evidence that anyone was ever killed in a quick draw showdown at high noon. We like to think that this is how all disputes were settled in the Old West, but it in fact has never been recorded as ever happening. Not once. Ever. But let's get back to that revolver…"

He pressed the button and once again Yul Brynner returned. "If Yul Brynner's character, Chris, was really a professional soldier of fortune looking to drive off aggressive bandits, and indeed was in possession of a firearm, then he most certainly would have preferred a shotgun or a rifle over a six-shooter. Six-shooters were just not very lethal. They didn't use bullets as we think of them today, but employed a cap-and-ball system with an effective range of around 40 feet. Also, they burned the back of your hand."

Dr. Rainey finally put down the projector controller and placed his hands on the podium, ready to give the same final statement that he had been giving to this lecture for twelve years. "So remember, kids, don't believe everything you see in movies. That's all for today."

With those words, the students began to pack up their laptops and shuffle their slipper-wearing feet out of the lecture hall. Dr. Rainey flipped off the projector and started to pack up as well.

"I don't care what history says," an older man's voice said in a thick Texas droll. "This cowboy prefers a Stetson."

Dr. Rainey looked over to see that someone was still sitting in the back of the now-empty room. It was a man in his sixties wearing a nice suit, a bolo tie, and a crisp white Stetson upon his head. A thick gray mustache dominated much of the man's face.

"Can I help you with something?" Dr. Rainey said.

"That was interesting, about Yul Brynner. People were right about you. You sure seem to know your stuff."

"People? I'm sorry, what's this about?"

"I read your book. Cover-to-cover. Was going to bring a copy for you to sign, but wouldn't you know I up and left it in the truck."

Dr. Rainey assumed the man was referring to *Untold Tales of the West*, a 782-page tome that detailed lesser-known events of manifest destiny lost to history. The book was required reading for Dr. Rainey's History 373 class.

"What say you and me go grab some grub at The Big Pig and have ourselves a chat?" the man said, referring to the hot new barbecue restaurant on the ground floor of a high-rise office building in downtown Austin. Some said it wasn't as good as Rudy's or Stubbs on Red River, but true Austinites like Dr. Rainey knew that The Big Pig was the real deal. It was always packed with college kids, tourists, and businessmen.

"First of all, I don't know who you are, but more importantly The Big Pig would have a good hour wait at this time of day."

"Oh, we won't have to wait," the Stetson-wearing stranger flashed a big smile. "My name's Ernie Swords. I own the place."

"You own The Big Pig?"

"Well, not really. I own the building it's in. But that's kind of better when you think about it."

CHAPTER 4

Valerie Trujillo was lost. Not emotionally nor spiritually, but literally physically lost. The delivery sheet on the two large two-topping pizzas that she was trying to deliver (one pepperoni and mushroom, one Hawaiian) said the address she needed to go to was 1806 Barton. The problem was that Austin, Texas had a Barton Court, Barton Lane, Barton Creek Drive, Barton Creek Trail, Barton Falls, Barton Hollow Lane, Barton Oaks Drive, Barton Oaks Lane, Barton Park Lane, Barton River Court, and the intersection of Barton Skyway and Barton Springs Road where she currently sat in her ancient Toyota Corolla and waited for a red light. All of these streets were named after William "Uncle Billy" Barton, one of the original settlers of the city in the early 1800s. Val assumed he must have been pretty well-liked to have half the goddamn streets in town named after him.

She placed a quick call to Lee, her manager at The Onion Pizza, to learn that the address was actually 1806 *Burton*, a street named after less-liked settler John Burton and also halfway across town. After hanging up with Lee and making a highly illegal U-turn in the middle of the intersection, Val glanced to her phone's home screen and noticed she had missed two calls. One was from Alissa Stone, the bass player in her band. The other was from Dr. Douglas Rainey, her grad school advisor. She was immediately concerned about the missed call from Alissa.

Her band, Wherefore Art Thou Juliet?, had recently been asked to go on a small Texas tour with another band named The Irish Goodbye, which Val's friend Kevin was in. The plan would be to hit the big three of Dallas, Houston, and San Antonio as well as a handful of other cities between, including Plano and Waco. Her dream since she was a kid was to go on tour with a band. Her own band, singing her own songs. While most little girls in her class were planning their weddings or trying on makeup, she was preparing a tour rider, which featured a bowl of only red Skittles. She started her first band, Rex Mundi, when she was thirteen years old, with a couple kids from her northeast Los Angeles neighborhood who, in retrospect, weren't very good at playing their instruments. All during high school she was the lead singer of Tuesday Tuesday, and her crowning achievement was getting to play the Senior Prom in lieu of attending it. In undergrad at the University of Arizona, she managed to be part of six different bands over four years. Brown Curtains, Fuck Stummies, Scott Beowulf, The Good Plenties, Manic Titanic, and finally Val and the Serpents. She had moved to Austin a year ago for grad school and formed Wherefore Art Thou Juliet? within three weeks of arrival. All the members were female, and also fellow grad students in the University of Texas History Department, including problematic bass player Alissa. Alissa was sweet and she meant well, but she couldn't remember a set list to save her life even when it was taped on the floor in front of her. After many secret back room meetings, the other band members were in agreement that Alissa needed to go, but none of them, including Val, had the balls to do it due to their shared fear of confrontation. They had already replaced the poor girl without her knowing it and the new bass player, a tattooed beast named Sweaty Jesse, was supposed to play a show with the band at Emo's tomorrow night. This is why Val had finally texted Alissa a few hours before the ominous message: WE NEED TO TALK CALL ME LATER.

Wanting to postpone the confrontation even longer, Val opted to call back Dr. Rainey first.

Dr. Rainey never left messages, which often drove Val insane. He claimed that it was just "something he didn't do," as if leaving messages was the equivalent to talking about how much money one makes at a dinner party. She dialed Dr. Rainey's number and after several rings he picked up.

"Hey, it's me, Dr. Rainey." His voice sounded strange. He sounded almost excited, which he never was.

"What can I help you with, Doc?"

"I need you to drive me someplace tomorrow."

She audibly sighed, hoping the sound didn't make it through her hands-free headset. When she had applied to become Dr. Rainey's research assistant as part of the grad program, she didn't know it also meant she'd have to be his personal chauffeur. Dr. Rainey apparently hadn't owned a car since the '90s and exclusively used Austin's public transportation system, which wasn't very good. She had thought about complaining to the chair of the department, but research assistant positions were so coveted she'd let it slide.

"To where?"

"A ranch. Near Pleasanton."

"Where's that?" In the year that Val had been in Texas, she had begun to realize that it was really, really big. She was pretty confident you could pick any word in the English language and it was a town in the Lone Star State. Orange? Coffee? Utopia? Happy? All towns in Texas.

"It's near San Antonio," Dr. Rainey said.

"San Antonio? That's an hour and a half away."

"Actually, Pleasanton is further south, so it'd be about two hours away."

Val now rolled her eyes. The Corolla could barely handle the pizza delivery job, let alone these car trips. "What time did you need to go?"

"We need to be there by four o'clock."

Val did the math in her head. Two hours there and two hours back. She didn't know where they were going, but had a sneaking suspicion she wouldn't make it to her gig at Emo's. "I kind of have a gig tomorrow night, Dr. Rainey."

"We'll be back in time."

She had heard that before. They were never back in time. He once made her drive him to Dallas for a book signing and she completely missed a headlining show at Red Eye Fly. She wanted to straight up tell him that her band and her music were more secretly important to her than her graduate degree, but she chose not to do so. "Are you sure you can't find another ride?" she said.

"It's not just that. I want you to come with me. You're going to want to see this."

"See what?"

"I can't tell you."

"You can't tell me what?"

"I can't tell you where we're going. I had to sign a non-disclosure agreement."

"Are you serious? Aren't you going to have to tell me so I can drive you there?"

"I have one for you to sign too. We need to stop by a FedEx Kinko's on the way and fax it to his lawyer."

"Whose lawyer?"

"I can't tell you. Pick me up at 2:00 from outside my office." Dr. Rainey hung up before Val had the chance to say any more. She audibly sighed again and tossed her phone back into her purse. She was annoyed. She had been looking forward to playing at Emo's since she first moved here. On the bright side, though, she no longer felt the pressure to call Alissa back.

CHAPTER 5

Huey and his daughter Jenny were in constant battle over the car radio. Every morning he gave the seventeen-year-old a ride to school, and every morning she tried to slyly flip the station from 97.1 The Point, Las Vegas's home of classic rock, to NPR. This morning was no exception, and Jenny pulled the move halfway through "Layla" by Derrick and The Dominoes. When she did this, Huey involuntarily made a noise that resembled a pig squeal.

"Dad, it won't kill you to hear what's going on in the world," Jenny said. She said this every morning.

"I know, but you just cut off 'Layla.' That's, like, a cardinal sin."

"It was over."

"It was not over! It was about to get to the second movement. A four-minute-long piano coda. A beautiful four-minute long piano coda."

"It sounded over."

"I have so much to teach you."

He turned his Jeep to pull up to the front entrance to Chapparal High School, home of the Chapparal Cowboys. A giant cartoon buckaroo holding two ears of corn, Silverado Stan, was painted across the side of the building, and Huey thought back to when he attended the very same high school and Silverado Stan was holding guns. After the Columbine tragedy, some parents complained that the mascot promoted gun violence and the school administration decided to turn the guns into corn, perhaps not realizing the nearest corn field is a thousand miles away.

Jenny opened the door to the Jeep to get out, then stopped

as she seemed to remember something. "Oh, can you take me to graduation rehearsal on Saturday morning?" she said.

"What do you need to rehearse for? Aren't you just walking across the stage?"

"That's what I said." She laughed.

"What time? I've got a flight at noon."

"It's early, like 8:00."

"Ugh. For you, I guess so."

She laughed again and flashed him a smile. "Thanks, Dad. See you tomorrow." She hopped out, then reached back in to turn the radio to 97.1, The Point. She did this every morning. Huey watched her walk up the steps and into the school and couldn't help but smile to himself. He was so proud of that girl. Had never been more proud of anything in his life, and would hate to do anything to disappoint her. This is why he had not yet revealed that he had blown his chance to send her to Northwestern University.

A few moments later, Huey was cruising up I-15 on his way to the Stardust Heliport for his first flight of the day. He exited Desert Inn Road, took a left, and pulled under the sign for 777 Tours. He parked in the employee parking lot in the space reserved for him.

777, which offered tours of Hoover Dam by day and the Las Vegas skyline by night, had been in the Palmer family for three generations, and Huey had worked there since he was fifteen years old. He had become sole owner of the company when his father passed away a few years before, and he still flew three to four tours a day in the same Bell 206 helicopter that his father had purchased in 1986 and taught him to fly on.

While it might sound cool to say one owned a helicopter tour company, it was certainly not a lucrative business. Office overhead, insurance, helipad rental, FAA certification, maintenance, and fuel added up to be quite a pretty penny, and the Las Vegas tourism business nosediving post-recession didn't help one bit. 777 had been scraping by for years, which is why Huey was forced to fly himself and not able to kick back and roll around in piles of cash. This was not a big issue for Huey, however, because he loved to fly. It was in his DNA. It was literally in his name. He was named after the Bell UH-1 helicopter that his father flew in Vietnam. The original designation of the UH-1 was the HU-1, and everybody called it the "Huey" for short.

Huey walked out of the parking lot and approached the ticket booth where Maggie Calvert, the blue-haired woman who had been working the booth since the 1960s, flashed him a smile.

"Morning, Huey."

"Morning, Maggie. How we looking today?"

"Eh. So far no one's signed up for the noon or sunset flights. But the 10:00 is all booked up." Maggie gestured to two large men sitting in the waiting area. Both men wore black jackets and read sections of the newspaper through dark sunglasses. They looked like they weren't used to getting up this early.

"Just two of them?" Huey said.

"Yep. Bought out the whole thing." This was a bit unusual. The tours were charged per trip and the cost split amongst the number of passengers, so usually all six seats were taken. Occasionally a couple would rent out the whole chopper for a romantic excursion or so that the guy could propose as they passed over the Bellagio fountain, but something told Huey that this would not be the case with these two gentlemen.

Huey grabbed a cup of coffee and did a brief safety inspection of the Bell, making sure it had enough fuel for the tour. With a full tank, the helicopter could fly for about four-and-a-half hours, so the ninety-minute round trip would be no sweat. Huey then walked over to the two men and introduced himself.

"Morning," Huey said. "My name is Huey and I'll be your pilot today."

"Aren't pilots for planes?" one of the men said, not looking up from the sports section.

"Pilots are those who control the flying controls of an aircraft. We who fly helicopters are indeed refereed to as pilots."

"Oh, really?" the other man said. "So the guy who drives the Goodyear Blimp is a blimp pilot?"

"Yes, actually. And piloting a blimp is quite difficult. It takes years of training."

The men laughed. Huey was not sure why this was so funny. "Anyway," Huey said, "I just need to go over some quick safety precautions and then we can get going." The two men didn't look up. Huey was beginning to grow impatient. "I'm going to need your full attention." The two men sighed, seemingly in unison, and lowered their newspaper sections. Huey thanked them and then went through the safety spiel he was legally required to give all passengers. What to do in case of an emergency and so on.

A few moments later, the three men had piled into the Bell and were lifting off. One of the men opted to sit in the passenger seat, and the other in the back. Both still wore their sunglasses, in addition to the massive headsets passengers needed in order to communicate over the noise. It took only about thirty minutes to reach Hoover Dam, and during that time Huey gave a brief history of the engineering marvel that the two men seemingly had no interest in hearing. Huey followed this up with some fun facts, his favorite being that the dam is filled with 3.25 million cubic yards of concrete, enough to pave a strip sixteen feet wide and eight inches thick from San Francisco to New York City. The men did not appear to find this fact very fun. Huey circled the chopper over the dam for a few minutes, and it was then that the man in the front decided to finally speak up.

"Has anyone ever hijacked a helicopter before?" the man in front said. He seemed genuinely curious. Huey found this question to be a bit odd. He had never been asked that before, and actually had to think about it for a moment.

"Sure," Huey said. "Usually for prison escapes. In 1973, three IRA members hijacked a police helicopter and had it fly them to freedom. Somebody even wrote a song about it."

"What about terrorists?" the man in back said. "Like 9/11 style to fly into a building?"

Huey was now beginning to grow uncomfortable with this line

of questioning. "We sort of don't like to talk about 9/11 while on flights," Huey said. "Kind of a bad omen."

"Just curious is all. I mean, it sure is easy to sneak a gun onto one of these things." The man in the back's matter-of-fact tone and use of present tense caused Huey to come to a realization.

The man in front pulled out a 22mm Glock and aimed it right at Huey's gut. All passengers were required to pass through a metal detector upon entering the heliport, but clearly these men had found a way to bypass it. This did not surprise Huey one bit, considering the security guard in charge of the metal detector was an idiot named Chet.

"Guys," Huey said, "I don't know what your plan is here, but me flying a 1986 Bell 206 into Hoover Dam is like throwing a glass vase against a brick wall. The only damage it would do is to us."

The men eyed one another and laughed. "We're not terrorists," the man in front said. "We were just genuinely curious about the hijacking thing. We work for Mark."

Huey's heart sank a bit. He now wished they were terrorists.

"We're here to intimidate you," the man in back said, not realizing how on-the-nose he sounded.

"In my helicopter? Couldn't you have done this at my apartment?"

"We've been wanting to check out Hoover Dam anyway. Seemed like a way to kill two birds with one stone."

"So what's your plan here? You going to shoot me in the kneecaps or something?"

"No, might pistol-whip you a bit," the man in front said before doing just that. He smashed the gun against Huey's head, causing Huey to wince in pain and let go of the controls. The helicopter tilted. "Jesus Christ!" Huey said as he quickly righted the aircraft. "Is that really what you should be doing right now?" The two men eyed one another. They clearly hadn't thought this out. "What does Mark want?"

"What do you think he wants?" the man in back said. "He wants his fucking $25,000."

"Plus 8% interest," the man in front said. "A total of $27,000."

"I know he wants his money," Huey said. "Of course he wants his money, that's what he does. But I have two weeks."

"Nope. Mark only allows one week for paybacks now."

"What? Since when?"

"Since April."

"I wasn't told about this."

"We're loan sharks, Huey. We don't have to send you update agreements in the mail whenever our account policies change."

"I beg to differ. This information should have been told to me as a precondition before borrowing the money in the first place." The man in front pistol-whipped Huey in the head again, once again causing Huey to momentarily lose control of the helicopter. "What is wrong with you?" Huey said, gripping his ear. "I'm flying a helicopter!"

"I don't like words like 'preconditions' thrown in my face."

"I am the pilot! If I lose control of this thing, then we will all die!"

"Well, I have poor impulse control so stop saying stupid shit!"

"Okay, look," Huey said. "This has been an honest misunderstanding. I really didn't know. If Mark will just make an exception this one time and give me the additional week, I'll have the full $27,000 for him."

"Really?" the man in back said.

"Yeah. I swear to God. I have it, I just need to get it together." This was not true. Huey had $344 in his checking account and no idea whatsoever where he would get the money.

The two men eyed one another, seeming a bit unsure. "We should call Mark and clear it with him," the man in front said. The man in back nodded and pulled out a cell phone. He tried to dial, but soon found he had no reception.

"I got no bars up here," he said.

"Of course not," Huey said. "We're 8,000 feet in the air in the middle of the desert."

The man in front pistol-whipped him again.

CHAPTER 6

Dr. Rainey gripped the handle above the door of Val's Toyota Corolla as she merged onto I-35, weaving between two pickup trucks in the process. He had always thought his research assistant was a bit of a reckless driver, and the half dozen dents on the side of the car seemed to support this theory. "Could you slow down please?" he said. "I'd like to get there in one piece."

"Your wish is my command, boss," Val said. She slowed the Corolla to the speed limit and gave him a glance. "Now you want to tell me what this is all about?"

The two had just left a FedEx Kinko's where Val had faxed in her non-disclosure agreement, so Dr. Rainey was finally able to fill her in on what exactly they were doing without fear of being sued. "You ever heard of Ernie Swords?" he said.

"I don't think so."

"Neither had I. Turns out he's one of the biggest real estate magnates in Texas. We had lunch at The Big Pig and he had said that he owned the building, but he meant the entire square block that building was on. He's responsible for half those new condo buildings going up downtown."

"So I'm supposed to hate him then?" Val said. Dr. Rainey knew she was joking, but not really. There had been a boom in Austin condo towers going up downtown, and many of the bohemian locals were none too happy about the wave of gentrification. The common joke was "How many Austinites does it take to screw in a light bulb? Well... what's wrong with the old light bulb?"

He recounted his lunch for Val beat-by-beat. After heaping praise on Dr. Rainey's book for half an hour, Ernie Swords revealed that he was himself was an Old West enthusiast and an avid collector of the era's artifacts. A few years before, Ernie had bought up a massive collection of memorabilia from the now-defunct Wild West Wax Museum in Denton, and it turned out that the museum's basement was filled with boxes and boxes of photographic negatives of Old West life that no one had looked at in over eighty years. He then hired a top-notch team of photography experts to develop the negatives, and would now be happy to donate them to the University of Texas, but only on the condition that Dr. Rainey himself drive out to his ranch to examine one of the photos in particular and verify its contents.

"And what are its contents?" Val said.

"I don't know."

"I signed the NDA."

"No, I really don't know. He wouldn't tell me. He just said that once I saw the photo, then everything would become clear. But I couldn't tell anyone I was coming." Dr. Rainey didn't care for all the cloak-and-dagger nonsense, but he knew that the donation could do wonders for the University and his standing within it. He would be willing to put up with a field trip if it meant getting the dean of the History Department off his back for a few years.

A little over two hours later, Val's Corolla turned onto a dirt road off of Highway 281 outside of Pleasanton. They drove for several miles and eventually reached two wrought-iron gates. The gates were adorned with giant crossed swords, each with the word "Sword" written on it, a detail that Dr. Rainey found a little redundant.

"This appears to be the place," Val said.

"Yeah. I wonder how we—" He didn't get to finish his thought, because the gates began to open on their own.

"This guy's not going to murder us, is he?" Val said. "Like, let us loose in the woods and hunt us for sport?"

"I seriously doubt it."

She put her foot on the gas and the car lurched through the gates. They drove for another few minutes onto a different dirt road, this time passing a handful of cows, and eventually a house came into view. It was a massive ranch-style home, and several sports cars and high-end pickup trucks were parked out front.

"How much do you think he's worth?" Val said.

"6.5 billion," Dr. Rainey said. "I looked it up."

They pulled up to the front of the house and parked. The front door opened and an older woman stepped out wearing a sparkling pantsuit and cowboy boots. She had big hair and Dr. Rainey suspected had spent a pretty penny on plastic surgery. "Howdy, y'all," she said. "Have any trouble finding the place?"

"Not at all," Dr. Rainey said.

"It's pretty hard to miss," Val said.

This caused the woman to let out a laugh. She stepped to them and shook their hands. "Name's Misty Swords, I'm Ernie's better half. Y'all need anything? Sweet tea?"

"No thank you," Dr. Rainey said.

"Actually I'd love a sweet tea," Val said. She gave Dr. Rainey a shrug. "I'm not going to pass up a sweet tea."

"Great," Misty said. "I'll have it brought to you in the armory. Now come on inside, Ernie's waitin' for ya." She turned and headed inside, gesturing for them to follow.

"The armory?" Val said to Dr. Rainey in a whisper. "We probably should have told someone where we were going." Dr. Rainey laughed.

A few moments later, Dr. Rainey and his research assistant stood in a large room surrounded by guns. A lot of guns. Thousands of guns from every period in history. Pistols, shotguns, rifles, machine guns, Gatling guns, Tommy guns, you name it. Each one hung on the wall on its own rack, and they all faced in the same exact direction.

"What you see before you is the largest privately-owned collection of firearms in the world," a voice said. They turned around to see Ernie Swords step out behind them, arms open like a carnival barker about to introduce the bearded lady. He was wearing a Western shirt tucked into jeans and the same Stetson he had on when he went to visit Dr. Rainey's class. "Over 22,000 pieces from every manufacturer known to man."

"This is so where I want to be during the zombie apocalypse," Val said.

Ernie couldn't help but laugh. "Wouldn't do you much good," he said. "I don't have any bullets. These pieces are not meant to be used as weapons, but rather stand as pieces of history. To stand as pieces of art. To trace the rise of man through his weapons. From this…" Ernie stepped over to a case against the wall that held a long, bronze, spear-like weapon attached to a bamboo tube. "A tenth century Chinese fire lance. Over a thousand years old. Considered by military scholars to be the first gun ever created, it used newly discovered 'gunpowder' to fire flames and shrapnel at intended target." Ernie then stepped to the very next case, strategically placed in a way that made it clear he had given this speech many times before. "To this…" he said. Inside was a high-tech, futuristic-looking metallic rifle with a red light panel on the side. "A prototype military rail gun, an electrically-powered electromagnetic projectile launcher based on similar principles to the homopolar motor."

Val leaned in and studied the rail gun closer. "Is this legal to own?" she asked.

"I make a lot of political contributions to some very well-connected people in the bag for the Military Industrial Complex," Ernie said with a chuckle. "Besides, it doesn't work. Half the guns in this place don't."

"We really appreciate you showing us around your collection, Mr. Swords," Dr. Rainey said.

"Please, call me Ernie."

"Ernie. But we're sort of pressed for time. Val has a gig to get back to." He pointed to Val, and she immediately shot him a surprised look. He could tell that she didn't like being used as an excuse to hurry this up, but did in fact appreciate the fact that he remembered her show in the first place.

"Ah, yes," Ernie said. "Of course. I was just getting to the reason I brought you here." Ernie stepped back out into the middle of the racks, surrounded by guns in every direction, a king standing amongst his treasures. "I have spent the last forty years, and a considerable amount of my fortune, tracking down each and every firearm in this room. My lifelong dream has always been to not only hold the biggest collection, but also the most complete. A model of every firearm ever made. But much like Captain Ahab, I have my white whale. A gun that remains elusive to this day, even after my considerable efforts."

Ernie gestured behind them. Dr. Rainey and Val turned around to see that there was a rack with no gun on it, but a framed drawing instead. The drawing showed a 19th century black revolver with a walnut grip and an ornate gold-inlaid barrel that showed several eagles.

"Do you recognize that firearm, Dr. Rainey?" Ernie said.

Dr. Rainey took a step closer, eyeing the drawing. He did, in fact, recognize the gun. He had read an article about it in an academic journal years before. "The Special Edition Colt Third Model Dragoon Percussion Revolver," he said.

"That's right," Ernie said. "Created as part of a set of three that Samuel Colt himself took to Europe in 1854. Do you know why?"

Dr. Rainey suddenly felt like he was being quizzed, and he sort of enjoyed it. It had been a long time since he had been on the opposing end of a history test. "Because that year saw the outbreak of the Crimean War, which pitted Russia against Turkey and her allies, Great Britain and France. Colt, who was a savvy businessman, attempted to sell guns to both sides. He presented the three gold-inlaid Special Edition Colt Third Model Dragoon Percussion Revolvers to Czar Nicholas I of Russia. One of them now sits in the Hermitage Museum in Saint Petersburg. Another is on display at the Metropolitan Museum of Art in New York City. I actually saw it a few years ago."

"And where is the third?" Ernie said.

"No one knows," Dr. Rainey said. "It just disappeared."

"Precisely. No one has seen the third Special Edition Colt Third Model Dragoon Percussion Revolver in 160 years. It has become the most sought-after firearm in the history of the world, and I have been searching for it for almost my entire life without a single viable lead."

A devilish grin crossed Ernie's face and he took a dramatic pause. "Until now, that is." Dr. Rainey gave him a look. Ernie officially had him on the edge of his seat. "Dr. Rainey, I mentioned to you at our lunch the photograph collection I purchased from the Wild West Wax Museum in Denton."

"Yes, you did."

"This was one of the photos included in that collection." Ernie reached into his coat pocket and pulled out an old black-and-white photograph for them to inspect. It showed a distinguished-looking man with a long gray beard wearing a nice 19th century suit and top hat. The man looked directly into the camera, a very serious expression on his face.

The man held a Special Edition Colt Third Model Dragoon Percussion Revolver in his right hand.

Dr. Rainey studied the man's face and recognized him instantly. "Oh my god," he said. "I don't believe it." He and Ernie shared a knowing glance.

"Who is that guy?" Val said.

Dr. Rainey slowly turned to Val and gave her a dumbfounded look, as if she had just asked him who a picture of Elvis Presley was. "It's Etienne Roux," he said.

"Who is Etienne Roux?"

His look gradually went from dumbfounded to utter disappointment. "Val," he said. "Have you not read my book?"

CHAPTER 7

An excerpt from the book Untold Tales Of The West
by Dr. Douglas Rainey. Essay entitled "Anarchy in the U.S."

The political landscape of the post-Civil War Reconstruction era was a volatile place. With the Confederacy fallen and the Union struggling to keep itself whole, many fringe political movements emerged from every corner of America, some stranger than others. There was Radicalism, a precursor to Communism that sought a redistribution of property and an abolition of titles. Progressivism, which asserted that advances in science, technology, economic development, and social organization would improve the human condition above all else. Populism, a political doctrine where one sides with "the people" against "the elites."

Perhaps the most fringe political viewpoint to gain popularity at this time was Anarchism, which advocated stateless societies based on non-hierarchical free associations. Anarchists believed the state to be undesirable, unnecessary, or harmful, and in the simplest of explanations, that people should be allowed to rule themselves. Despite the modern perception of the term "anarchy" that one might associate with punk rock and its use in the common vernacular to describe any chaotic situation (usually by the mass media to describe riots), in the mid-to-late 19th century Anarchism was a viable movement with well-educated and well-respected leaders. The negative reputation truly began in 1901, when self-proclaimed anarchist Leon Czolgosz assassinated President William McKinley, shooting him twice at point blank range with a .32 caliber revolver.

Forty years before that assassination, the most popular Anarchist voice in America was a man by the name of Etienne Roux. Roux was a French nobleman who studied philosophy at the University of Paris and, along with his Anarchist contemporary Pierre-Joseph Proudhon, had been witness firsthand to the French Revolution of 1848 and the political reforms it brought to Europe as a whole. While Proudhon eventually joined the French Parliament, Roux opted to emigrate to the United States soon after the Civil War with a desire to spread his message to a nation in disrepair.

Charismatic and handsome, Roux traveled up and down the East Coast preaching a political ideology that he felt was perfect for the American sensibility: Anarcho-Capitalism. Anarcho-Capitalism, an offshoot of Anarchism of Roux's own design, advocated the elimination of the state in favor of individual sovereignty in a free market. In an anarcho-capitalist society, law enforcement and the legal system would be provided by privately-funded competitors rather than through taxation, and money would be privately and competitively provided in an open market. Therefore, personal and economic activities under Anarcho-Capitalism would be regulated by privately-run law rather than through politics.

Roux gathered many followers, and he gathered them quickly. By 1872, only two years after setting foot on American soil, Roux's Anarcho-Capitalist Party had a recorded 17,000 members from all strata of society, including many women and freed slaves who felt the laws of American government weren't necessarily doing them any favors. Roux was pleased with his following, but dismayed by the lack of attention he was getting in Washington, DC, where Republicans and Democrats were the two parties of choice and the Anarcho-Capitalists looked down on as a joke. Roux, not one to be laughed at, devised a bold idea to show the nation's leaders and the nation as a whole that Anarcho-Capitalism could in fact work and create a utopian society if only given a chance.

In 1877, Roux purchased a 200-acre tract of land in Northern

Louisiana, a state which he was fond of due to its own French heritage. He established what he called "an anarcho-capitalist commune," to which he invited any American citizen who wanted to live free of the burdens of the state. The Louisiana newspapers soon dubbed it "Roux City." The commune had an estimated 300 citizens at its inception and within six months had ballooned to over 2000. Details of life within Roux City are sparse save for the writings of Roux himself, which tell of a place where people lived in harmony and indeed ruled themselves.

Not everyone was pleased about the formation of Roux City, however, especially not the US Marshals Service. In addition to not paying taxes, the Marshals suspected that Roux and his followers were also practicing polygamy (which had been made illegal by the Morrill Anti-Bigamy act of 1862) and accumulating a large amount of firearms. While there is to this day no proof of the first allegation, there is much documented evidence that Roux and his followers certainly acquired many, many guns. Roux was a very strong believer in the Second Amendment, and not only supported but encouraged his followers to carry firearms with them at all times. He was once asked at a rally why this was the case since Anarcho-Capitalism was supposedly a peaceful movement, to which Roux replied "Because not everyone in this country believes in me. Not yet, anyway."

In October of 1878, the US Marshals received approval from the Department of Justice to raid the commune and find out for themselves what exactly was happening in Roux City. Roux must have gotten wind of this plan, for when the Marshals arrived they found that Roux and every single follower, including women and children, was gone. Crude wooden buildings still stood on the land, but much like the lost colony of Roanoke, the people and their possessions had vanished into thin air. The Marshals were baffled, but upon further investigation discovered that Roux and his followers had spent the previous weeks buying up every horse and covered wagon from Little Rock to New Orleans, clearly planning an escape. The disappearance would have remained a mystery forever if Roux himself had not mailed a letter to *The New York*

Times on the day before the raid that was received weeks later and subsequently published.

> *To Whom It May Concern,*
>
> *My followers and I attempted to make lives for ourselves, but have learned that the government of these United States is displeased with our peaceful existence and plans to disrupt it. We will not abide by laws which we do not believe exist, and have thus decided that we will go to a place where lawlessness is not an aberration but the norm.*
>
> *We will go west.*
>
> *- Etienne Roux. October 15, 1878*

Roux, along with every single one of his followers, was never seen or heard from again. No trace of his expedition has ever been found.

CHAPTER 8

The text message from an unknown number had been sent to Huey's cell phone at 9:45 that morning. He had been out on a Hoover Dam flight, so he didn't notice it until he returned to the heliport and was heating up a cup of Top Ramen in the microwave for lunch.

MR PALMER. YOU MAY FIND THIS MESSAGE UNUSUAL AND I APOLOGIZE FOR THE COYNESS, BUT I WAS GIVEN YOUR NAME AS A RECOMMENDATION BY GRANT HOLIDAY AND WISH TO SPEAK WITH YOU REGARDING THE PRIVATE RENTAL OF YOUR AIRCRAFT. IF YOU ARE INTERESTED IN DISCUSSING THE MATTER, I AM STAYING AT THE PALMS CASINO IN THE HARDWOOD SUITE. BE THERE AT 5PM AND ALL WILL BE EXPLAINED. - ERNIE SWORDS

Huey had no idea who Ernie Swords was, so he used the computer in the office to look him up online. The first hit that came up was the man's Wikipedia page, and the highlights were that Swords was a billionaire real estate developer, owner of The San Antonio Swordsmen, and founder of something called the South Texas Objectivists Society. What the man wanted Huey for was anybody's guess, but it was fairly common to have rich types want to rent out the helicopter for the day for some bizarre purpose. About ten years before, he had been paid $10,000 to fly incredibly low over a gun range so that a billionaire could fire an M-16 assault rifle at targets and relive his days from Vietnam. There were now three separate companies in Las Vegas that officially offered this service, mostly used by bachelor parties.

Grant Holiday, the man that Ernie mentioned in his text, was the owner of a local establishment called The Aviatrix. Despite sounding like an S&M club, The Aviatrix was actually a bar by the airport frequented almost exclusively by current and former pilots. The walls were covered with old propellers and photos of WWII bombers, and it was the go-to gathering spot for any man or woman in town who flew for a living. Commercial pilots, military test pilots from nearby Nellis Air Force Base, crop dusters, and folks like Huey. If anyone was ever looking to hire a helicopter for a legitimate purpose, they went to the phone book. For illegitimate purposes, they went to Grant Holiday.

Huey didn't really have time for mysterious messages and visits to penthouses, because there was still the matter of $27,000 he didn't have. He had spent the last few days going over his options, the main one being selling the 1986 Bell. It was in pretty good shape, but was still almost thirty years old and had clocked a fair amount of miles. He figured he could get about $75,000 for it. The sale would destroy the business and force him to let go all of his employees, but at least he wouldn't be murdered in an alley or whatever it is Mark was planning to do. While time was of the essence and Huey had much bigger fish to fry, it did occur to him that a visit to Ernie Swords could potentially be the answer to his financial issues and therefore might be worth the time. He canceled the final two tours for the day, which no one had signed up for anyway, and headed towards the Strip.

He parked in the garage at The Palms and headed through the lobby in search of the elevators. The hotel and casino had been built in the early 2000s as a hip alternative to the more stuffy haunts of old Vegas, and they had even shot a season of *MTV's The Real World* there. The Cosmopolitan had stolen a bit of The Palms' thunder when it opened in 2010, but the place had still managed to retain its reputation as a hot spot for the young club crowd. Huey had visited it a handful of times to hit up the sports book, but he was never a big fan of their setup because they tended to blare dance music over the speakers instead of the game sound, a detail any true sports fan would find maddening.

It took him forever to find the elevators, casinos being designed to be purposefully disorienting, and he soon discovered that he had to check in with a security guard in order to access the elevator bank for the penthouses. His name was already on a pre-approved list, and the guard said, "Mr. Swords is expecting you," in a very ominous tone. He took the elevator up to The Hardwood Suite, where he rang the doorbell and waited. He thought it was funny that a hotel room necessitated a doorbell, but when the door opened and he saw the massive size of the suite he understood the need.

An older man wearing a proper butler's outfit stepped into the doorway. "Mr. Palmer?" the butler said. Huey was surprised he didn't have a British accent and momentarily wondered if that was somehow racist.

"Yeah," Huey said. "That's me."

"Please, come in."

Huey headed inside and soon learned why it was called "The Hardwood Suite." The massive penthouse contained a regulation-sized basketball court and a full professional locker room. The court was currently occupied by two young women who looked no older than twenty-one spilling out of outfits that didn't seem appropriate for playing basketball in. The women were playing H-O-R-S-E, and they seemed to find it hilarious that one of them currently had "ho" and the other "hor."

"Mr. Palmer!" a voice said. "Thank you for coming!"

Huey turned to see Ernie Swords standing behind a bar mixing a cocktail, Huey recognized him from the photo on his Wikipedia page. The old man was wearing a Western shirt tucked into jeans and a bolo tie. Huey thought the outfit sort of resembled the one that the dealers wore at Lucky Pete's Gambling Saloon. Ernie seemed genuinely excited to see Huey and quickly walked around the bar to shake his hand. "Would you like a drink?" Ernie said.

"Sure. Whiskey on the rocks if you've got it."

"Oh this place has everything. What brand?"

"Buffalo Trace?"

"Coming right up. Hey, also do you mind signing this?" Ernie reached over to the bar and grabbed what appeared to be a thick contract of some sort. He handed it to Huey along with a pen that had The Palms logo emblazoned on the side.

"What is it?"

"It's a non-disclosure agreement. What I want to talk to you about is something I'm trying to keep on the hush hush. It just says you won't go telling anybody about it. You can read it over if you want." Huey eyed the front page, and the document seemed pretty standard. He had signed a few NDAs before when dealing with rich clients who wanted to take their mistresses on private flights, and he knew there was no point in reading it over because he didn't speak legalese. He assumed the gist was that if he spilled the beans about whatever it is they were going to talk about it, he'd owe Ernie Swords his right arm *and* first born.

"Why not?" Huey said.

Ernie smiled and stepped back behind the bar to prepare the drink. Huey signed the contract, then momentarily watched one of the girls attempt to make a free throw. She missed wildly. "Your friends need to bend their knees when they shoot," he said.

"Oh they're not my friends. They come with the room. Like I said, this place has everything," Ernie handed over the drink and gave Huey a wink. Huey would never understand rich people. Ernie then lifted up a tray with three other drinks on it, a martini and two beers, and gestured to a hallway. "Come on, the others are outside."

"Others?"

Ernie started to walk, so Huey followed. They headed down the long hallway, which was lined with basketball jerseys autographed by NBA superstars, and reached double doors leading out to a private balcony. The door opened automatically and Huey followed Ernie out, noticing the sweeping view of the Las Vegas Strip at sunset. Most people would have described the view as "breathtaking," but since Huey looked at beautiful views of Las Vegas for a living he was a bit over it.

"I'd like you two to meet Huey Palmer," Ernie said. "He's the pilot I was telling you about." Huey looked over to see that a middle-aged man and a younger woman were already sitting on the balcony, taking in the view. The man wore a brown corduroy jacket and glasses. The woman wore ripped jeans a very old-looking Smiths t-shirt. "Huey, this is Dr. Douglas Rainey and his assistant Valerie Trujillo,"

"*Research* assistant," Val said.

Ernie handed the martini to Val and one of the beers to Dr. Rainey, keeping the other for himself. He set the tray down and gestured to Huey to take a seat. Huey did so.

"A doctor?" Huey said. "So is this like an intervention or something?" Ernie did Huey the favor of laughing at his bad joke.

"I'm a PhD," Dr. Rainey said. "In American History."

"He's the world's foremost expert on the Old West," Ernie said. "You should read his book." Huey noticed that this statement caused Dr. Rainey to shoot his research assistant a look.

"Okay," Huey said. "So what can I do for you guys?"

"Before we get to that," Ernie said with a smile. "I'd like to tell you a story."

It took an hour and another round of drinks, but Ernie Swords told Huey the whole tall tale. The legend of Etienne Roux and his connection to the missing Special Edition Colt Third Model Dragoon Percussion Revolver. Huey had never heard of the man nor the gun, his breadth of Old West history coming from the walls of Lucky Pete's, and he actually found the story quite interesting. He was, however, left with a burning question.

"So how'd this Roux guy get the gun?" Huey said.

"If I had to make an educated guess," Dr. Rainey said. "I'd say that he probably got it directly from a Russian royal. The Romanov family loved to hobnob with European intellectuals and we know that Etienne Roux made several trips to Moscow. I could imagine a scenario where some prince or princess wanted to impress the great political thinker by giving him the gun as a gift, never stopping to realize that Roux's ideology called for the destruction of their very way of life."

"And nobody really ever saw his group again after they left Louisiana?" Huey said.

"Many wagon trains out west vanished," Dr. Rainey said. "Granted, none were nearly as big as Roux's. Pioneers would set out with grand ambitions to find a new life, but not bother to hire a professional guide or research proper routes, ending up face-to-face with aggressive native tribes, harsh weather conditions, even angry bears. An overwhelming majority of the terrain was unexplored at the time, and a wrong turn could put you in a very unforgiving place. Even to this day, there are parts of the American West that no one has ever truly explored on foot due to their sheer remoteness."

"Huh," Huey said as he took a sip. The exploration of the West is admittedly something he had never thought much about. "So what exactly does this have to do with me?"

The other three exchanged a glance. Ernie almost seemed giddy to continue. "The Roux expedition could have been lost just about anywhere west of the Mississippi," Ernie said. "And I have been determined to figure out where. Find the expedition, and you find the Special Edition Colt Third Model Dragoon Percussion Revolver." Huey began to wonder if they were always going to use the full name when referring to the gun. It was a mouthful.

"As Dr. Rainey just mentioned," Ernie said, "there are indeed parts of America that no one has ever explored on foot, but that doesn't mean we can't explore them from the sky." Ernie pointed up dramatically. "Now it would take forever to fly over the most isolated parts of America to peek around, but in 2008 we were handed a gift from the gods. Google Maps. Google struck a deal with GeoEye Inc, a private satellite imagery company, to be provided high-resolution photos of the world that they would throw up on the internet for all to see. I immediately hired a team of researchers, who signed NDA's like the three of you, to scour Google Maps looking for any sign of Roux's expedition out west. They spent day and night looking in every nook and cranny, but they didn't find a damn thing." Huey could tell that Ernie was getting a kick out of telling this story.

"We soon learned that there were two massive limitations to the satellite images due to government espionage laws," Ernie said. "First was that all the images had to be fairly low resolution. So you could see that a red car was parked outside of some fella's house, but you wouldn't be able to read the license plate or zoom in any closer than a few hundred yards away. This made spotting the remnants of a 130-year-old wagon train a bit tough. The second and more important limitation is that you couldn't publish any images that the National Security Agency didn't want you to see. If you looked up a military base or government compound on Google Maps, you were met with pixilated images of nothingness. This was of course to prevent any bad guys from knowing the layouts of these places in order to plan an attack."

Huey now knew where this was going. Growing up in Nevada, you learn at a very young age that the biggest landowner in the state is the federal government. Uncle Sam owned a whopping 85% of the Silver State and did whatever the hell it wanted with the place. Then again, a large portion was an inhospitable wasteland probably best suited for atomic weapons tests anyway. Smack dab in the middle of it all was the Nevada Test and Training Range, a 5,000-square-mile piece of land that consisted of Nellis Air Force Range, Area 51, and the National Wild Horse Management. It was bigger than the state of Connecticut, and no American could set foot there without proper authorization, which wasn't easy to get.

"There are huge portions of the country that we could never see because of NSA regulations," Ernie said with a smile. "But after I pulled some strings under the table, we were finally able to." Huey thought it interesting that Ernie was so proud of something that could probably land him in jail for the rest of his life.

"What kind of strings?" Huey said.

"It's best you don't ask," Ernie said.

"Now you know why you signed the non-disclosure agreement,"

Val said. She flashed Huey a wry smile. "And it's about to get a lot worse." Huey was starting to put it all together.

"You found something?" Huey said.

"We found something, all right," Ernie said. Ernie grabbed a folder off the table and opened it up to reveal a collection of satellite photos. Huey leaned in closer to inspect them. The photos showed a heavily wooded area in the middle a dense mountain range, but nothing seemed too out of the ordinary to his eyes.

"Right here," Ernie said as he pointed to a particular spot on the photo. Huey looked closer at what appeared to be a brown square.

"It's a barn," Dr. Rainey said.

"You sure?" Huey said. "Could be a big boulder."

"A perfectly square boulder? That just so happens to be a thousand yards from more perfectly square boulders?" Dr. Rainey pointed to another spot on the photograph and sure enough, there were other brown squares. A row of them. "It's ruins, Mr. Palmer. It's ruins where there shouldn't be anything at all. It's ruins in a place where no American is known to have set foot in hundreds of years, especially not the kind who build wooden structures."

"Where is this?" Huey said.

"Near Reveille Peak," Ernie said. "About 200 miles northwest of here. Smack dab in the middle of land set aside in the 1940s for potential future nuclear testing and untouched since."

"Which means it's restricted airspace," Huey said.

"Correct."

"Which means you need someone to fly you there illegally."

"You came highly recommended."

"Why not just ask the government for permission?"

"It would take years and I'd have to explain what I was doing, which I'd rather not do. What if it's not Roux's expedition, but some other random group of pioneers who built that barn? I would have revealed my secret to the world and opened the hunt for the Dragoon to anyone. Plus, my daddy always taught me it's better to ask for forgiveness than permission."

Huey was relieved that the gun had now been shortened to just the Dragoon. He glanced over to Dr. Rainey and Val. "And you two are down for this?"

"You're only handed a once-in-a-lifetime opportunity once in a lifetime," Dr. Rainey said. Huey thought Dr. Rainey sounded like a fortune cookie, and it occurred to him that this was the first time he'd seen the man smile.

"I think it sounds pretty fucking awesome," Val said. "I mean, I'll either be part of an amazing historical discovery or get arrested by the military and become a symbolic political prisoner. It's really a win-win."

Huey looked to Ernie, who had leaned back in his chair and was clasping his hands together like a Hollywood agent about to close a big deal. "How much you looking to pay?" Huey said.

"How much would you like?"

"$139,900."

Dr. Rainey and Val shared a glance, clearly surprised both by Huey's complete lack of hesitation and incredibly specific dollar amount. What they did not know was that this number had been floating around his head for weeks. That this was the number that would pay back Mark, send Jenny to four years at Northwestern, and make all of his problems go away.

"Done," Ernie said.

CHAPTER 9

Huey sat across the table from his daughter as she stared at him with the fiery intensity of a thousand suns. Or at least that's how he felt. "You what?" Jenny said.

"I can't take you to graduation rehearsal tomorrow."

"Why not?"

"It's a little complex."

She continued to stare as she set down a slice of pizza and folded her arms. The two sat in a corner booth at Salvaggio's, a hole-in-the-wall Italian place in a strip mall near Fremont Street. Jenny stayed with Huey every other weekend, and it had become tradition that he would pick her up from his ex-wife's house on Friday evening and the two would hit Salvaggio's to split a large pie and a basket of their famous Provolone rolls. "Good thing I understand complexities," she said.

"I have to take a job."

"You have to take a job? You have to take a job that will make you to miss your daughter's high school graduation, an accomplishment you should be proud of considering Nevada has the third lowest graduation rate in the country?" Jenny loved to throw statistics at her father about their home state. She had recently informed him that there is one slot machine in Nevada for every ten residents.

"I didn't say I was going to miss the graduation. I said that I couldn't take you to rehearsal. I'll be back before sundown with plenty of time to make it to the school." He had done the math in his head over and over just to make sure this was not a lie. Even if Ernie Swords and the others wanted to fly around those ruins all day, they'd be unable to because the Bell would eventually run out of fuel. They'd have to come back to Vegas after a couple hours whether they wanted to or not. Of course there was the possibility that the helicopter would be spotted by the military and they'd be forced to land and all arrested, but at that point he'd have much bigger problems than missing his daughter's graduation.

"What is this job?" Jenny said.

"I can't tell you. I had to sign a non-disclosure agreement, and it's for the best that you don't know anyway. In case there's a trial."

"A trial?"

"I'm just kidding." He wasn't really.

Jenny continued to stare at her father, skeptical. And she had reason to be. Huey hadn't been the most "present" when she was younger, and he had missed out on many of her crowning achievements. Dance recitals, gymnastics competitions, softball games. He had also managed to miss both her kindergarten and eighth grade graduations, the latter of which was something he didn't even know existed until he was informed it was already over. He had used the excuse of needing to go out on a job often, but a large majority of those times he was actually going off to go on a bender, hit the sports book, or both. The divorce from Terry and subsequent custody hearings had been a huge wake-up call to Huey. He had always known deep down that he was a bad father, but hearing it read back out loud by a court stenographer will really do something to a man's soul.

"Jenny, trust me when I say the only reason I'm taking this job is because it's going to help us both out."

"Let me guess," Jenny said. "You're not going to explain what that means?"

"Nope. It's going to be a graduation present. I'll tell you tomorrow night." He was hoping for a smile, but it didn't come. He knew from years of experience that mere words wouldn't comfort Jenny in her skepticism of her father. She finally unfolded her arms, though, and picked the pizza back up to take a bite.

"I just really want you to be there, Dad. It means a lot to me."

"I know. And I will be there. I wouldn't miss it for the world."

CHAPTER 10

When Ernie Swords was a teenager, he was obsessed with trains. He grew up dirt poor on the outskirts of San Antonio, in a neighborhood on the wrong side of the tracks. Literally, his house was right next to railroad tracks. His father worked in the train yard, and Ernie spent countless hours visiting him to watch the massive steel locomotives pass by. Ernie saw himself working there one day, putting in an honest day's work for an honest day's pay in order to provide for the family he didn't have yet. His sophomore year in high school, he had to write a paper on an aspect of the transportation system, so he picked the railroads and went his local library to do research. This trip would change his life forever. Someone had accidentally misfiled Ayn Rand's 1957 novel *Atlas Shrugged*, the plot of which did in fact entail the railroad industry, into the non-fiction transportation section. Ernie checked the book out, based on the cover's stark image of tracks leading into a tunnel, and got home to discover that he was now in possession of the magnum opus on the philosophical system of Objectivism. Objectivism argued that there is no greater moral achievement than living by one's own efforts to pursue happiness, and that the ideal man does not give or receive the undeserved. This spoke to the impressionable sixteen year-old. Ernie read the 1200-page book three times, and soon after decided he no longer wanted to work in the train yard. He wanted to own it. He wanted to acquire anything and everything that would make him happy.

As the 1986 Bell 206 lifted off from the Stardust Heliport and headed north over the Las Vegas strip, Ernie looked upon the sunrise and thought about how this might have been the happiest moment of his life. After a lifetime of searching, he knew that he was at the finish line of his quest.

He sat up front beside Huey, who was manning the controls. Dr. Rainey and Val sat in the back. Val appeared a bit hungover behind a pair of sunglasses. She had mentioned the night before that this was her first time in Las Vegas, and Ernie suspected she had celebrated that fact a little too hard.

They passed the Stratosphere tower and soon were over the sprawling suburbs of North Las Vegas. A few minutes after that, the landscape changed from tracks of identical stucco houses in gated communities to nothing but vast desert as far as the eye could see. "Man this town is really in the middle of fucking nowhere, isn't it?" Val said.

"Las Vegas existed merely as a stopover on the pioneer trails to the West," Dr. Rainey said. "And it was a staging point for mines in the surrounding area that shipped goods to the rest of the country. It probably would have stayed that way forever if it wasn't for the mafia and the invention of air conditioning."

"My two favorite things," Val said.

"All right, ladies and gentlemen, we've now reached our cruising altitude of 8,000 feet," Huey said in his best smooth airline pilot voice. "We will soon be starting in-flight beverage service."

"How long until we're there?" Ernie said.

"If I can maintain this speed, we should be there in about an hour."

"Can we go faster?" Ernie eyed the speedometer on the control panel to see that the Bell was moving along at 135mph.

"We can, but we won't."

"Why not?"

"Because it's dangerous." Huey shot Ernie a look. "Leave the flying to me, Mr. Swords." Ernie accepted this, although he wasn't thrilled about it. A week before, he had actually looked into taking flying lessons himself and buying his own helicopter in order to be the one behind the controls, but he abandoned the idea when he realized it's a skill that apparently takes years to master.

They flew and flew, and Ernie noticed that the terrain below seemed to become more and more bleak. Huey shared some of what he called "fun facts" with the group, telling them that Nevada was predominately rocky and inhospitable, but was also home to the topographical phenomenon known as "sky islands." These were mountains isolated by surrounding lowlands of a dramatically different environment, in this case dry arid desert, but because of atmospheric conditions resulted in a completely different ecosystem which had significant implications for natural habitats. This meant that there were lush forests filled with wildlife randomly peppered throughout the driest state in the union.

It was not too far past one of these sky islands that Ernie spotted a chain link fence below them. "Is that it?" he said.

"That's it," Huey said. "The point of no return." They had officially just crossed into restricted airspace, and if caught would be in a heap of trouble.

Ernie had treated his expedition team to breakfast at The Peppermill, an old diner across from Circus Circus filled mostly with partiers who hadn't gone to bed yet, to go over the cover story which he had devised months before and dubbed "Operation A Simple Misunderstanding." If caught, they would claim that Dr. Rainey had hired Huey to fly him, his research assistant, and his new benefactor Ernie Swords out to look at an abandoned nuclear test site on Nellis Air Force Base for a book about the Manhattan Project that he was working on. Dr. Rainey would claim that he had received authorization from the military for this trip, and even be able to present a letter from the Pentagon confirming this. The letter was real, but in actuality granted Dr. Rainey to visit Altus Air Force Base in Altus, Oklahoma, where Dr. Rainey actually *had* asked for permission to visit and it been granted, since Altus was a training academy that offered daily tours to the public anyway. When military investigators would bring this fact to Dr. Rainey's attention, he would state that the woman on the phone at the Pentagon must have misheard him, confusing "Nellis" for "Altus," and then blame Val for not double-checking the authorization letter itself. It was all to be chocked-up to a simple misunderstanding. The four would probably be held for a while as their backgrounds were thoroughly checked, but eventually be released as to avoid a negative story in the press about the military trying to impede on academic research. Or at least that's what they hoped would happen.

There was of course another scenario that Ernie was well aware of, but he had chosen to keep it quiet not wanting to scare any of the others: that the Air Force could just straight up decide to shoot the helicopter down. The military didn't take too kindly to unknown aircraft entering into restricted federal airspace, and Ernie wouldn't put it past them to shoot first and ask questions later. This scenario was highly unlikely, though, because the bad press of killing four innocent civilians with a missile would be much worse than detaining four idiots who got lost in the wrong neighborhood.

"You ever thought of being a military helicopter pilot, Huey?" Ernie said.

"Oh my father wanted nothing more," Huey said. "For me to follow in his footsteps and join the Air Force. To sit behind the controls of an Apache or Black Hawk. But I had no interest in the career choice, mostly from listening to the stories that he would tell about Vietnam and the shit he had seen there."

"I was drafted myself," Ernie said.

"You serve?" Huey said.

"No, I got a deferment. Had a bad knee from playing high school football."

"Yeah, well my dad never let me hear the end of it," Huey said. "One of the last times I saw him before he died, he told me that I was 'not a real man.'"

"Sounds kind of like a dick," Val said. "No offense."

"None taken," Huey said. "He was."

The Bell continued deeper into the heart of darkness of central Nevada for what seemed like forever, and the further it went the further away from civilization Ernie felt. He hadn't seen a car or a building in quite a while, and now there wasn't even a road on the horizon in any direction.

"I take back what I said about Vegas," Val said. "*Now* we're really in the middle of fucking nowhere." Ernie knew she was absolutely right. No human being had probably been to this part of America in a hundred years, if ever.

Ernie pulled out a handheld GPS device and checked their location in relation to the coordinates of the barn spotted on the satellite images. He looked ahead and grew excited. "We're getting close," Ernie said. "Very close." Dr. Rainey and Val pressed themselves against their respective windows to get a better look as Huey descended the helicopter's altitude to a thousand feet. "I feel like Captain Ahab," Ernie said. "About to finally track down Moby Dick."

"Have you ever actually read that book?" Val said.

Ernie wasn't sure what that was supposed to mean, but assumed she was trying to kill his buzz. He looked back out to the horizon to see that helicopter was slipping between two large mountains into a canyon that was surprisingly green, filled with thousands of trees. A sky island. Ernie looked ahead and pointed. "Up here. Get lower." Huey obliged and lowered the Bell to 600 feet.

The Bell cleared a thicket of trees and Ernie could now see that a small river winded its way through the canyon. "Hey! It's a river," Val said.

"An ideal place for pioneers to have set up camp," Dr. Rainey said. The Bell soared over the river and approached what appeared to be a clearing ahead.

Then Ernie saw it.

"Oh my god." he said. "There! Look to the left!" He pointed to the horizon.

A wooden barn stood in the middle of the clearing. The structure had seen better days and succumbed to the elements long ago--the roof completely caved in--but it was clearly a barn nevertheless.

"I've found it!" Ernie said. He clapped his hands together and pumped his fist into the air. "I've found it!"

"We've found a barn," Dr. Rainey said. "Let's keep looking around."

"Let's land and look around on foot," Ernie said.

Huey gave him a look. "Come again?"

"Land in the clearing."

"I'm just flying you over. That was the deal."

"And now I've changed my mind, so the deal has changed with it. I want to check out the barn." Ernie knew there was no way he'd let them turn back. They were so close. He could already feel the cold steel grip of the Dragoon in his hand.

"I'm not landing, Mr. Swords. It's not safe."

"You want your money or not, Mr. Palmer? Land this helicopter right now or I will—"

Ernie didn't get to finish his threat, because the Bell 206 violently jolted as if it had been struck by something. The entire helicopter spun to the left, and Huey pulled on the controls to counteract the movement.

"What was that?" Ernie said.

"I don't know," Huey said.

"What do you mean you don't know?"

Ernie eyed the controls to see the needle on the fuel gauge dropping. They were losing fuel and they were losing it fast. He looked out the window to see a stream of gold liquid pouring out of a hole in the helicopter's belly.

"Oh no," Huey said.

"Oh no?" Ernie said. He gripped onto his seat. "Oh no what? Pilots shouldn't say 'oh no.' That can't be good."

"It's not."

The Bell jolted again, and the front window cracked into pieces. The helicopter again spun to the left, this time faster, and Huey attempted to counteract, but something was wrong. Something was very, very wrong. They just kept spinning, the controls were useless. Huey gave Ernie a look as the helicopter spun flipped upside and fell towards the earth.

"We've been shot down," Huey said.

CHAPTER 11

The birds were chirping very loudly. That's what Val first thought as she regained consciousness. She had never thought of there being birds in the desert, not except for the Road Runner from the old Looney Tunes cartoons. She opened her eyes to see the trees gently swaying above her in the breeze. The sun was shining, its rays casting a warm comfort on her skin. She could just lie here all day, she thought. Then she remembered why she was on the ground in the first place.

She sat up to see the twisted wreckage of the 1986 Bell 206 before her, and it took her a few seconds to realize it was upside down. The helicopter appeared to have crashed into the side of the mountain and been torn open like a tin can, pieces of it littering the area. She looked down at her own body to see that she seemed to be completely fine, not a scratch on her. She wondered how the hell she got thrown from the helicopter in the first place, considering she was wearing her seat belt like everyone else. She slowly stood up and got her bearings, realizing she was a bit dizzy. She wondered if she had a concussion. She had never had one before, but had heard about them during football broadcasts and assumed from the description of symptoms that it was probably something like this.

She made her way over to the wreckage and peered inside. Huey and Ernie still remained strapped to their chairs, dangling upside down. Both were bloody and bruised, and neither was moving. The back seat was empty. Dr. Rainey was nowhere in sight.

She crawled over to Huey, and he didn't seem to be breathing. She wondered if he was dead. "Huey?" She shook him. "Huey, are you dead?" She then wondered if maybe he was unconscious with a concussion, and she was actually making it worse by shaking him. She wished she had paid more attention during those football broadcasts. Huey's eyes slowly opened and she felt a wave of relief wash over her. He wasn't dead, and that was a very good thing.

"What happened?" Huey said. "What's going on?"

"We crashed."

Huey looked around to get his bearings. "Oh, right," he said. "You okay?"

"Yeah, I'm fine."

Huey slowly looked to Ernie sitting next to him. Ernie was hanging very awkwardly, his left arm twisted around the back of his head. "Ernie? Ernie, you okay?" Ernie didn't respond.

Huey looked down to his seat belt and pressed the button, sending him crashing to the glass-covered floor, which was actually the glass-covered ceiling. He winced in pain. "Didn't really think that through," Huey said. He crawled over to Ernie and looked him over. Ernie's arm was in nasty shape. It was bent the way an arm should not be bent

"Ernie? Ernie, wake up." Huey slapped Ernie across the face.

"Is that a good idea?" Val said. "What if he's had a concussion?" She was genuinely concerned, and felt that in the last three minutes she had grown into a concussion expert.

Ernie's eyes slowly opened and he looked around. Huey gave Val a look and shrugged. They were both relieved.

"My arm," Ernie said. "It hurts like a son-of-a-bitch."

"You should see how it looks," Huey said. "Let's get you down." He gestured to Val, and together they undid Ernie's belt and lifted him to the floor as he winced in pain. They then carried him out onto the grass and set him down in a clearing.

Huey looked over and for the first time was able to soak in the wreckage and the scope of what had happened. "Jesus Christ," he said. "She's done for." Val couldn't help but think Huey's tone was that of a man looking at the family pet he knew he was going to have to put down.

"Where's Dr. Rainey?" Val said. She gestured to the back of the helicopter, and Huey looked in to see that it in fact was totally empty.

"You didn't see him when you woke up?" Huey said.

"No, I woke up way over there." She pointed to the spot in the grass where she came to.

"Then maybe he was thrown too?"

Ernie winced in pain again. Huey bent down and took another look at his condition. "We need to make a splint for his arm," Huey said. "There's an emergency kit in the cockpit. Can you do that and I'll look for Dr. Rainey?"

"I have no idea how to make a splint," Val said. "I mean I was in the Girl Scouts for like a week, but all we did was sell cookies and shit so I quit."

"Okay, then I'll make the splint and you look for Dr. Rainey."

Val nodded and stood up as Huey headed back to the cockpit. She started to look around, noticing that the wreckage went out for almost fifty yards in every direction. There even seemed to be some pieces stuck up in the trees. She walked among the twisted metal pieces, searching.

"Dr. Rainey?" Val said in a loud voice. "Dr. Rainey, where are you?" She momentarily felt silly calling the man Dr. Rainey at a time like this, but wondered if he would even respond if she started yelling Doug. "Dr. Rainey? Are you okay?" There was no response, and she started to grow concerned. She tried to think positively. Maybe he woke up and went to go get help? Maybe he was taken by whoever shot them down?

She accidentally kicked something on the ground that felt like a heavy soccer ball. She looked to down to see a hairy blob that appeared to be a dead animal of some sort. She was confused. "What the fuck is that?" she said, taking a step back. She used her foot to kick it over, and it was at that moment all the blood drained from her face.

It was Dr. Rainey's head.

CHAPTER 12

The birds were chirping very loudly. That's what Val first thought as she regained consciousness.

She quickly realized that she had already had this thought mere minutes ago. She must have been dreaming, right? She must have imagined waking up in a field to find a crashed helicopter and her boss's decapitated head. She was probably lying on the grass of the South Mall of the University of Texas right now, catching a quick nap between classes. The bell from the clock tower would start ringing any second.

"You okay?" Huey said.

Val opened her eyes to see Huey kneeling over her, his face bloody and bruised. She hadn't been dreaming after all. She was indeed lying amongst the wreckage of the 1986 Bell 206.

"Shit," Val said. "Did I pass out?"

"Yeah. You fainted after seeing…well…" Huey gestured over to a small blue tarp that had been placed over Dr. Rainey's head. Sadness immediately washed over her. Dr. Rainey was an oddball and a bit of a jerk, but she liked him.

"You find his body?"

"Yeah, over there." Huey gestured over to another, larger blue tarp about fifty feet away. "I thought about putting them together, but I wasn't sure if I should move anything."

Val stood up and looked around. Ernie was now leaning against a tree, his arm in a splint. He had his eyes closed and seemed to be in pain. "Is Ernie okay?" she said.

"Not really," Huey said. "His arm's in pretty bad shape. I gave him some acetaminophen from the emergency kit, but I don't think it's doing much." They walked over to Ernie, who opened his eyes and looked up to them. He was out of it.

"How long until they get here?" Ernie said.

"Who?" Huey said.

"The rescue people."

"What rescue people?"

"Don't you have like an emergency beacon or something?"

"I have a radio. I *had* a radio. It's busted." Huey pointed to the cockpit of the helicopter. "Everything is busted. We're lucky the emergency kit survived."

"So no one knows we're here?" Ernie said with an accusatory tone.

Huey stared at him for a moment, unsure of how to respond to this. "You wanted this to be a secret, remember? You paid me to not write down a flight plan. You paid me to not tell anyone where we were going. Therefore, I didn't."

"So you didn't tell anyone?" Ernie said. "Anyone at all?"

"What did I just say, Mr. Swords? No. No, I didn't. The only person who knows we're here is whoever shot us down."

"And where are they?"

"I don't know. Maybe they didn't see where we crashed."

"Oh this is perfect, Huey. This is just perfect. You've really fucked us now."

"Look, you're in shock and you're getting upset—"

"I'm not in shock. I'm not in fucking shock. I'm just fucking pissed off right now. I can't believe you didn't tell anyone where we were going."

"Excuse me?" said a gruff man's voice from behind them.

Val perked up. She really, really hoped that Dr. Rainey's decapitated head hadn't decided to start talking.

"Over here."

She turned around to see a man standing in the woods staring at them. He looked to be in his seventies, had a long graying beard, and was dressed head-to-toe in what appeared to be animal pelts. He held a walking stick in his hand and had a toothpick jutting out of his mouth. A coonskin cap sat atop his head, and Val remembered about how Dr. Rainey once told her Davy Crockett did in fact wear a coonskin cap, and it was one of the few things about the Old West that the movies got right.

"You folks all right?" the man said.

The three stared at him for a very long time. No one was sure what to say. The man just stared back at them, waiting for an answer. He seemed to be growing impatient. "I asked if you folks were all right?"

"Who are you?" Huey said.

"Name's Rawlings. James Rawlings, but most people call me just Rawlings. How about you, stranger?"

"Huey. What are you doing here?"

"I heard all the commotion earlier so I thought I'd come over to see what the ruckus was. Looks like you all had an accident of some kind." Rawlings eyed the helicopter, confused. "What the hell did that used to be?"

"Are you with the Army?" Huey said.

"The Army? No. Are *you* with the Army?"

"No, we're not."

"I'm a trapper" Rawlings said. "Like my daddy and his daddy before him and his daddy before him. Beaver mostly. The occasional bear or wolf here and there. Best not to mess with the wolves, they don't take too kindly to you skinning 'em and if you kill one you make the whole rest of the pack mighty mad at ya'. I tell you, one thing you don't want is a whole mess of wolves mad at ya'. Those bastards are mean. I offer really good prices if you all are in the market."

"Maybe later," Huey said. "Does the government know you're out here?"

"Government?" Rawlings laughed more. "Government?" He found this very funny for some reason.

"Sir, do you have a phone?" Val said.

"A what?" Rawlings said.

"A phone. To call for help."

"When I call for help, I use this." Rawlings pointed to his throat and laughed some more.

Val gave Huey a look. "I'm getting a serious Ted Kaczynski vibe right now," she said in a whisper.

"Where you folks from?" Rawlings said. "Ain't never seen no clothes like that before." Rawlings gestured to their outfits, everyday jeans and T-shirts that had become dirty and speckled with blood. "You from San Francisco? I hear they dress all funny in San Francisco."

"Las Vegas," Huey said.

"Las Vegas? Didn't know nobody lived there. Thought people just passed through."

Rawlings noticed Ernie's arm and took a step closer to inspect it. "That's a nasty break you got," Rawlings said. Ernie just stared at Rawlings, and Val suspected that he was unsure if the bearded fur trapper was a hallucination brought on by shock.

"Is this guy real?" Ernie said. He looked to Val and Huey. They nodded that he indeed was.

"If you want," Rawlings said, "I can take you folks into town to see the doctor. He should be able to get this arm fixed up. He's good. Pricey, but good."

Rawlings's offer very much got Val, Huey, and Ernie's attention. The three shared a knowing glance.

"Town?" Val said. "Did you say town?"

Rawlings pointed behind them, and she turned to see that he was gesturing to the top of a ridge. She and Huey walked over so that they could stand atop it and look down into a valley below.

Their jaws both dropped.

Before them was a thriving town straight out of the Old West. A long main street was lined with wooden buildings. Houses and farms dotted the landscape surrounding it for miles in every direction. The town was filled with hundreds and hundreds of people going about their day.

Val blinked several times to make sure that what was before her eyes was real. It was. The town was there.

"Where are we?" Val said.

"Why, you're in New Roux City," Rawlings said.

CHAPTER 13

It took Huey about an hour to put together a makeshift stretcher so that he and the others could carry Dr. Rainey down the mountain. He used the blue tarps, and Rawlings seemed to have no issues whatsoever picking up Dr. Rainey's head and putting it with the rest of the body. Rawlings had remarked, "Ain't the first time," when he did it, and Huey didn't care to ask what that meant. Huey gathered up any supplies from the helicopter he could salvage and the group headed for a trail that winded down the mountain. He and Val carried the stretcher, Ernie unable to because of his broken arm. Rawlings had offered to do the heavy lifting instead of Val, commenting it was a "man's work," but she instantly shot down what she referred to as his "old timey macho bullshit." So instead Rawlings led the way, since he knew the trail. When the old fur trapper was far enough ahead out of earshot, Val began to conjecture.

"Okay, so this is secret government property right?" she said. "What if there was like a weird time travel wormhole project going on that we passed right through? Shot us back to the 1800s."

"That's ridiculous," Huey said.

"Oh is it? You ever hear of the Philadelphia Experiment? The army has been messing around with metaphysics since World War Two. There was an *X-Files* episode about it."

"Maybe the girl's right," Ernie said. He trailed behind them and seemed to be a bit dazed, still wincing in pain from his arm. "I mean stranger things have happened."

"What stranger things have happened?" Huey asked. He received no response.

"There has to be some explanation," Val said. "We've either

traveled through time or we're all dead and this is heaven and heaven is fucking terrible."

Huey knew she was right. There had to be some sort of explanation for why they were currently walking towards a fully populated 19th century Old West town. He didn't know what the explanation was just yet, but couldn't help think of the old Sherlock Holmes line he read as a kid. "When you have eliminated the impossible," Huey said, "whatever remains, however improbable, must be the truth."

"What the fuck are you talking about?" Val said. She then raised her voice so Rawlings could hear her. "Hey Rawlings, what year is it?"

"You don't know the year, ma'am?"

"Humor me."

"It's 85."

Huey shot Val a glance. Maybe she was right after all? "Look," Val said returning her voice to a whisper. "We have to remember not to do anything to alter the future. We might screw something up and we get back to the present and there are robot overlords or some shit. And don't tell them anything that hasn't happened yet, like who wins the 1886 World Series or something."

"The World Series wasn't played until 1903," Ernie said.

"You get my point," Val said.

Huey spotted something ahead and gestured to the others. They were approaching a wooden sign that read WELCOME TO NEW ROUX CITY. WHERE ALL OPEN-MINDED ARE WELCOME. Rawlings had already reached the sign and was waiting for the rest of them to catch up. "Good thing we're open-minded," Val said. "At least I think we all are. I barely know you guys."

"Here we are," Rawlings said as they reached him. He gestured to the street about a hundred yards away. "The doc's set up shop down on the end of Main Street, so it ain't too much further."

They continued to walk, and for the first time Huey was able to really get a good look at New Roux City. Main Street seemed to be centered around a three-story clock tower that told him it was 1:03

in the afternoon. Some of the wooden buildings looked to be in better shape than others, the run-down ones overgrown with weeds and littered with garbage that spilled out into the street. He could see signs for a general market, a clothing store, a gunsmith, a bank, several saloons, and something called Madame Jackson's House of Pleasures.

"Holy shit," Val said. "Is that a brothel?"

"Sure is," Rawlings said. "Madame Jackson's got the prettiest girls in town. Will cost you an arm and a leg, though." Rawlings looked to Ernie and laughed. "No offense."

Huey took a closer look at Madame Jackson's House of Pleasures and noticed that several young women, all wearing fairly scandalous dresses, sat in the upper windows and stared at him and the others entering town as if they were Martians. "You know my graduate thesis is about brothels," Val said to him. "I'm examining the relationship between showgirls and prostitutes in frontier towns, and how they were often the same job. I'm comparing this situation to modern day pop stars and their willingness to sexualize their own images for profit and attention. The title is *From the Old West to MTV: Once a Singing Whore, Always a Singing Whore.*"

"Looks like you'll get to do some firsthand research," Huey said. Just about all the people on Main Street had stopped what they were doing and stared at them. The populace appeared surprisingly multicultural. White, black, Hispanic, Asian, and a fair amount of those of mixed race whose exact ethnicity was unclear. The fashions seemed to be an eclectic mixture of styles from the late 19th century. Leather coats, vests, bolo ties, all sorts of hats, an abundance of gloves, and so on. The girls in the brothel window actually seemed to be the only ones wearing dresses, as all the other women in town were dressed just as utilitarian as the men.

"Don't mind all these folks staring at ya'," Rawlings said. "There hasn't been a stranger come to town in quite some time." Rawlings laughed. Huey was beginning to suspect that Rawlings laughed at everything he ever said.

Ernie walked up to keep pace with Huey and lowered his voice.

"They're all carrying," Ernie said. "I mean all of them." Huey hadn't even realized it, but Ernie was right. Every single person on Main Street wore a holster with a six shooter tucked into it, even most of the children save for the very young ones. "But I don't see the Dragoon anywhere," Ernie said. Huey gave him a look, a bit in disbelief that that's what was on the billionaire's mind at this moment as he walked next to the beheaded corpse of his history expert. But Ernie just shook his head, seeming upset with himself. "Damn it," he said. "I should have brought my piece. Why did I listen to you?" Ernie had boarded the helicopter that morning packing a loaded Colt M1911, which he claimed he brought everywhere he went and even had a special permit to take into church. Huey had kindly reminded Ernie that if the group happened to be caught by the Army both trespassing *and* in possession of a firearm, the federal shit storm would be amplified tenfold. Ernie had reluctantly come to his senses and left the pistol in 777's office safe.

They continued to walk down Main Street, the focus of the town's attention as if they were a funeral procession or incredibly boring parade, until Rawlings finally stopped before a small wooden building with a sign that read DOCTOR beside a red cross. "Well, here we go," Rawlings said. He walked over and knocked on the door. "Let's see if the doc's in."

A moment later, the door opened and an old Native American man stepped out. He was thin, and his skin looked weathered. He wore an ornately designed robe and a headdress that seemed to be made of bird feathers. He stared at the group, expressionless.

"Hey, Doc," Rawlings said. "Meet the strangers. Strangers, meet Dr. Thundercloud."

CHAPTER 14

Ernie had never liked doctors. He thought half of them were crooks and the other half quacks. This why he hadn't gone in for a checkup in fifteen years, despite having a wing at St. Luke's Hospital in San Antonio named after him. The charitable contribution had been Misty's idea, she was always bothering him to give to some organization or another, and he had only attended the dedication ceremony in protest. So it wasn't the fact that Dr. Thundercloud was Native American nor that his office looked like a cross between Frankenstein's lab and a voodoo shop in the French Quarter that made Ernie skeptical of the man, it was the mere fact that he was a doctor at all.

After examining Dr. Rainey's body and giving the obvious diagnosis that the poor bastard was dead, Dr. Thundercloud had laid Ernie down on his examination table and started prodding and poking him every which way. Huey and Val watched on from across the room, intrigued by the office's décor. There were dozens of taxidermied animals and jars filled with powders cluttered amongst 19th century medical devices and crudely drawn anatomy charts. A glass case sat on the top shelf that seemed to have live snakes inside of it, and Ernie wondered what medical purpose they could possibly serve.

After a few moments of prodding, Dr. Thundercloud twisted Ernie's arm, this caused Ernie to scream out in pain.

"Did that hurt?" Dr. Thundercloud said.

"What do you think?" Ernie said.

Dr. Thundercloud didn't respond, just continued with his examination. The arm did hurt Ernie like a mother, but it was a pain he had felt several times in his life. He had broken that particular appendage twice before, once when he was a boy and fell off a bull and once when he was in his twenties and he fell off of a surfboard while trying to impress a girl in Galveston. He supposed surviving a helicopter crash blew those two experiences out of the park.

"I didn't realize Roux's wagon train had Native Americans," Val said.

"What is a Native American?" Dr. Thundercloud said.

"An Indian," Ernie said.

"My people, the Cherokee, encountered Etienne Roux in Oklahoma as he journeyed west. We had been forced to leave our land by the government years before, and Roux's message that we should rule ourselves rang true in our hearts. We were accepted into his fold."

"Right, The Trail of Tears," Val said. "You guys really got screwed."

"Screwed?" Dr. Thundercloud said.

"Fucked," Ernie said. "You guys got fucked."

"Yes. We got fucked." Dr. Thundercloud finally stepped away from Ernie and looked them all over. "The ulna is fractured. The bone needs to be set and the wound stitched up."

"Is that something you can do?" Ernie said.

"Yes. We will need to discuss payment."

"Payment?" Huey said.

"Medical treatment is not free."

"Nor would I expect it to be," Ernie said. "This is America after all. Now I can pay you a lot. And I mean a lot. Just not right now. I can get it to you soon, though."

"I need payment up front," Dr. Thundercloud said. He pointed to the 24-carat Movada Series 800 on Ernie's wrist. "That timepiece will suffice."

"This was a gift from my wife."

"You are welcome to visit another doctor."

"Is there another doctor?"

"No."

Ernie took off the watch and handed it over. He wasn't too upset, knowing his wife had bought him two more just like it on the same ski trip she acquired this one. Dr. Thundercloud took the watch and placed it in a drawer. He then grabbed a crude 19th century metallic syringe off of a table and began to fill it with a with a white liquid that had been cooking over a flame. "What is that?" Ernie said.

"It's a natural remedy. We call it Tears of the Moon. A compound extracted from the poppy plant and combined with several other extracts."

"Are you talking about heroin?" Val said. "Are you giving him heroin?"

"Heroin?" Dr. Thundercloud said.

"It pretty much sounds like you just described heroin."

"Tears of the Moon will take the pain away," Dr. Thundercloud said. He screwed the top onto the syringe and tapped it several times. Something seemed to occur to him and gave Huey and Val a look. "Do either of you want some? I can give you a good price."

"Are you now trying to sell us heroin?" Val said.

"I am still unfamiliar with this term heroin."

"Tears of the Moon, whatever. Is that legal for you to just sell it to people who don't need it?"

"Legal?" Dr. Thundercloud said, then laughed for the first time since they had met him. "Nothing is legal here. Nothing is illegal either."

Ernie then realized that in all the commotion and confusion of traveling back in time and walking into New Roux City, he had completely forgotten about the bizarre anarcho-capitalist ideology upon which the place was founded. "So you really have no laws?" Ernie said. "At all?"

"No," Dr. Thundercloud said. "We do not."

"No government of any kind?"

"None whatsoever. We rule ourselves. It's the freedom that Etienne Roux gave us."

It now occurred to Ernie that he had seen neither a jail nor a courthouse when they were walking down Main Street. He hadn't seen a Sheriff, a constable, or any other lawman either. "You're really doing it?" Ernie said. "You're really—"

Ernie was unable to finish his question as Dr. Thundercloud stuck the syringe into his leg and pressed on the plunger. Within seconds, a wave of calmness washed over him and the pain in his arm did in fact go right away. He slumped back onto the bed and looked up to the other three, finding himself unable to speak. All he could do was watch as Huey walked over to the window and pointed out.

"Is Etienne Roux here?" Huey said. "In town?"

"Of course," Dr. Thundercloud said. "Right at the end of Main Street. Feel free to pay him a visit."

CHAPTER 15

Huey stood on a hillside and looked up to Etienne Roux, who leered down at him from on high. Etienne wore a three-piece suit, a wide-brimmed hat, and a holster on his hip.

Etienne was nine feet tall and weighed forty tons. He was a statue erected atop a grave in the center of New Roux cemetery. An inscription was chiseled across the statue's base.

"Authority Does Not Grant Freedom. Freedom Grants Authority."
—Etienne Roux

April 4th, 1832 – July 19th, 1931.
Died of Natural Causes.

"We didn't travel back in time, Huey." Val said. She stood beside him, her eyes locked on the statue of Etienne Roux.

"I've realized that," Huey said.

"So why did that Rawlings guy say it was '85?"

"I have no idea." A lot was racing through Huey's brain, but he was at least relieved that they hadn't traveled through some electromagnetic wormhole but instead were still in the present. This made going home a lot simpler than solving the mysteries of the space time continuum.

"So these people?" Val said. "They've just been out here alone for 135 years?" She looked to the town in the distance. "How is that possible?"

"I don't know. I mean, you do read all the time about tribes in the Amazon or Indonesia or wherever that people are still discovering." Huey thought of a newspaper article tacked behind the bar at The

Aviatrix that he had stared at countless times. It showed a photo taken from a helicopter of a tribe in the Acre region of Brazil, the tribesmen throwing spears at the helicopter, thinking it some sort of winged dragon creature. Drunk pilots found this photo hilarious and probably symbolic of something about aviation.

"But that's the Amazon or Indonesia," Val said. "We're in fucking Nevada. We're two hours away from a Cirque Du Soleil show about The Beatles. How has no one ever found them in 135 years?"

"This land has been restricted for the past *eighty* years."

"The government never spotted them?"

"Maybe the government wasn't looking. What are the odds they're scouring satellite photos of the Nevada desert for no reason whatsoever?"

"But if the Army doesn't know we're here, then who shot us down?"

Huey shrugged. It had to have been someone here. Perhaps it was a native who thought they were a winged dragon creature. Val sat down on the ground and leaned against a tombstone, trying to process. "This is blowing my mind right now, Huey," she said. "This is fucking blowing my mind." He felt the sentiment.

He looked out over the cemetery to the long rows of graves, all of which were pointed to face the statue. There were hundreds and hundreds of them, some in better shape than others. These people had been here a long time. He eyed one nearby.

Clyde Perret
October 14, 1865 – February 3rd, 1915.
Killed by Glen Brighton.

He found it a bit crass that credit on a man's grave was given to the one who put him there, but then nothing was really surprising anymore about this place. He eyed another.

Bernadette Cooper
January 6th, 55 – April 15th, 83.
Killed by Cook Woodson.

He noticed that the tombstone didn't look that old, especially not like it had been there since 1983. He read the inscription again, and then a third time. "So Rawlings said it was '85, right?

"Yeah," Val said.

"Look at dates on this tombstone. 55 to 83. I think… I think they just started counting over."

"Counting over from what?"

He did some quick math in his head and it all made sense, or least as much sense as anything could right now. "85 years ago, it was 1931. According to that statue, Etienne Roux died in 1931."

"The guy died and they just started time over? Roman emperors used to do that, man. Are we dealing with some Julius Caesar-level shit here?"

"I don't know what level shit we're dealing with here," Huey said. He looked to the next tombstone.

Marcus Crider
March 3rd, 30 – November 24th, 71.
Killed by Cook Woodson.

He noticed that the same name, Cook Woodson, was listed as the killer. He wasn't sure whether or not to be impressed by this fact. For a brief moment, he thought that maybe Cook Woodson was a lawman of some kind, then he remembered there were no lawmen here in New Roux City. He looked to the next tombstone.

Walter Chow
December 13th, 65 – March 28th, 81.
Killed by Cook Woodson.

Another notch in Cook Woodson's belt, this one a sixteen-year-old. Huey looked to Val, who was still sitting on the ground leaning against the tombstone and staring into the void. "I'm going to take a look around for a minute."

"Okay. I'll be right here contemplating," Val said.

He walked down one of the long rows, eyeing the names.

He counted seventeen more tombstones giving credit to Cook Woodson, the last of which was covered with fairly fresh dirt.

Pauline Hancock
June 30th, 25 – May 18th, 85.
Killed by Cook Woodson.

May 18th had been only a week before. Whoever this Cook Woodson was, he was still racking up a lot of points. Huey was about to move on to the next grave, but something caught his attention and he stopped in his tracks.

He smelled smoke.

He sniffed the air. It was tobacco smoke.

He looked over to see a woman in her thirties sitting atop a tombstone with her arms folded, a hand-rolled cigarillo dangling from her lips. The woman wore a red wool coat, a red hat, and red gloves.

She stared at Huey for a moment, expressionless, and sucked on the cigarillo. "You taking a little tour of the bone orchard?" she said. She circled her finger in the air. "Seeing the sights?"

"Uh, yeah." Huey said. "Just looking around."

"Not too pleasant of a view, I'd think. Why, in fact, one might say it's downright foreboding." She took another drag and blew a fairly impressive smoke ring into the air. "You in here all by yourself?"

Huey wasn't sure how to respond, unsure of the woman's intentions. He glanced over to see that Val was out of view across the cemetery, probably still seated on the ground with her blown mind. "Yeah," he said.

"How rude of me, I neglected to make an introduction," the woman said. "I'm Pearl, and these are my associates Rose and Maria." He then heard footsteps and turned around to see that two more women now stood right behind him. These women seemed equally as humorless and were also wearing red coats, hats, and gloves.

Pearl flicked the cigarillo to the ground and stomped it out with her red boot. She took a step closer to Huey, then slightly opened her coat to reveal a holstered silver revolver. "Now how about you come with us?" she said.

CHAPTER 16

Ernie slowly opened his eyes and looked around to discover that he was still lying in Dr. Thundercloud's office. He was groggy, but felt pretty damn good all things considered. The Tears of the Moon worked like a charm. He had never really been a drug user, legal or illegal. Sure there was a hot moment in the '80s when he dabbled in cocaine, since everyone else was doing it and no one knew it was bad for you yet, but he preferred to have his wits about him at all times. A cold Coors Light was all he needed to take the edge off.

He glanced down to his arm, which was now set in a crude cast hung in a sling around his neck. He knocked on the cast, and it was indeed very stiff.

"Don't do that," Dr. Thundercloud said. Ernie looked over to see that the old man was sitting at a desk in the corner lighting a gas lamp.

"How long was I out?" Ernie said. The sun was beginning to set out the window, casting an orange glow over the room.

"A couple hours," Dr. Thundercloud said as he walked over to him. "The arm should heal. Don't move it. If you feel pain, you can take this. It is included in the price of treatment." Dr. Thundercloud placed a vial of white powder into Ernie's hand, and Ernie noticed that the 24-carat Movada Series 800 was now on the doctor's wrist. Ernie shook his head, then eyed the vial.

"Is this more Tears of the Moon?" Ernie said.

"A lower dosage." Dr. Thundercloud gestured to the door. "You will need to leave soon. Lodging was not included in the price of treatment."

"What happened to the people who came in with me?"

"They left to look around. They have not returned."

"Is there a hotel you would recommend?"

"There are no hotels in New Roux City."

"What kind of town doesn't have ho—?"

Ernie did not get to finish his query, because the office door was kicked wide open and a large, burly man walked into the room. The man donned a thick beard and a well-worn brown duster over a black shirt and black pants. A revolver hung in a holster around his waist. Ernie took notice of crisscrossing bullet belts that the man wore over his chest forming an "X." He had always associated this with Pancho Villa, the Mexican revolutionary who also had a chain of Tex-Mex restaurants in San Antonio named after him.

"Shit," Dr. Thundercloud whispered under his breath.

"Where is it?" the man said.

"I told you," Dr. Thundercloud said. "You can have it when you pay me for it."

The man didn't care for that response. He stepped closer and looked Dr. Thundercloud right in the eyes. "Or how about you give it to me now, and we'll chalk this up as an IOU situation?"

"That's what you said last time."

"And did we pay you?"

"No. No, you didn't. You haven't paid me in months. You cannot keep doing this."

"Are you in the business of telling us what we can and cannot do now, Doc?" The man took another step closer. "Tell me, can I do this?" The man held out his hands, showing off two black leather gloves. He began to remove one of the gloves, but Dr. Thundercloud reached over and stopped him.

"It's all right," Dr. Thundercloud said. "I'll get it for you. It will be an IOU situation."

"I was hoping you'd say that," the man said.

Dr. Thundercloud turned and walked to a cabinet in the corner. It was filled with a dozen glass jars, each filled to the brim with marijuana buds. "Which kind did he prefer?" Dr. Thundercloud said.

"Not the stuff from the last time, but the time before. The stuff last time made him all antsy."

Dr. Thundercloud selected one of the jars and began to transfer some of the buds into a smaller metal box. "I don't understand why you cannot pay me on time," Dr. Thundercloud said. "Roux is the richest man in town."

This caught Ernie's attention and he perked up. "Roux?" Ernie said. "Etienne Roux?"

The bearded man with crisscrossing bullet belts looked over, confused. He hadn't noticed Ernie lying there. "Who the fuck are you?" the man said. He then looked to Dr. Thundercloud. "Who the fuck is this?"

"He's a stranger," Dr. Thundercloud said.

"A stranger? Since when are there fucking strangers in town?"

"Rawlings found three of them up near the pass. Says they crashed in some sort of flying locomotive contraption."

"What? Where the fuck they from?"

"Why don't you ask him? He's sitting right there."

The man turned to Ernie. "Where the fuck you from, stranger?"

"San Antonio," Ernie said.

"San Antonio?" The man looked back to Dr. Thundercloud. "Why was Roux not told about this?"

"They just arrived a few hours ago," Dr. Thundercloud said.

Ernie could tell the bearded man was not pleased with this response. He grabbed the box of marijuana buds from Dr. Thundercloud and turned to leave. "We're supposed to be kept abreast of things," the man said. "He's not going to like this." The man walked out, leaving the door open.

Dr. Thundercloud walked over to close the door, discovering it no longer sat correctly on the hinges after being kicked open. He sighed.

Ernie sat up a little more. "So that guy works for Etienne Roux?"

"Etienne Roux has been dead for eighty-five years. He was referring to Miller Roux, Etienne's great-great-great-grandson."

Ernie thought about this, slowly putting it all together. "I thought you said your family met up with Etienne Roux in Oklahoma and was welcomed into the fold?"

"Yes, my ancestors. But I was born here in New Roux City, just like everyone else."

Huey had been right with that Sherlock Holmes quote that Ernie could no longer remember. They hadn't traveled back in time at all. Ernie rubbed his eyes, then pointed at the door. "And so then who was that?"

"That was Miller Roux's right-hand man," Dr. Thundercloud said. "A real asshole by the name of Cook Woodson."

CHAPTER 17

Huey counted twenty-seven prostitutes currently staring down at him from the interior balcony of Madame Jackson's House of Pleasures, far more than he had ever seen in one place at one time. Growing up in Las Vegas, he had actually been exposed to his fair share of women of the night. Because of a 1971 ordinance, prostitution was legal in the state of Nevada, but only in counties with a population under 400,000. This meant that Las Vegas was technically ineligible, and sex workers there lived in a grey area where they referred to themselves as "escorts" and advertised in the yellow pages or on fliers handed out by day laborers. Pretty much everyone, including the police and the casinos, had decided to turn a blind eye to these women knowing that they were fairly harmless and provided what some considered a service to the community. If a potential john was ambitious, however, he could drive to a different county and visit one of the twenty-eight licensed brothels in the state. Huey had only done this once, when he was nineteen and his friends thought it would be a good idea to drink several cases of beer and take Benny Portnoy to the Rooster Coop Ranch so that he could lose his virginity to two girls at the same time. After arriving to the brothel, the group of teenagers quickly abandoned this plan when they learned that fifteen minutes alone with one girl cost $150, and two at the same time cost $500. Collectively they had only raised $70, an amount that the girls of the Rooster Coop Ranch found rather insulting.

The twenty-seven women currently staring down at Huey as he stood in the ornately decorated parlor were more morbidly curious. He couldn't help but feel like he was on trial, and the women sat in the gallery of the courtroom waiting to hear the verdict. He glanced over to Pearl, Rose, and Maria who stood against the wall with a half dozen other women wearing the same all-red outfit and thought they resembled bailiffs. Before him sat Madame Josephine Jackson in a red velvet chair, and she was clearly the judge.

Madame Jackson was a distinguished black woman in her fifties who wore a fitted mid-19th century business suit and not too much makeup. She carried herself very, very seriously. Huey noticed that she had amazing posture, something he never noticed about anyone, which meant it must have been exceptional.

"A helicopter?" Josephine said. "A flying machine?"

"That's right," Huey said. "Been flying one all my life."

"Not very well, apparently."

The prostitutes laughed, as did Pearl and her red-clad associates. Huey had learned on the walk over from the cemetery that Pearl's group referred to themselves as the "Crimson Guard," and they were under Madame Jackson's employ to provide security and "whatever else she required." He remembered from when he was a kid that the Crimson Guard was the name of an elite group of evil soldiers in the *G.I. Joe* comic books, but he chose not to bring this up in fear that one of the women would shoot him.

"Are helicopters common in Las Vegas?" Josephine said.

"Well, they're pretty expensive. It's not like everyone has one parked out front of their house."

"Are you able to fix it? Do you plan on flying out of here?"

"No, it's destroyed."

Josephine thought about this for a moment, then nodded. She slowly stood up and walked over to Huey, looking him right in the eye. "Look, Huey," she said. "Can I call you Huey?"

"Sure."

"Let me be straight with you. I don't believe a single goddamn word that you say."

"Excuse me?"

"Etienne Roux passed on many words of wisdom from his struggle to start a new life. The most important being what?"

Josephine looked up to the prostitutes on the interior balcony like a schoolteacher looking to call on a student for the right answer. "Trixie?"

Trixie, a young blonde woman wearing too much lipstick and a pink negligee, stepped up. "If strangers ever come to town," Trixie said, "then don't believe a goddamn word they say."

"That's right," Josephine said. She looked back to Huey and smiled. "You see, our founders knew that it could take five years or it could take five hundred, but eventually people would discover us, and then try to fill our minds with how our way of life was wrong or sinister. How things were better out there in the 'real world.' We would need to understand that they would be 100% full of Grade-A bullshit."

"Grade-A bullshit," Pearl said. The other Crimson Guard members nodded in agreement.

"So are you the one in charge of New Roux City?" Huey said, looking Josephine in the eye.

"No one is in charge of New Roux City, Huey. We have no leaders. No mayor. No town council. We are in charge of ourselves. And me? I'm just a businesswoman who asked you here today to tell you face-to-face that I don't want any trouble."

"There won't be any trouble," Huey said. "We don't exactly plan on sticking around. If no one comes looking for us in the next couple of days, I'll go out on foot to get help." This comment caused just about everyone in the room to laugh. Huey felt like there was an inside joke that he certainly wasn't part of.

"Go out on foot?" Josephine said. "We are smack dab in the middle of a desert. An unforgiving desert. If the heat doesn't kill you, then the thirst will. You can carry ten gallons of water on your back, but you will perspire twenty by the end of the day."

"What about horses?" Huey said. "I could borrow one. Pay you back." He had ridden a handful of horses in his life, and while not an expert, was fairly confident in his abilities. Especially if it meant getting out of this place.

"Horses?" Josephine laughed. "Have you seen any horses, Huey?"

Now that she brought it up, it seemed glaringly obvious. He hadn't seen a single horse since they arrived, and he hadn't even spotted one from up on the ridge when they first saw the whole town. There were no hitching posts, no stables, no signs of horses anywhere.

"We have no horses," Josephine said. "We have chickens. We have cows. We have pigs. Perhaps you could ride a pig out?" The women in the room laughed again.

"Etienne Roux's wagon train had horses," Huey said. "What happened to them?"

"He killed them all."

"Who did?"

"Etienne Roux."

He gave Josephine a look. That's not the answer he was expecting. "What?" he said. "Why?"

Josephine once again looked up to the row of prostitutes above them, choosing someone to give the right answer. "Tell them why, Margaret."

Margaret, a young Asian woman wearing a silk robe, stepped up. "Because once he found this valley, far removed from the rest of the world, Etienne Roux knew he had found a place to build a perfect utopia. He knew it could only exist over time, and that would require patience. He knew that some wouldn't hold that patience and would want to abandon the dream, so he made sure abandonment was impossible."

Huey thought Margaret sounded like a high school student reciting a poem in front of the class that she had memorized but never once thought about figuring out the meaning of. "By killing all the horses?" Huey said. "That's insane."

The room grew very, very quiet.

Huey could immediately feel the daggers that were being stared at him. It was if he had walked into the middle of Sunday morning mass and insulted Jesus.

"Etienne Roux was a complicated man," Josephine said. "But he was a great man."

"I'm sorry," he tried to save face. "I'm sure he was in fact wonderful. But you're saying there's no way to leave New Roux City?"

Josephine leaned back in her chair and put her hands in the air. "Nope. Not unless one of your flying helicopter friends comes looking for you."

Huey closed his eyes and let out a sigh. It was finally beginning to dawn on him that he probably wouldn't make it back in time for Jenny's graduation.

CHAPTER 18

It took Val a good half an hour to notice that Huey had disappeared from the cemetery. She was often one to daydream, especially when working on song lyrics or cutting up toppings at The Onion Pizza, and as she leaned against the tombstone and reflected on the ramifications of her current situation, the time just flew by. Once she realized that Huey was in fact missing, she searched the entire graveyard up and down and could find no trace of him.

She decided to head back into town to check on Ernie. She walked towards Main Street, and as she got closer she noticed that some shop owners were closing up for the night while others were lighting up gas lamps and torches to throw light on their establishments. There were no centralized street lamps, and Val wondered if this was a result of the lack of a civic government to erect them.

"Hey there, pretty lady," a voice said.

Val looked over to see a young man wearing a bowler hat and big smile. He couldn't have been more than fourteen, and his three-piece suit seemed a size too big. He held a couple books in his hands and wore a revolver around his waist. "What's a beautiful flower like you doing out all alone on a beautiful evening like tonight?"

Val looked around, a bit confused. "Are you talking to me?"

"Who else would I be talking to?" The young man took a step closer and looked her up and down. "I heard there were strangers in town, but not no one mentioned how straight up beautiful they was. At least how beautiful one of them was, that is."

"Thanks," Val said. She felt like one of her friend's kid brothers was putting the moves on her.

"My name's Walt. You?"

"Valerie." She gestured to the books he was holding. "You just get out of school, Walt?"

"Sure did. Been a long day. How about I buy you a drink?" Walt gestured behind him to a saloon with a sign that read "The Prospector" hanging out front. "You like whiskey?"

"How old are you?" Val said.

"Just turned fifteen, as a matter of fact." He was very proud of this.

"Are you old enough to be—?" she didn't bother to finish, realizing that of course he was old enough. This kid must have been old enough to do whatever he wanted in a town without laws. There must be no drinking age, no gambling age, and from what she saw at Dr. Thundercloud's, recreational drugs aplenty. She assumed that New Roux City would have been a blast for spring break when she was an undergrad.

"Come on, just one." Walt gestured over to the Prospector and gave a wink. "For starters, at least."

Val thought it over, eyeing the saloon. She knew this probably wasn't a good idea and that she should probably check on Ernie and/or find Huey. "Sure," she said.

Walt nodded and led her over by the hand, holding open the swinging doors so she could step inside. The Prospector was a big place and Val's first impression was that it looked just like she imagined an Old West saloon would. There was a long bar with a row of wooden stools before it and an older barkeeper standing behind. Several tables scattered the room, and Val spied a group playing what appeared to be poker. An old upright piano sat in the corner looking like it hadn't been played in years.

This all met Val's expectations, but what she never could have imagined was the abundance of children in the place. One of the poker players looked to be about ten and had a cigarette dangling out of his mouth. A couple tweens in the corner were smoking out what looked to be a 19th century bong and laughing at god knows what. A little girl who looked around twelve sat at the bar with a slew of empty shot glasses before her.

Walt gestured for Val to sit at one of the bar stools and she did so. She noticed that people were staring at her, but not nearly as many as she was expecting. Perhaps the exotic allure of strangers had already passed, or perhaps they were too drunk to even notice if a giraffe was taking a seat at the bar.

"Evening," the old barkeeper said.

"Evening, Shaky," Walt said. "Two whiskeys, please."

"Coming right up." Shaky nodded and disappeared.

"Hey, you're one of the strangers, right?" a voice said. Val realized it was the twelve-year-old girl sitting at the bar with the slew of shot glasses before her. Val could now clearly see that the girl was cradling a bottle of what looked like moonshine and was extremely drunk.

"You're from out there," the twelve-year-old girl said. She pointed to nowhere in particular.

"Yeah," Val said. "I'm from out there, I guess."

"What's it like?"

"Um, It's—"

"Liar!" the twelve-year-old girl said. "You're a fucking liar!" The girl laughed uproariously.

"Be nice, Claudia," Walt said.

"Fuck you, Walt." The little girl turned away from them, returning to her stupor. Val found herself strangely more surprised by the girl's liberal use of f-bombs than the fact that she was drunk on moonshine.

Walt shook his head. "I apologize for that. She'll learn how to hold her liquor soon enough. Shit, I was a bad drunk until I was thirteen."

"Good God, where are her parents?" Val said in a whisper.

"Dead," Walt said.

"Then who looks after her?"

Walt gave Val a look, confused. Shaky returned and set down two whiskeys before them. "There you go," Shaky said. "That'll be 100,000."

Val's eyes widened and she gave Shaky a look. "100,000? Dollars? For two whiskeys?"

"No," Walt said and laughed. "100,000 roux." He pulled out a handful of copper coins from his pocket and Val eyed them. The coins had been crudely engraved with the image of Etienne Roux's profile and "25 MILLION ROUX" was written across the front.

"Wow," Val said. "Guess you guys don't have anyone to regulate inflation, huh?"

"Inflation?"

"Nevermind."

Walt raised his glass of whiskey and they toasted. They both took the shots, and Val thought it actually went down pretty smooth. Walt didn't even flinch and slammed down the shot glass upside down on the bar. "That's what I like," he said. "That's what I fucking like."

Val gave him a smile, but deep down she couldn't shake the feeling that this whole situation was all very, very wrong. Being able to drink and smoke and do god knows what at any age sounded good in theory, but now seeing it in practice it was just sad.

She looked around the bar to try and get this out of her mind and just do as the Romans do, despite the unsettling nature of Rome. She noticed an oil painting of Etienne Roux hanging above the fireplace. They were really fond of this guy. She noticed something else hanging next to the painting, and it caught her attention mostly because she had no idea what the hell it was. It looked to be a giant monthly calendar made of slate, and a different combination of names was written on each of the next four days.

SATURDAY MAY 21st – HAWKINS/CHAVEZ
SUNDAY MAY 22nd – WANG/LEE
MONDAY MAY 23rd – BIENVENU/WOODSON
TUESDAY MAY 24th – MACKENZIE/CHAMBERS

Val tapped Walt on the arm, then gestured to the calendar. "What's that?" she said. He looked over.

"That's our Showdown schedule."

"Your what?"

"Oh, right. You're a stranger. I forget, since it seems like we've known each other forever." She couldn't help but roll her eyes. "It's a bit complicated to explain," he said "It's when…" He trailed off, as if having a realization. "Actually…" He grabbed one of the books he had been holding and pushed it over to her. She looked down to see that it was a schoolbook entitled *The Showdown and You: A Guide For Young People.*

"You should just borrow this," he said. "You might need it."

CHAPTER 19

An excerpt from the book The Showdown and You:
A Guide For Young People, 3rd Edition *by Hannah Hancock.*
Chapter entitled "The Showdown Conditions"

As was discussed in Chapter Three, The Showdown was created by
Etienne Roux in 1880 after Henry Brown was accused of stealing
one of Alexander Washington's sheep. The founders understood
that even though the town was an idyllic community that existed in
harmony, occasionally an injustice may occur and need to be settled.
It is important to understand that The Showdown is not a law, but
an understood set of conditions that the city's founders agreed upon
and the residents have upheld ever since.

The conditions were inspired by the Irish Code Duello, a
series of prerequisites addressing the practice of pistol dueling and
its codes of honor, which was written in 1777 and prescribed for
general adoption throughout Great Britain. Etienne Roux admired
the Code Duello, but he understood that one hundred years had
passed since its inception and there had been advancements in both
firearm mechanics and the general American code of civility. He set
out to draw up a set of twenty-one new conditions, referred to only
as "The Showdown Conditions," and the founders unanimously
agreed upon them. The conditions have remained the same ever
since, and all the citizens of New Roux City agree that it is by far the
fairest system of justice for our community.

The conditions are thus…

1. Upon a child's fifteenth birthday, he or she is to carry a firearm at all times. The firearm may be concealed or unconcealed. The firearm is to be purchased from the gunsmith shop by the child's parents. If the child's parents are deceased or unable to afford the firearm, then a credit arrangement may be drawn up between the child and the gunsmith.

2. All citizens over the age of fifteen are to carry a pair of gloves at all times. The gloves may be made of any material that the citizen chooses. The gloves do not need to be worn on the hands, but must be on the citizen's person.

3. If at any time a citizen feels that an injustice has been committed against him or her, he or she (henceforth "The Offended") may approach the person that they feel committed the injustice (henceforth "The Offender") and initiate a Showdown.

4. A Showdown is initiated by The Offended removing one of his or her gloves and throwing it to the ground before The Offender. The words "I demand satisfaction" must be spoken loudly and clearly so that The Offender understands that a Showdown has been initiated.

5. The Offender may allow the glove to remain on the ground and apologize for the injustice, offering to make any reparations if it is deemed appropriate. If The Offended accepts the apology, he or she is to reclaim the glove and shake the hand of The Offender. There will be no Showdown.

6. If the Offender wishes to further pursue The Showdown, he or she is to pick up the glove and strike The Offended once upon either side of the face with it. The words "I accept your showdown" must be spoken loudly and clearly. The strike is not to be so hard as to cause any injury that would affect the Offended's performance in The Showdown.

7. A Showdown is to be scheduled for noon the following day to allow for a cooling-off period. If a Showdown is accepted by The Offender after midnight, then it is to be scheduled at noon on the day after the following.

8. The Offender is permitted to apologize to The Offended at any

point during the cooling-off period. If The Offended accepts the apology and the two parties shake hands before a witness, then The Showdown will be called off. The cooling-off period is to last until one hour before The Showdown, after which no apologies may be offered or accepted.

9. Only one Showdown is allowed per day. If a Showdown is already scheduled for the following day, then the second Showdown is to be postponed until the day after the following. If a third Showdown is accepted, then it is to be postponed until two days after the following and so on.

10. Upon The Showdown being accepted by the Offender, both duelers are to name a "second." The second may be any citizen over the age of fifteen who accepts. The responsibilities of the second are as follows.

    A. Attempt to reconcile the two duelers and reach an apology if possible.

    B. Ensure that his or her dueler arrives to The Showdown on time and properly armed.

    C. If his or her dueler is injured as a result of The Showdown, ensure the dueler receives proper medical care.

    D. If his or her dueler is killed as a result of The Showdown, ensure the dueler receives a proper burial.

11. The clock tower at the center of Main Street is to be the official time for The Showdown.

12. Showdowns are to take place on Main Street. All citizens not participating in The Showdown are to be clear of the street by 11 a.m. Spectating from the sidewalks is permitted and encouraged.

13. The duelers are to take positions on Main Street at 11:54. They are to stand at a distance of twenty paces apart. The Offended is to face north and The Offender is to face south.

14. Between 11:55 and 11:59, both The Offended and The Offender are allowed to make final statements regarding the injustice which spurred The Showdown. The Offender may speak first and not exceed two minutes. The Offended may

have the last word and also not exceed two minutes. No one else, whether spectator nor the other dueler, is allowed to speak during this statement period.

15. At 11:59, the two duelers are to hold their hands over their respective holsters without physically touching their firearms. Between 11:59 and 12:00, the two duelers are to remain silent.

16. When the clock tower chimes 12:00, the two duelers are to retrieve their firearms and fire upon one another.

17. If neither dueler is injured after the first shot, then the duelers may do one of the following.
    A. Agree that The Showdown is a draw. This is done by both duelers saying the words "satisfaction has been brought" in a loud and clear voice and shaking hands. The Showdown is now complete.
    B. Continue firing.

18. If one dueler is injured and unable to further fire his or her firearm, the non-injured dueler may declare that The Showdown is complete. The non-injured dueler may do this by reholstering his or her firearm and saying the words "satisfaction has been brought" in a loud and clear voice.

19. If both parties are injured and unable to further fire their firearms, then The Showdown is complete. If one or both parties is killed, then The Showdown is complete.

20. Upon the completion of The Showdown, the winner—if still alive—may take possession of the loser's firearm as a spoil.

21. If any of the prior conditions are not properly followed by The Offended, The Offender, their respective seconds, or any citizen, then he or she will be considered to be in violation of The Showdown Conditions. The violator is to be shot dead on sight by any other citizen of New Roux City over the age of fifteen.

CHAPTER 20

Huey sat before the fireplace in an abandoned one-room house a mile from town and stared into the burning embers. Madame Jackson had told him that he and his friends were free to squat in any of the dozens of abandoned houses littered around New Roux City whose owners had passed away. They had chosen this one, because other than a thick layer of dust, the house looked just the way that a schoolteacher named Jeb Gant left it three months before, when he walked down to Main Street to get shot down by his ex-wife.

He shifted his gaze to Val, who sat beside him wrapped in a handmade quilt. She had just finished reading aloud the chapter from *The Showdown and You: A Guide for Young People* and closed the book. "The inmates are running the asylum," Huey said.

"Yeah. We need to get the fuck out of here," Val said.

"Like I said, we can't. According to Madame Jackson there's no way out."

"And you believe her?"

"Well, the sample size for people successfully leaving New Roux City seems to be zero, so yeah I'm likely to believe her."

Val stood up and started to pace back and forth. She glanced over to Ernie, who sat in a rocking chair by the window and seemed a little out of sorts. "When will your people realize something has gone wrong?" she said.

"What?" Ernie said through his fog.

"Your people. Your wife. Your executive assistants, I don't know. Were you supposed to call anyone tonight?"

"How am I supposed to call my wife? We're stuck out here. My phone doesn't get any reception."

Val studied his eyes. "Are you fucking high right now, Ernie?"

"Yeah," Ernie said. "I'm pretty sure. My arm started hurting so I took some of this stuff." Ernie revealed the vial of white powder that Dr. Thundercloud had given him. "He didn't really say how much to take. He really doesn't say a lot."

"We know you can't call your wife," Huey said. "But was she expecting you to call her tonight?"

"I wasn't supposed to call my wife tonight. And I can't call her because I'm not getting any reception." Ernie's words were starting to slur. He pulled an iPhone out of his pocket and showed it off, and Huey noticed that the screensaver was the logo for the San Antonio Swordsmen arena football team. "It's also about to die," Ernie said. "I haven't seen a charger anywhere in this whole goddamn town."

"Okay, let's think about this," Val said. "Misty Swords or whoever will realize Ernie never got back to Vegas, if not tonight then tomorrow. Then she'll probably call the Air Force, right? They'll send a search party to the coordinates of the barn to look for us, right? So basically we're stuck here until your people realize you've disappeared." Val looked to Ernie for confirmation, only to see that he was now asleep in the rocking chair. She sighed.

A blood-curdling scream rang through the air.

It was a woman's voice and sounded as if it was coming from the distance. Ernie didn't seem to notice, off in slumberland. Val turned to Huey. "What the fuck was that?"

Huey ran over and threw open the door. It was incredibly dark outside, with only the moonlight dimly illuminating the landscape. He could make out the silhouettes of several houses in the distance, some with lit oil lanterns hanging out front.

The scream rang out again, and Huey realized it was coming from a house about fifty yards to this left. He started to run as Val stepped into the doorway. "Huey, where are you going?"

"Where do you think?" Huey disappeared into the darkness, and a moment later Val followed. They ran up a dirt road and approached the front porch of the house to see that the door was open.

"Hello," Huey raised his voice. "Are you okay?"

There was no response. He looked back to Val. He could tell that she was scared. "Maybe we should call the police?" she said. Then, "Oh, right."

"Hello?" Huey said again. There was no response. He stepped to the doorway and peered inside. It was a cozy place that appeared to be a family residence. He spotted a few wooden children's toys on the rug before a crackling fireplace. He stepped in and looked around. The place seemed to be empty.

"What do you see?" Val said, still standing on the porch.

"Nothing. I don't think there's anyone here."

"Then who was screaming?"

Huey then heard a rattling behind him. He turned around to see a man in his thirties pointing a shotgun. The man's hands trembled. He didn't seem to be comfortable holding the weapon. Behind the man was a woman and five children huddled together under the kitchen table.

"What are you doing here?" the man said.

"I heard a scream," Huey said. "I apologize for coming into your home. I just wanted to help." The man gave Huey a look as if he'd never been offered help in his entire life, then lowered the shotgun.

"You're not it," the man said.

"I'm not what?" Huey said.

"The Silk Specter."

Val, still standing on the porch, laughed. Huey shot her a look, having no idea what could be so funny.

"Sorry," she said. "It's just there's this graphic novel called *The Watchmen* and the Silk Specter is…you know what, I'll tell you later." She flashed an awkward smile.

"Is it gone?" one of the children under the table said.

"Looks like it," the man with the shotgun said. He set the weapon down and helped his wife up off of the floor. She eyed Huey and Val.

"You all must be the strangers," the wife said. "You're not going to give us any trouble, are you?"

"Our reputation precedes us," Huey said. "No, we're not going to give you any trouble."

"Hey, sorry to interrupt," Val said. She stepped into the doorway. "Cute kids, by the way. But if I could jump back for one second, what exactly is the Silk Specter?"

"It's a phantom," one of the children said. "It comes in the night and sucks your soul."

"It ain't no phantom, dummy," one of the other children said. "It's just a bandit who dresses like a phantom. Wears all black and a black mask and everything. He comes into houses at night and steals your linens."

"Your linens?" Val said.

"That's right," the wife said. She gestured to a wardrobe in the corner that looked like someone had recently rummaged through it. "Tablecloths. Sheets. Napkins. Just the silk and cotton. Always leaves the wool."

"Why would a bandit be stealing your napkins?" Huey said.

"No one knows," the man said. "But he started robbing folks a few years back. Hit a quarter of the houses in New Roux City by now." Huey found this very strange, but still at the bottom of the strangeness totem pole of his last twelve hours.

"Well, sorry again if I scared you all," Huey said. "We'll be on our way." Huey nodded to the family and they all nodded back. He and Val headed out through the door.

They made their way back down the dirt road to the dead schoolteacher's house. Ernie was still passed out in the rocking chair, so Huey gave Val the bed and he lay himself down on a rug on the floor.

As Huey lay there and listened to the crackling fireplace, he gazed out the window at the thousands of stars in the sky. It was a sight one never saw in Las Vegas due to the light pollution, and he really hadn't seen at all since he and Jenny went camping when she was thirteen. He looked at his watch to see that it was only 9:30 even though it felt so much later. Jenny's graduation ceremony had started at 8:00. He assumed that the principal would have given a speech, as would have the valedictorian, and that would have taken about twenty minutes. That meant that because of her position in the procession and the fact that there were about 400 kids in her class, Jenny very well could be walking across the stage to receive her diploma at that exact moment.

CHAPTER 21

Miller Roux sat in the gunsmith workshop and put the finishing touches on his latest custom six-shooter revolver. Miller was a craftsman, and he believed in making every firearm he sold by hand, and by his hands alone.

It was an elaborate process that took days, if not weeks. Miller would start by shaping and machining the gun's frame. He mainly went off of designs created by Etienne Roux or one of his other ancestors. He would then carve the cylinder, cutting slots for ammunition and notches for rotating the cylinder after a shot is fired. After filing down any rough edges, he would then screw the curved trigger guard and the grip to the frame. He would then assemble the wooden grip casing to the metal back strap and attach them to the grip. Once he had confirmed that it was a good fit, he would remove the casing and carve the gun's serial number inside. He would stamp a matching serial number onto the grip, then polish it along with the gun's frame to a glossy finish. Next up was to roll the gun's model number and identifying information onto the gun's barrel, in this cased "Roux Sunfire Special Edition." He would dip the parts into hot salts followed by cold water in a process called "color case hardening," a reaction that both stiffens the pieces together and gives the metal a bronze finish. Once the frame was dry, he would install the cartridge-loading gate onto it and file down the mechanism for rotating the cylinder to make the dimensions perfect. He would then insert a bushing and a pin into the cylinder's center, using that pin to install the cylinder into the gun frame— the pin also serving as the axis for the cylinder to revolve on. If the revolver spun nicely, he would slide a few test slugs into the chambers to confirm that the gap between the cylinder and the frame was correct. He would then affix the gun barrel to the frame and, using a special measuring rod, check the alignment of the cylinder and barrel. If everything checked out, he would tighten the barrel to the gun frame. Miller would then aim the assembled gun at a target across the shop to eyeball the alignment of the barrel to the frame. Once the alignment seemed literally right on target, he would install the gun's hammer and trigger. He would then pop the cylinder back into the gun frame and insert the rod for ejecting spent ammunition. He would then screw a spring into the side of the hammer and cock it into its three different positions to make sure that it was in working order. He would then reattach the grip and assemble a flat spring to it; this was the main spring that transfers energy from the trigger to the hammer to cause the revolver to fire. He would finally take the finished gun behind the shop to the outdoor firing range and make sure everything was in working order with live ammunition. If everything worked precisely as it should, it was time to put the gun up on the shelf for sale.

Miller was about 95% finished with the gun he was currently working on, in the process of attaching the main spring to the grip. He was having a bit of trouble focusing, however, with Josephine Jackson and her red-clad bodyguard staring at him from across the room.

"I haven't laid eyes on the other two yet," Josephine said, "but my girls saw them from the window. An old man and a pretty girl. Something was wrong with the old man's arm. They were carrying a stretcher of the one who died. They left his body with Dr. Thundercloud."

Miller said nothing and didn't look up to her, instead focusing on his work. He had held enough of these little chats with the madam to know that eventually she'd get to the point.

"Are you listening to me, Miller?" she said. She used the schoolteacher tone that worked on her girls, and Miller knew she did this merely to annoy him.

"Of course I'm listening to you, Josephine," he said. "Unlike your whores, I can do two things at once." His man Cook Woodson, leaning against the wall picking his teeth with a nail, laughed at this. Miller always took a small amount of pleasure in making Cook laugh. The man was a rock.

Josephine rolled her eyes and shared a glance with Pearl, the bodyguard standing beside her. "I sat one of them down," Josephine said. "Told him I didn't want any trouble."

"Thank you for your public service to the community," Miller said. "I will deal with the strangers tomorrow."

"Deal with? You don't seem very concerned that these people just waltzed into—"

He slammed the gun down and finally looked up to her, his patience worn thin. He didn't care for anyone to question his role and responsibility to New Roux City, most of all Josephine Jackson. Of course the news of the strangers concerned him, but it was up to him to decide how and when they would be dealt with. "Is that all you wanted to see me about?" he said.

"Actually, no," Josephine said. "We need to discuss the matter of the Hancock farm."

Pauline Hancock was a chicken farmer who lived on the south side of town. She had been shot dead by his man Cook Woodson in a Showdown the week before. He couldn't remember why. "I wasn't aware that there was a matter to discuss," Miller said.

"The matter is that ever since your trained monkey here murdered her, the farm is sitting empty." Josephine gestured to Cook, who seemed to find her description of him amusing. "There are hundreds of chickens on that farm and they need tending to. One of my girls, Suzanne, she's retiring soon so I figure she can take it over and—"

"Retiring? Retiring from what?"

"She'd prefer to spread her legs in the private sector," Josephine said. "Now, Suzanne grew up on a farm and is used to—"

"My men are gonna slaughter those chickens," Miller said.

"Slaughter? You know how many eggs they provide?"

"The Feast is in a few days, and my chef thought roasted

chicken would be a mighty scrumptious dish to serve the guests."
He gave Josephine a look. "Do you not think the people of New
Roux City deserve a scrumptious dish of roasted chicken?"

"I think a good, honest young woman deserves a nice place
to live and find a station in life," she said. He found Josephine's
definition of good and honest mighty suspect.

He finished attaching the spring to the gun and gripped it in his
hand. He eyed the barrel and aimed it at a target across the room.
"It's unfortunate that I don't give a fuck what you think," he said.
"And it's even more unfortunate that I don't give a fuck if one of
your busted whores needs a new job."

"How about you send her over here?" Cook said. He grabbed
his crotch and tugged on it. "I bet I could find a station in life for
her." This made Miller laugh.

"She doesn't work charity cases," Pearl said. Cook shot Pearl
a look.

Josephine took a step closer to Miller, and he looked up to her.
He could tell she was angry, a point she always came to eventually
in these little chats. "It's not up to you to decide what happens with
that farm," she said.

"Huh," Miller said. He then lifted up the gun he had been
working on and aimed it right at Josephine's chest. Pearl instinctively
inched her hand closer to her holstered revolver. "You're right. It's
not up to me."

He pulled the trigger. In the blink of an eye, Pearl pulled out
her revolver and aimed it at him. Cook pulled out his revolver and
aimed it at Pearl.

Click.

The new gun wasn't loaded.

Josephine stared him down, seemingly unfazed. Pearl and Cook
lowered their revolvers. Miller smiled and placed the gun down on
the table.

"Guess it's up to the chickens," Miller said.

CHAPTER 22

Ernie, still feeling a little out-of-sorts courtesy of Tears of the Moon, stood on the corner of Main Street and, for the first time, got a good look at the entire population of New Roux City. There must have been at least 3,000 people lined up waiting to see today's Showdown, crammed into every available space on the sidewalk and pouring out of every open window. Huey and Val had managed to work their way to the middle of the crowd to get a better view, but Ernie had resigned himself to stay in the back and get up on his tiptoes.

"Morning," a voice said. He looked over to see Rawlings sitting on the ground in an alley, leaning against a barrel with a bottle of whiskey in his hand. "How's the arm?"

"Not too bad," Ernie said. "Thanks for asking."

"Dr. Thundercloud give you some Tears of the Moon?"

"He did."

"Whew, keep an eye on that business. It's a snake that'll bite you. Bite you real good." Rawlings laughed at himself and then gestured out to the crowd. "You here for The Showdown?"

"Had to see what all the fuss was about."

"You really got to show up early to get a good spot."

"Yeah, I can see that." Ernie was reminded of The Tournament Of Roses parade, which his wife had dragged him to countless times over the course of their marriage. People would start lining up on the streets of Pasadena at four in the morning just to get a good view of the flower-covered floats and marching bands from around the world. Ernie always just purchased VIP seats in the grandstand

and would have gladly done the same here today, but New Roux City hadn't apparently caught on to the VIP concept yet.

Rawlings slowly stood up and walked over to him, taking a swig from the bottle. "Me, I've seen enough of 'em. Really only come down 'cause everyone else does. Plus I like to lay down a bet here and there." He gestured to a building a few doors down that had a sign reading "Kooper's Card Room" out front.

"You can bet on The Showdown?" Ernie said.

"Oh yeah. It's one of the finest forms of entertainment here in town. Heck, sometimes folks challenge each other to Showdowns just to give people something to wager on. You can bet straight up who you think will win, but the odds aren't always so good. You can also bet on some propositions—if one dueler will just wound the other and if so then where, will one dueler just fire into the air, and so on."

"Why would you just fire into the air?"

"Sometimes folks challenge each other to a Showdown over something trivial. They stand in the street staring each other down and realize the offense isn't really worth maiming or killing somebody over. No harm, no foul."

"Watch yourselves!" a voice said from behind them.

Ernie turned around to see that four large men were moving through the crowd. Each man held onto the end of a pole that was supporting a large metal box with slits cut into the side. "What is that thing?" Ernie said.

"That's Mr. Roux's litter," Rawlings said. "He rides in it for protection."

"Miller Roux is *inside* that box?" Ernie's interest was perked. If there one man in this town who could help him locate the Dragoon, it would be the great-great-great-grandson of the previous owner.

"Yeah," Rawlings said. "That's how he gets to and from Castle Roux up on the mountain." Rawlings pointed to a mountain trail on the edge of town and laughed. "Castle Roux, that's what we all call his house."

The men holding the litter passed by them. Ernie attempted to see inside of it, but the slits were too small and all he could see was darkness. The men reached the gunsmith shop and carried the litter inside, shutting the door behind them.

"Miller Roux doesn't watch The Showdown?" Ernie said.

"Nah," Rawlings said. "Hasn't in years." Rawlings then noticed something out in the street and pointed. "Quiet down. They're about to begin."

Two men were now walking into the street. Both were Asian and looked to be in their early twenties. Ernie glanced to the clock tower to see that it was just about 11:54. The duelers were right on schedule. "What's with these two?" he said to Rawlings in a whisper. "Why are they Showdowning?" He wasn't sure if this was an actual term.

Rawlings squinted at the two men to get a better look, apparently not remembering who exactly was taking part in The Showdown that day. "Oh, these two. This is a classic lover's quarrel. Henry Wong and Gordon Lee. They're engaged and got into a big argument over whose last name they're gonna take once they're married."

Ernie gave Rawlings a look, confused. "Engaged? To each other?"

"I for one think they make a mighty sweet couple," Rawlings said. "If they could just get over this silly surname issue."

"So, gay marriage is le—" Ernie cut himself off, remembering where he was. Of course gay marriage was legal here, since it wasn't not legal.

The clock struck 11:55 and a hush fell over the crowd. Henry Wong, standing in the middle of Main Street facing south, took a step closer to the fiancée he had allegedly offended and began to shout. "Now you listen up, Gordon," Henry said. "I love you to death and you know that. I love you more than all the stars in the sky. You mean everything to me, goddammit."

"That's so sweet," Val said from the middle of the crowd. She was promptly shooshed by an old woman standing next to her. Now that The Showdown had begun, spectators were expected to keep quiet.

"But this is one issue I just can't drop," Henry said. "I'm the last male Wong and it's very important to me that my family name lives on. I don't mind your name, Gordon. I don't mind it at all. Lee is a very fine name. But you got a whole mess of kin with that name and there'll be no shortage of Lee heirs. This is why I feel so passionate about the issue and have refused to budge. That is all I got to say." Henry nodded and stepped back, finished with his speech.

Ernie, along with all the other spectators, eyed the clock. The moment it struck 11:57, Gordon stepped forward.

"Oh Bullshit, Henry!" Gordon said. "The last male Wong? First of all, you up and hated your folks and done nothing but complain about 'em since you and me been together. Second, we're two fellas who can't have no babies therefore we ain't gonna be passing on our name to nobody anyhow! You just want to control me. You want to be the top in the bedroom, and you want to be the top in our marriage. You want to fuck me two ways." Ernie noticed that this statement caused some parents in the crowd to place their hands over the ears of the younger, more impressionable children. "Now I'll say it again," Gordon said. "I'm fine with us just keeping our names how they is. You keep Wong and I'll keep Lee and that's the end of it." Gordon nodded and stepped back, finished with his speech.

The clock struck 11:59 and the street got extremely, extremely quiet. The only thing Ernie could hear was some wind chimes hanging outside a barber shop across the street.

Henry and Gordon both placed their hands over their respective revolvers, staring one another down. The seconds ticked by, and every single citizen of New Roux City waited with baited breath.

The clock continued to tick.

The seconds seemed like hours.

The clock struck twelve and a bell rang out, filling the quiet air. Henry and Gordon pulled their guns and fired.

Bang. Bang.

Gordon dropped his gun and screamed out in pain. He fell to the ground, gripping his left leg, grazed by a bullet. The crowd began to murmur, and there were several cheers from those who had placed bets on Henry Wong.

Henry slowly approached Gordon, a smoking gun still in his right hand. The crowd, unsure of what would happen next, got quiet again. Henry stood over Gordon, casting a shadow over his bleeding future husband, and nodded. "Hope that don't hurt too bad, Mr. Wong," Henry said.

Gordon just shook his head and sighed. "You're a son of a bitch, Henry."

Henry holstered his gun and looked out to the citizens of New Roux City. "Satisfaction has been brought," Henry said in a loud and clear voice. The crowd began to applaud. Ernie wasn't sure whether to join in with the applause and opted not to. A moment later, the crowd began to disperse and return to their daily routines as the show was now over. Ernie noticed that Henry was helping Gordon to sit up, as was a young Asian woman who must have been Gordon's second.

Huey and Val emerged from the crowd to join Ernie, and he thought they looked like they had just gotten off of a rollercoaster. "Did you see that, Ernie?" Val said. "That was fucking intense."

"Oh that was nothing," Rawlings said. "You should see when—"

"Excuse me, strangers?" a man's voice said from behind them. "Could I have a moment of your time?"

They all turned around to see Cook Woodson standing with his arms folded. He wore the same outfit that Ernie had seen him wearing the day before, and from the looks of it he hadn't bothered to bathe in the time since. Rawlings' eyes widened and he gave the three strangers a look. "I'll be seeing you around," Rawlings said. He walked off and disappeared into the crowd.

"I notice you three are unarmed," Cook said. "I know you're new to town, but we here in New Roux City follow what's known as The Showdown Conditions. Are you familiar with them?"

"We are," Huey said. "We read them last night."

"Then you're familiar with Condition #1 that states all citizens of New Roux City over the age of fifteen be armed at all times.

Now, I'm not a medical doctor, but I'm sure as shit you're all over the age of fifteen."

"We're not citizens of New Roux City," Val said. "We're strangers."

"Then congratulations," Cook said. Cook placed one hand over his heart and one in the air as if he was swearing them in. "Because by the authority vested in me, you have just been granted citizenship." He lowered his hands and pointed across the street. "Now I recommend you head on over to the gunsmith shop toot sweet and acquire yourselves three pieces."

"Are you joking?" Val said.

"Do I look like I'm joking?"

"We don't have any money," Huey said. "We can't afford to buy guns." Val shot Huey a glare. She seemed to be in disbelief that he was even entertaining the idea of arming himself.

"Not a problem," Cook said. "You can make an arrangement with the gunsmith."

"What kind of arrangement?"

"That'll between you and Mr. Roux."

"Mr. Roux?" Ernie said. "The gunsmith is Mr. Roux?" Cook nodded. Ernie grew excited and gave the others a look. "Let's do what the man says."

"Are you fucking kidding me?" Val said. "I'm not buying a gun."

"You don't need to buy it," Cook said. "You and the gunsmith can make an arrangement."

"I'm not arranging anything and I'm not carrying a gun. I am a staunch anti-gun advocate and I'm not going to pick up a gun just because of some insane 'condition' written by some insane man 135 years ago."

Ernie could immediately tell that Cook didn't care for Val's statement. Not one bit. Cook took a step towards her and slowly placed his hand on his hip, right next to his holstered six-shooter. "Now you listen to me, you dirty cunt," Cook said with clenched teeth. Val's face went white, and Ernie realized that taunting a mass murderer might not have been the best of ideas. "I also feel the need to remind you of Condition #21, which states that myself, or any citizen of New Roux City, is to shoot you dead in the street for violating any of the other Conditions, including #1." Cook stared Val down. No one moved for what seemed like forever.

"Look," Huey aimed to diffuse the situation. "We'll get guns. We'll all go get guns. Right now. We're not here to cause trouble." Ernie was beginning to feel like they should all get business cards with "we're not here to cause trouble" printed on them.

"Great to hear," Cook said. He took a step back and flashed Val a smile. "And I'm sure you and me'll meet again real soon." Cook turned and walked away, heading down the wooden sidewalk. "And get some new clothes. You all look like goddamn circus clowns."

Huey let out a breath and looked to Val, who stood there in a daze. "You okay?" Huey said.

"I'm fine."

"Let's just go over to the gunsmith and—"

"No," Val cut him off. "Fuck that guy. And fuck Etienne Roux. I'm gonna go eat lunch." She marched across the street to The Prospector Saloon.

Huey shook his head and looked to Ernie. "What about you?" Huey said. "You want to go get a gun?"

"Are you kidding?" Ernie said. "I can't wait."

CHAPTER 23

Val sat in The Prospector at a table near the window and finished up her lunch. She was still upset, and she always ate when she was upset. When she was a teenager, she once took a quiz in *Seventeen Magazine* and learned that she was what's called an "emotional eater." Of course most of her stress at that time came from being picked on by popular girls at school, not threatened by gun-wielding psychopaths. She wasn't sure which one was worse.

She really did feel passionate about guns. She grew up in a rough neighborhood in Los Angeles, and she had attended the funerals of several classmates who thought joining a gang was a viable after-school activity. When she was a kid, her father bought a .22 caliber pistol for protection and wanted Val to learn how to use it. Val refused, saying that if their house needed protecting they should have just gotten a dog. She had always wanted a dog. She still had never had one.

She looked down to the plate in front of her, trying to think about anything else. She had ordered the daily special, which from what she could tell was the only thing that The Prospector offered. It was called "The Kid Pie," and she had to admit it wasn't half bad. She had tried meat pies before, she once had a boyfriend who was really into Middle Eastern food and always brought her Fatayers, a flaky golden pastry usually stuffed with lamb.

"Why do you call this a Kid Pie?" Val said to Shaky as he passed by her table holding a tray of dirty dishes.

"Because it's got kid in it," Shaky said. By the look on his face he wasn't kidding.

"Holy shit. What?" She eyed the bite on her fork and thought about how the taste was unlike anything she'd experienced before. "Like a Donner Party situation?" she said.

"No," Shaky said. "Kid. A baby goat."

She let out a deep breath, relieved that she wasn't eating a small child. She then became mildly upset that she was eating a baby goat, but shrugged it off to a cultural difference and took another bite. "It's pretty good," she said.

"Thanks," Shaky said. "I need to ask you, ma'am. How do you intend to pay for this?" He gestured to the half-eaten pie still on the plate.

"Oh, right. Uh. I actually hadn't thought about that. I mean, I could owe you."

"I don't run tabs here. Not since Chester McGinty refused to pay up and I had to Showdown him. Perhaps you could provide me some kind of service?" Shaky looked Val up and down. "You look able-bodied."

"I'm not a whore," she said. She had said this statement probably a hundred times to her mother in the midst of heated arguments, but had never actually had to say it in a context where someone thought she was a legitimate prostitute.

"That ain't what I mean." Shaky held up his hand to show off a wedding ring. "I'm happily married, ma'am. Got two little ones at home."

"Sorry. I've just seen a lot of whores around here."

"Perhaps you could help me out around the saloon. Maybe wash some of these dishes." He gestured to the tray that he was holding and Val eyed the dishes piled on top of it. She glanced back up, and at that moment the dusty old piano in the corner caught her attention. Something occurred to her.

"What about the piano?" She pointed to it.

"That don't need washing."

"No, what if I played it?"

"Played it?" Shaky thought about this for a moment. "Huh, we ain't had a piano player in years."

"It's awfully quiet in here. Some music could really liven up the place."

"Sure, okay, I guess," he said with a shrug. "Give it a shot." Val smiled and gave him a nod.

She finished up the Kid Pie and then walked over to the piano, wiping off a layer of dust with her napkin. She sat down and thought about what to play. She knew she could easily do one of her originals, but as she looked out over the handful of New Rouxians scattered around the establishment, she realized that none of these people had ever heard any popular music created after 1878. If she were to play a cover, then they would be hearing the song for the first time.

She immediately began to play Alicia Keys's "Fallin'". It was the first song that she had ever learned to play when she was a ten-year-old, and it had remained one of her favorites. She opted to sing the lyrics as well, feeling that it was her duty as The Prospector's new entertainer. She knew she didn't have the greatest voice in the world, but she could hold her own and had actually once won a karaoke competition at a bar in Austin singing this very song while wasted. It felt good to play. She had always used music as a way to release frustrated feelings, and after her recent encounter with Cook Woodson she definitely felt frustrated.

When she was finished with the song, she turned around to gauge the response of The Prospector's patrons and was surprised to see them staring as if they had just seen a ghost. She wasn't sure how to read this. A few seconds passed, and finally an old man with a thick grey beard stood up and began to applaud. One-by-one, all the other patrons stood up and began to applaud as well. Val felt a wave of relief wash over her. The old man walked over, took out a 50,000 roux coin, and placed it in a jar that sat atop the piano. "How about another?" the old man said with a wink. She flashed him a smile.

Over the next few hours, Val played the entirety of Alicia Keys's *Songs in A Minor*, Fiona Apple's *Tidal*, and Tori Amos's *Little Earthquakes*. She made just over one million roux in tips.

CHAPTER 24

Huey tried the door to the gunsmith shop only to find that it was locked. This made sense as a security measure, he supposed, since he was pretty sure this was how every gun shop worked. He had only been in one once before, when he and Terry first got married and Huey decided to buy her father a shotgun as a birthday present since the man was a self-described hunting enthusiast. A few years later, after a nasty late-night fight that found Terry crashing on her parents' couch, his father-in-law threatened to shoot Huey with said shotgun. Huey had always found this ironic.

Huey knocked three times and stepped back next to Ernie to wait. They heard two separate dead bolts unlock and a moment later the door opened to reveal a large, scruffy, duster-wearing guard brandishing a rifle. He looked them both over, then turned back to speak to someone inside.

"It's them," the guard said.

"Send them in," a voice said. Huey hadn't realized that they were expected. The guard stepped aside, and Huey and Ernie headed into the shop.

Miller Roux sat behind the counter, smiling at them. He was thin and dressed very dapper, his clothes fitting perfectly and mustache precisely waxed. Huey noticed a copy of *Great Expectations* by Charles Dickens in the man's hands and was momentarily reminded that the people of New Roux City did in fact have some of their culture, just nothing that had been made after 1878.

Miller laid the book down and eyed the two men. "Ah, the strangers," he said.

"Yes, we're the strangers," Ernie said. Ernie walked over and shook Miller's hand, awkwardly with his left, since his right was in the sling. "I'm Ernie Swords. It's an honor to meet you." Ernie then noticed something, and Huey realized it was an entire wall of the shop covered with guns on display, each with a price tag. Huey quickly scanned them all, looking for the Dragoon. It didn't seem to be there.

"How about you?" Miller said. "You got a name?"

"That's Huey," Ernie said. "Mr. Roux, I have to ask you something. Do you know anything about a Special Edition—"

"Where is the girl?" Miller said, cutting Ernie off. Miller's eyes were still focused right on Huey. "I was told there were three strangers, and one of them was a pretty girl. Where is she?"

Huey thought about this for a moment, not really sure how to answer. He certainly didn't feel like explaining what it meant to be a staunch anti-gun activist. "She's chosen not to follow the conditions," Huey said.

"Has she read the conditions?" Miller said.

"She has."

"So she's aware she could be shot dead in the street?"

"She is."

"Let me rephrase that. She *will* be shot dead in the street. I advise you to pick out a firearm for this girl, and she and I can arrange payment later."

"What exactly is this payment arrangement system we keep hearing about?"

"It's quite simple." Miller gestured to the wall of guns. "You may choose to purchase any gun, they are priced from five million to twenty-five million roux, and we can set up an installment plan. Installments are due once a week, collected by one of my men. If you are unable to pay an installment, then I may add interest to the following week's doubled payment or have you do some work for me to pay off the debt."

"What kind of work?" Huey said.

"Whatever I need done at the time. Perhaps build a fence around my corn field. Perhaps empty out my latrine. Perhaps give me a foot massage. But I doubt I'd ask either of you to do that," Miller said. "Maybe your friend, although I'd want to take a look at her first." Huey squinted his eyes at Miller, put off by the man's crassness.

Huey shifted his gaze to the guns on the wall and something occurred to him. "You made all of these yourself?" he said.

"I did," Miller said. "Each one by hand. A family trade passed down for generations. Every firearm you see there was made on the same machinery that my great-great-great-grandfather Etienne Roux brought with him from Louisiana."

"So Etienne Roux was the first gunsmith here?"

"That's correct."

"So the man who wrote The Showdown Conditions, which say that every citizen must carry a gun, also sold all the guns?"

"What are you implying?" Miller said.

"Nothing." Huey smiled. "I'm just fascinated by history." Miller and Huey stared each other down for a moment.

Miller laughed. "I think I like you strangers," he said. "You've got spunk. And speaking of history, I'd be remiss if I didn't invite you to The Feast tonight."

"The Feast?" Ernie said.

"The Feast of Roux. A gathering held once a year at my home to celebrate Etienne Roux's birthday. The whole town is invited and everyone looks forward to it all year. We're going to have roasted chicken."

"Well, thank you for the invitation," Ernie said. "We'd love to come." Huey shot Ernie a look. He didn't like other people speaking on his behalf.

"Great," Miller said. "Make sure you bring your lady friend. And you might want to get some new clothes, it's a bit of a dressy affair. You'll want to pick up gloves anyway, in case you want to throw down the gauntlet and challenge someone to a Showdown. Did you know that's where the expression comes from? To 'throw down the gauntlet?' Medieval knights would wear long gloves, gauntlets, with their armor and when wanting to sword fight with another knight, they would throw one of the gauntlets down on the ground."

"Fascinating," Huey said. "But I don't really plan on challenging anyone to a duel during my stay."

"You never know," Miller said as he gave Huey a look. "Now, let's pick you out some weapons and get you on your way."

Miller came out from behind the counter, and Huey immediately noticed two unexpected things about the man.

The first was that Miller had the Special Edition Colt Third Model Dragoon Percussion Revolver in a holster around his waist.

The second was that Miller Roux was confined to a wheelchair, paralyzed from the waist down.

CHAPTER 25

Val stared at her reflection in the mirror and thought that she actually looked pretty bad-ass. She had never been into the Austin nouveau-Western scene, plaid shirts tied at the waist complemented by daisy dukes and cowboy boots, thinking it reserved for sorority girls and/or girls actually from small towns in Texas who didn't know any better. But she wasn't in Austin now, and the brown pants and coat combo she was currently modeling just made her look like everybody else.

She was standing inside Darling's Haberdashery, a clothing store on Main Street that offered top-quality handmade boots, pants, shirt, hats, dresses, gloves, belts, and holsters. The proprietor, an excitable young woman named Clementine Darling, had taken the opportunity during Val's fitting to give her the history of the establishment. Clementine's ancestors had thought ahead to bring with them all the supplies they would need to dress an isolated community for all of eternity. Cotton seeds, hemp seeds, sheep, silk worms, and cows for materials. Gins, sewing machines, and irons for production. Clementine had taken over the store from her mother, who had taken over the store from her mother, who had taken over the store from her mother. The styles hadn't changed much in New Roux City over the last 135 years, though, because according to Clementine, folks felt like the way the founders dressed was the way they should continue to dress forever. Clementine had never understood this, and the few times she tried designing more eclectic pieces they stayed on the sales rack forever. Occasionally one of Madame Jackson's whores would purchase one, but they weren't necessarily trendsetters around town. Clementine said that she herself had once tried wearing a short skirt to The Prospector for dinner and ended up with a glove thrown at her feet by Reverend Hallister, something about her "offending god by showing off her snatch." Clementine had apologized and promised not to show her snatch in public any more, so a Showdown was ultimately averted.

Val could tell that today was a big kick for Clementine, because she was getting to dress the strangers. Huey and Ernie were off in the main showroom picking out hats while Val got Clementine's full attention here in the changing room.

"So what do you think?" Clementine said.

"Not bad," Val said.

"And of course don't forget this." Clementine turned and grabbed a holster off of a stool. Val looked down to see her brand new black metal revolver nestled inside of it. Huey had bought both her and himself the cheapest gun available, the "Roux Snapdragon," which was five million roux. Ernie had gone for the "Roux Thunderbolt" which cost considerably more.

Val shook her head and looked back into the mirror. "This is such bullshit," she said.

"I think you look great."

"No, the clothes are fine. I'm talking about that." Val gestured to the Roux Snapdragon. "The fucking gun."

"Oh," Clementine said. "I see."

"Apparently if I don't carry it then I'll be shot dead."

"Yeah, you will."

"You're telling me in the history of New Roux City there hasn't been a single anti-gun activist? There hasn't been a single citizen over the age of fifteen who refused to pick up a weapon as protest?"

"Oh no, there have been plenty."

Val gave her a look, a bit surprised by this. "And what happened to them?"

"They got shot."

Val sighed and returned to the mirror, adjusting her coat. In the reflection, she noticed Clementine step to the changing room entrance and draw the curtain tighter.

"Actually," Clementine said in a whisper. "There is something you can do. To protest, I mean."

Val gave her a look, confused. "What do you mean?"

"Put out your hands."

Val did as she was told. Clementine pulled out her own revolver and showed it off. It was an ornate silver piece. "This is my pistol," Clementine said. "I carry him with me everywhere I go. He's part of me. I call him Rupert." She opened up the cylinder and dumped the bullets from the chamber into Val's hand. "But Rupert is harmless."

Val looked at the bullets closer. They were just empty shells. "Blanks?" Val said.

"Blanks," Clementine said. "And that's what we call ourselves. Blanks. Those of us who don't believe in all of this craziness."

"But you're still carrying a gun?"

"Yes, I am. This is true. To protect myself from Condition #21 so some asshole doesn't shoot me in the street. But this is not a weapon that could kill. This is merely an accessory."

"What happens if someone challenges you to a Showdown?"

"Then I hope the person that challenged me shows me compassion and chooses to fire into the air."

"And if they don't?"

Clementine gave Val a look, then put the blanks back into Rupert and closed the cylinder. She spun the gun around and holstered it.

"Val?" Huey said from the other side of curtain. "You decent in there?"

Clementine pulled the curtain open. There stood Huey and Ernie, both now completely decked out in Western gear. Huey was in a brown rawhide jacket and Ernie wore a black suit. Both wore wide-brimmed hats, leather gloves, and their new guns in holsters.

"How do we look?" Ernie said.

"Like you're at one of those stupid photo places in the mall," Val said.

"Yeah, well, this ain't so stupid," Ernie reached for his revolver, but momentarily forgot his arm was in a sling and couldn't grab it. He used his left hand instead, but awkwardly fumbled the gun, which fell onto the floor.

"Watch out there, Jesse James," Clementine said. The others laughed as Ernie bent down to pick the gun back up.

"How much is this all going to cost?" Huey said.

"About half a million roux"

"We don't really have any money. Do you have some sort of credit system?"

"Actually, I think I can cover that," Val said. She reached into her backpack and pulled out a handful of coins, which she set down on a table. The coins were of different sizes and shapes, but each one had a picture of Etienne Roux's face on the side.

"How the hell did you get all that?" Ernie said.

"Same way I did when I was sixteen," she said. "I busked for it. Played piano at The Prospector. Shaky actually offered me a residency." She smiled. Being offered a residency was a big step for a musician. This was her first.

"Congratulations," Huey said. He then noticed Val's gun sitting in its holster and gestured to it. "And, look, I know you really don't want to—"

"It's okay," Val said. "I'll carry it." She flashed Clementine a smile, and Clementine returned the favor.

"You should name him," Clementine said.

Val eyed the lug of black metal in her hand and thought for a moment. "I think I'll call him Dick."

Bang.

A gunshot rang out, and their smiles quickly faded.

Val looked over to see someone standing in the middle of the store. It was a figure wearing all black and a black mask covering the entire face. The figure held a gun in each hand, one aimed at the ceiling and the other at the group.

"Shit," Clementine said. "He's back."

"Who?" Val said in a whisper.

"The Silk Specter."

The figure took a step closer and gestured one of the guns to a counter. Clementine, seeming more annoyed than scared, took off her holster and placed it down on the spot the figure pointed to. She looked to the others. "Go ahead," Clementine said. "Put your guns down here."

"Has this happened before?" Huey said.

"Third time this year." Clementine shot the Silk Specter a glare. "I'd love to hire some security, but been a little low on funds lately due to the stolen inventory and all. It's a bit of a vicious cycle."

Val, Huey, and Ernie all placed their guns on the counter. The Silk Specter then gestured for them to sit on the floor, back-to-back, and proceeded to tie them up using a string of belts, which were in abundant supply inside the store. Val remained fairly calm. She had actually been in a holdup before, at a convenience store in Highland Park when she was thirteen. The guy who robbed the place was clearly holding a squirt gun, and the Korean store owner beat the shit out of him with a baseball bat.

The Silk Specter went shopping, and after a few minutes had collected a large stack of gowns and robes. The figure threw the garments into a burlap sack, then slipped out through a back window, all without ever speaking a word. The Silk Specter didn't take a single roux from the cash register or touch the pile of them that Val left sitting on the table.

The four sat in silence for a few moments, still tied to one another. Val finally spoke up. "I don't get this Silk Specter guy. Why steal a bunch of dresses?"

"Maybe he's a cross dresser?" Huey said. "Like the Old West Tootsie." Val laughed at this.

"What's a Tootsie?" Clementine said.

"It's a movie."

"Oh," Clementine thought for a moment. "What's a movie?"

It took a little over three hours for someone to discover the captives, during which time Val was able to explain most of film history, or at least her version of it, to Clementine. She spent a considerable amount of time on *Star Wars*, which spurred an argument between she and Huey about whether or not anyone living in an isolated community ever needed to be told about the existence of the prequel trilogy. Right as the argument was getting heated, a pair of young women looking for new boots walked through the front door and were nice enough to untie them.

CHAPTER 26

Ernie trailed behind Huey and Val, along with the rest of the citizens of New Roux City, up a path on the west side of town. This path led to Castle Roux, where The Feast of Roux would soon begin. Ernie noticed that the townsfolk, who had dressed in their finest for the occasion, weren't paying the strangers much attention anymore. He wondered if it was because their new digs were truly amazing camouflage, or if the strangers were now just yesterday's news.

"Do we really have to go to this thing?" Val said.

"Probably," Huey said. "Or I'm sure they'll threaten to shoot us. Or maybe they'll threaten to shoot us for going, who the fuck knows anymore."

"You're probably right. Did we need to bring a bottle of wine or something?"

"I'm sure we'll be all right."

They continued to walk, and after a few moments Huey glanced back at Ernie with a curious look. "You all right, Ernie?" Huey said. Ernie realized he hadn't spoken for a while. Not since they had escaped Darling's clothing store. "How's the arm?"

"It's fine," Ernie said. "Hurts a little."

"You got any of Dr. Thundercloud's magic powder left?"

"Yeah." This wasn't true. Ernie had finished the last of the powder up earlier in the dressing room at Darling's, right before the Silk Specter had shown up. He would have to figure out how to get more later, but right now his mind was on the Dragoon. Earlier, when Ernie saw that Miller Roux wore it as his personal revolver, he was caught off guard and opted to keep his mouth shut. He understood that in business you never want a seller to know how badly you want to buy their commodity, because then you'll never get a good price. You want to pull off what grifters call "the long con." Make the seller think that giving you exactly what you want is *their* idea. Now that they were going to Castle Roux, Ernie's mind was racing with ways to pull a long con off.

The three turned a corner on the path, following the lead of everyone else, and stopped in their tracks at the sight before them. Ernie immediately understood why the locals called the home "Castle Roux."

Because it was an actual castle.

The place was gigantic, the size of a square block, and built entirely of stone. A large spire stuck up out the middle of the structure, and a series of towers lined the roof. A moat surrounded the building, a drawbridge currently lowered over it to allow visitors up into the torch-lined entranceway.

"This is great," Ernie said. He himself had thought of building a castle on a plot of land he owned out near Marfa, Texas. Partly for the fun of it, but more importantly to use as a doomsday prepper location in case the shit ever went down.

He started to walk up the entranceway, a new spring his step, and the others followed. They passed under a giant coat of arms emblazoned above the castle entrance that read "Roux" over a shield. The shield was segmented into four sections, respectively depicting a revolver, a fleur-de-lis, a bear, and a key. Below the shield was written "Concessiones Libertatis Potestatem."

"Man," Val said. "These Rouxs don't fuck around."

Ernie noticed that on each tower, there was a guard standing watch. Each one wore a black duster, a black hat, and held a rifle in his hands. "They sure don't," Ernie said.

They approached the entranceway and were greeted by a young woman in her mid-twenties wearing a 1880s-era dress. "Hello," the woman said in a fairly monotone voice. "Welcome to our home." She did not make eye contact with them.

"Your home?" Ernie said. "Are you a Roux?"

"I am, sir. I am Number 5."

"Number 5? That's your name?"

"Yes, sir."

"May I take your coat?" a different voice said. Ernie turned to see another young woman in a similar dress, also not making eye contact with them. "It would be my pleasure to take your coat."

"You Number 6?" Ernie said. He smiled, thinking the joke pretty funny.

"I am Number 9, sir," the woman said. Ernie's smile faded and he glanced back to Huey and Val, confused. Neither woman had yet to make eye contact with them.

"So you're Miller Roux's servants?" Val said.

"No ma'am," Number 5 said. "We are his wives." Val clenched her teeth in response.

"May I take your coat now?" Number 9 said. "It would be my pleasure to take your coat."

"Sure," Ernie began to take his coat off. Number 9 thanked them, then walked off as yet another young woman in the same style of dress appeared. She looked to be about sixteen and also made no eye contact.

"Hello," she said. "I am Number 14. Please follow me."

"How many wives does Miller Roux have?" Val said.

"Seventeen," Number 5 and Number 14 said in unison. Number 14 began to walk down a long torch-lined hallway, and the three followed her as instructed. Ernie wondered if Miller Roux skipped calling a wife "Number 13" the way that most hotels didn't have a 13th floor.

Val leaned over to Huey as they walked. "This is disgusting," she said. "Are you okay with this?"

"Of course I'm not okay with it," Huey said. "I just want to get this over with without causing a scene. We can call social services or whoever we need to call when we get home."

"Look, I get that," Val said, "but if the next wife we meet is like nine years old, then I'm going to lose my fucking mind."

"You won't be the only one."

Ernie's attention was taken by a series of paintings that lined the walls of the hallway. Each was a portrait of a member of the Roux family, going all the way back to Etienne Roux himself. The men all looked fairly similar, especially since each one wore the same exact thick mustache. What really caught Ernie's attention, though, was that in every portrait the man held the Special Edition Colt Third Model Dragoon Percussion Revolver in his hand. He was beginning to suspect that Miller Roux might be a little more attached to the gun than he initially thought.

Number 14 reached a large curtain and grasped the end of it with her hands. She turned back to the three, yet still didn't make eye contact. "Welcome to The Feast of Roux," she said. She pulled the curtain aside to reveal a massive courtyard decorated for a celebration. Large banners depicting Etienne Roux's face hung from the inside walls of the towers. There were dozens and dozens of long tables surrounding a stage, each one filled with New Rouxians consuming roasted chicken and copious amounts of wine. Ernie noticed Cook Woodson sitting at a table in the corner with some of Miller Roux's other men.

"Hello," a voice said. Ernie turned to see yet another young woman in a nice dress not making eye contact with them. She looked to be the youngest so far. "May I show you to a seat?"

Val looked the girl up and down. "How old are you?" Val said.

"Sorry, ma'am?"

"What's your age?"

"I'm fifteen, ma'am."

Val shot Ernie and Huey another look. "Sure, fifteen-year-old girl," she said in a sardonic tone. "Please show us to a table." The girl turned and led them to a table in the corner that was already full except for three chairs. Ernie sat down and eyed his eating companions, an assortment of townsfolk from all walks of life. The only trait they seemed to have in common is that none of them looked like they really wanted to be there.

"Evening," Ernie said to them. No one said anything back. He noticed a bottle of wine on the table and eyed the label, "Roux Vineyards," an 81 merlot. They even had a winery. Maybe this place wasn't so bad. He uncorked the bottle with his good hand and poured himself a large glass. He then handed the bottle to Huey, who poured a glass for Val and one for himself. Ernie took a sip and licked his lips. "Hey, that's pretty good. Has a nice oak finish." He had once owned a high-end wine bar in downtown San Antonio called "Wine-Ho Silver" and thought himself quite the expert.

They sat there for a few minutes, and Ernie started to feel like a guest at a wedding where he didn't know anyone at all, including the bride or groom. He attempted to strike up a couple conversations with their tablemates, but no one seemed to be in the mood to even talk to each other let alone him.

"For being a party, these people don't seem too happy to be here," Val said to him in a whisper. He looked around at the well-dressed dinner guests, and sure enough the antisocial behavior wasn't limited only to their table. No one at the feast was really speaking to one another, and the mood actually seemed rather somber and wake-like. The fact that there was no music whatsoever didn't help.

"Ladies and gentlemen!" a voice shouted. Ernie looked up to see Miller Roux sitting in a private viewing box on an upper balcony, wearing a nice suit and flanked by what appeared to be two more wives. Miller held a glass of wine in his hand and immediately had the room's attention. "Welcome to The Feast of Roux!"

Everyone applauded. Ernie applauded as well, but Huey and Val apparently didn't feel the need. "We are of course here to celebrate the life of a great, great man," Miller said. "The grandfather to us all. And here tonight to remind us of the struggle that that great, great man went through are the children of New Roux Elementary!"

The crowd applauded again and Miller gestured down to a curtain which was pulled aside by one of his wives. Standing behind it were a dozen children, all dressed in period costumes. The children walked to the stage in the center of the courtyard and proceeded to put on a one-act play entitled "Roux The Day."

CHAPTER 27

Script for the one-act play Roux the Day *by the children of New Roux City Elementary to be performed at the 85 Feast of Roux.*

SCENE 1 – A FRENCH STREET

(Several POOR PEOPLE sit on the street and beg for change. ETIENNE ROUX and a CLASSMATE enter.)

CLASSMATE: Disgusting. Would you look at all these poor people? I wish they would get jobs.

ETIENNE: Perhaps they cannot get jobs, classmate. Perhaps they cannot get jobs because the monarchy has passed laws that forbid it.

CLASSMATE: Hogwash, Etienne. The monarchy is here to serve the people, not hold them down. And even if the monarchy was bad, there's nothing you or I could do about it because they are so strong.

(CLASSMATE and POOR PEOPLE freeze. An ANGEL appears.)

ANGEL: Etienne Roux, I am an angel from heaven.

ETIENNE: An angel? But what do you want with me?

ANGEL: I am here to tell you that God wants you to rise up against the king. Only you can save the people of France.

(ANGEL exits.)

ETIENNE: I must listen to the angel. The monarchy needs to be defeated. I know this and shall lead the way. I will rally the people of France and lead them to revolution.

(ETIENNE ROUX exits)

SCENE 2 – VERSAILLES DINING ROOM

(THE KING and THE QUEEN sit and eat a fancy dinner.)

KING: This meal is delicious, my queen.

QUEEN: Agreed, my king. And to think that the people of France have nothing to eat.

(THE KING and THE QUEEN both laugh.)

KING: It is a good thing that you and I were born into royalty and do not have to worry about the laws of government holding us back. It is also a good thing that the people of France are too poor and stupid to ever rebel against us.

(ETIENNE ROUX and three CLASSMATES enter with swords.)

ETIENNE: Hold it right there, Louis Phillipe.

KING: You must call me Your Majesty, royal servant.

ETIENNE: No, I do not. For majesty comes from the Latin word "maiestas" meaning "greatness" and you are not great. You use laws and government to oppress the people of France.

QUEEN: Oh no, King. This man Etienne Roux is on to us.

KING: I must kill him. And it will be no problem for me since I am the greatest swordsman in all of Europe.

CLASSMATE #1: He is right, Etienne. You are no match for the king. He will surely defeat you.

(THE KING, THE QUEEN, and THE CLASSMATES freeze. THE ANGEL appears.)

ANGEL: Fear not, Etienne Roux. God will act through your sword and give you the speed and agility to dispense justice.

*(THE ANGEL exits. ETIENNE ROUX and
THE KING fight. ETIENNE ROUX kills THE KING.)*

ETIENNE: The King of France is dead! I have killed him!

CLASSMATE #2: Perhaps you should be the new king, Etienne?

CLASSMATE #3: Yes, I agree. All of France agrees that you being
so wise and brave should be king.

ETIENNE: No thank you. I believe no man should be king, not even
me. Authority does not grant freedom. Freedom grants authority.

CLASSMATE #1: That is so smart, Etienne Roux.

CLASSMATE #2: What will you do now?

ETIENNE: Now that I have freed France from oppression, I will
do the same for the United States of America.

(ETIENNE ROUX exits.)

SCENE 3 – ROUX CITY, LOUISIANA

*(ETIENNE ROUX is surrounded by
three CITIZENS and a WIFE.)*

CITIZEN #1: Wow. It's so amazing how great life is here in Roux
City, Louisiana.

CITIZEN #2: I agree. I would not have thought before that living
in a place with no laws or government would be so peaceful,
but Roux City is truly a utopia.

WIFE: And I, your wife who loves you deeply, am glad that I can
share you with the other sister wives who also love you equally
as deeply as I do.

ETIENNE: I am glad that you feel this way, citizens. I hope that all
Americans will feel this way.

*(PRESIDENT RUTHEFORD B. HAYES
and two US MARSHALS enter.)*

PRESIDENT: Not so fast, Etienne Roux. The US government is
just as corrupt as the French monarchy and I, Rutheford B.
Hayes, and the Congress pass laws to keep good people down.

ETIENNE: Oh no. This is my worst fear.

PRESIDENT: Hold him down, boys.

*(The two US MARSHALS strip ETIENNE ROUX
of his shirt and push him to his knees. PRESIDENT
RUTHEFORD B. HAYES whips him.)*

PRESIDENT: Scream in pain, Etienne Roux. Scream in pain as I whip you.

ETIENNE: No, I will not scream. My body may be in pain, but my desire for freedom is not.

PRESIDENT: Etienne Roux's resilience is making me so angry.

CITIZEN #1: Etienne! Catch this gun!

*(CITIZEN #1 tosses ETIENNE ROUX a gun.
ETIENNE ROUX kills the two US MARSHALS.)*

PRESIDENT: You may be able to kill two US Marshals and you may even kill me, Etienne Roux. But you will never be able to hide from the corrupt American government.

ETIENNE: You are wrong about that last part. But right about the first two parts.

*(ETIENNE ROUX kills PRESIDENT
RUTHEFORD B. HAYES.)*

CITIZEN #2: What do we do now, Etienne Roux? Surely a new president and more US Marshals will come and once again try to disrupt our peaceful way of life.

ETIENNE: I do not know.

(THE ANGEL enters.)

ANGEL: Go west, Etienne. Go west.

(THE ANGEL exits.)

ETIENNE: Yes, we will go west where we can be free

.

SCENE 4 – NEVADA DESERT

*(ETIENNE ROUX is surrounded by five CITIZENS.
BIG CHIEF INDIAN bows to him.)*

BIG CHIEF: Thank you, Etienne Roux, for allowing my Indian tribe to join with your people and also thank you for leading us all the way to Nevada. One of my daughters would like to be one of your wives, a practice that I along with all the other men of New Roux City approve of.

ETIENNE: You're welcome, Big Chief Indian.

CITIZEN #1: But Etienne Roux, are we safe here? What if the US Marshals find us here? Won't they try to kill us all and destroy our way of life?

ETIENNE: No one will ever find us hidden in the mountains.

CITIZEN #2: But what if someone leaves here on a horse and goes and tells the US Marshals where we are?

ETIENNE: That is a good point, citizen.

(THE ANGEL enters.)

ANGEL: This is quite a dilemma, Etienne. God suggests that you kill all the horses.

ETIENNE: But aren't horses God's majestic creatures?

ANGEL: God is fine with it, as all the citizens will be.

SCENE 5 – MAIN STREET, NEW ROUX CITY

*(HENRY BROWN and ALEXANDER
WASHINGTON enter.)*

ALEXANDER: Now you listen to me, Henry Brown. You stole one of my sheep and now you better pay for it.

HENRY: I did not steal one of your sheep, Alexander Washington.

ALEXANDER: Then why are you wearing a brand new wool coat and eating lamb chops?

HENRY: All right, I confess I did steal one of your sheep, but since we have no laws there is nothing you can do about it. Nanny nanny boo.

(ETIENNE ROUX enters.)

ETIENNE: I heard your argument and think it is unfortunate that Henry Brown is a bad person. We must stick to our beliefs, however, and not make laws.

(THE ANGEL enters.)

ANGEL: Etienne, it is me the angel. I will appear to you this one last time. God thinks you know already exactly what to do.

(THE ANGEL exits.)

ETIENNE: I have a solution that you two should have a quick draw showdown on Main Street.
ALEXANDER: I think that is a great idea, Etienne Roux. Although I must point out that won't the man who is more proficient with a gun win?
ETIENNE: One would think that, but God will pass justice down from heaven into the man who deserves to win The Showdown and allow him to draw his gun quicker.
HENRY: I agree to this arrangement.
ALEXANDER: So do I and the whole town does too.
ETIENNE: Shoot on the count of three. One. Two. Three.

(ALEXANDER kills HENRY.)

ETIENNE: God has spoken. Justice has been served. May The Showdown be our way of life so that all citizens can live in prosperity.

THE END

CHAPTER 28

Miller watched from his private box as the children of New Roux City Elementary took a bow and the crowd applauded. He was proud of the youth of this town and the respect it had for its ancestors. They understood the importance of the Roux family, and this assured him that the future was bright.

He looked down to the table where the strangers were sitting, curious as to their reaction to the performance. The younger man applauded along with everyone else, but the girl sat there stoically. Perhaps theater was not something she took pleasure in. Miller noticed that the older man was missing. His chair sat empty, a half-filled wine glass and uneaten chicken set before it.

He then heard talking outside of his private box's door. Two guards were placed outside, as they always were, and he had given them strict instructions not be disturbed. He snapped his fingers and Number 7, the wife sitting on his left, looked to him. He gestured to the door, and she quickly stood and pushed his wheelchair over to it. He could hear a conversation being held out in the hallway.

"No one sees Mr. Roux when he's in his private box," one of his guards said.

"It will only take a second," a voice said.

"No one sees Mr. Roux when he's in his private box," the guard said again in the same exact tone. Miller looked to Number 1, his other wife who had remained seated, and gestured for her to open the door. She promptly stood up and did so.

Ernie Swords stood there with his two guards. Upon seeing Miller, Ernie's face lit up. "Mr. Roux, hello," Ernie said. He took a step closer, but his guards did not like this, aiming their rifles at him.

"It's okay," Miller said. The guards backed off. "Did you enjoy the show, stranger?"

"Yeah, the kids were adorable. Look, could I possibly speak to you for a moment? I have a business matter I would like to discuss."

"Go ahead."

"Actually could we talk in private?"

Miller eyed Ernie for a moment, then looked to his wives. "Number 1 and Number 7, prepare the elevator." The women nodded and hurried off down the hallway. Miller slowly rolled himself past Ernie in the same direction. "Walk with me," he said. Ernie walked alongside the wheelchair and the two guards followed not too far behind. "Now what sort of business matter would you like to discuss?"

"First I need to tell you a little bit about me," Ernie said. "Not to brag, but back in San Antonio I'm a man of great power and influence. A man like yourself. Now, are you familiar with the concept of a hospital?"

Miller shot Ernie a look, a bit dumbfounded by the stupidity of the question. "Of course I am. We are not cave men, despite what you and your friends may think."

"Yes, of course. I didn't mean to insult you. Just had to make sure. Anyway, I sit on the board at St. Luke's Hospital in San Antonio. I'm one of their biggest contributors, even have a wing named after me."

Miller reached the large door which was the entrance to his elevator. Number 1 and Number 7 stood holding ropes, ready to release the weights so that the elevator could descend. He waited for a few seconds, then gave Ernie a look. "It's not going to open itself," he said.

"Of course." Ernie opened the door and followed Miller inside. The two guards stood at the door, eyeing them.

"It's all right," Miller said to the guards. They nodded to him and backed away. Ernie closed the door, and a moment later the elevator began to slowly descend as the wives pulled on the ropes.

The guards headed down the stairs to meet the elevator when it arrived on the first floor. "As you were saying?" Miller said.

"As I was saying. I sit on the board of St. Luke's Hospital, and St. Luke's is on the forefront of advancements in spinal surgery. They've got the top specialists in the country."

"Spinal surgery?"

"That's right. There was this teenager. He was a quarterback for the Port Neches Cherokees. He wasn't an Indian, though, I know that probably sounds confusing to you. There's this game we play in Texas called football, and anyway it's real rough and this kid got plowed into and found himself paralyzed from the waist down. Similar to your situation here." Ernie gestured to Miller's wheelchair. "All the doctors told him there was no hope. That he'd never walk again. Then he went to St. Luke's and met with the top guys there. He underwent this new spinal surgery they developed that involved lasers, spent a little time in physical therapy, and the next thing you know he's out jogging the streets of Port Neches as if nothing had ever happened."

Miller considered this story. He found it to be quite interesting. "I'm not hearing a business arrangement," he said.

"Mr. Roux, I love what you and your family have done with this town. I really do. People seem happy. I mean, you've got seventeen smoking hot wives for Christ's sake. But I know there's one thing that you want. You want out of that chair. One call, and I can make that happen for you."

"And in return?" Miller said.

"I don't know. A simple token of appreciation. Something that you think would be a fitting exchange." Ernie glanced down at the gun in Miller's holster. "I collect guns, for instance. That one's beautiful. What is that, a Colt?"

Miller reached down and pulled out his gun, gripping it in his right hand. "It is indeed," he said. "Good eye. It's a Special Edition Third Model Dragoon Percussion Revolver. It was given to my great-great-great-grandfather by the Czar of Russia and has been passed down in my family for generations."

"Wow," Ernie said. "I'd love something like that."

"In exchange for allowing me to walk again?"

There was a ding as the elevator reached the ground floor. The two guards opened the door and waited along with two more of Miller's wives, Number 2 and Number 3. Miller eyed the Dragoon in his hand for a moment, then slowly looked back up to Ernie. He flipped the gun around so that he was holding the barrel instead of the grip.

He pistol-whipped Ernie across the face, sending Ernie falling against the elevator wall. The old stranger winced in pain and grabbed his nose, gushing with blood. Miller calmly placed the Dragoon back in its holster and wheeled himself out of the elevator. "Get the stranger something for his nose," he said to Number 2. She hurried off as Number 3 took control of the wheelchair and pushed him towards the courtyard. "And don't believe a goddamn word he says."

Miller now realized that the lies these strangers told were far greater and more complex than anything he would have expected. He had hoped that handling them would be an easy task, but was now beginning to fear it would be a challenge. He was so very grateful that Etienne Roux had had the foresight to warn of their plan.

He reached the courtyard to see that the other two strangers were still seated, enjoying their chicken dinner and Roux Vineyards 81 merlot. "I'll take it from here," he said to Number 3. He grabbed the wheels and rolled himself across the room to the strangers' table. Huey flashed him a forced smile. The girl did him no such favors. "Enjoying the festivities?" Miller said.

"Yes," Huey said. "It's been very informative. And this wine is great." Huey lifted the glass and took a sip.

"We're all about hospitality here in New Roux City," Miller said. He gave the girl a look and his smile grew bigger. She was beautiful, but looked to be one of those women who goes out of her way to hide that fact "I don't believe we've had the pleasure of meeting, young lady."

"My name is Valerie," she said. "Unless you don't like calling any woman by her name. I guess I could be Party Guest #35." Miller could immediately tell that the girl was drunk. He hoped this was the reason for her unnecessarily confrontational attitude.

"I know some of our ways may seem unusual to you," Miller said.

"They're fucking unusual, all right," she said in a loud voice that was beginning to get the attention of some of the other party guests.

"Val, you're drunk," Huey said.

"Of course I'm drunk. But in vino veritas, right?" she took another sip from her glass and looked to Miller. "I'm curious, Mr. Roux. How young is too young?" She pointed to someone behind Miller. It was one of the girls from the pageant, the one who played the Queen of France. "How about her? Maybe she could be wife Number 18?"

"That is my daughter," Miller said.

"So what?" Val said. "Nothing is illegal here right? Not even fucking your daughter?"

He slapped Val, hard.

The sound of the slap echoed off the stone courtyard walls, and everyone who heard it looked over. All eyes were now on their table. Val immediately put her hand to her face, in what appeared to be utter disbelief that a man had really just slapped her. Miller wondered if she had ever been put in her place before, or if she had always just been allowed to run her mouth off whenever she wanted.

The girl stranger then did something he wasn't expecting. She started to raise her own hand, apparently with the intention of slapping him back.

"Val, no!" Huey said. He jumped up, stepped between Val and Miller, and grabbed Val's raised hand. Huey accidentally bumped into Miller's wheelchair, causing it to tip over, sending Miller tumbling out of the chair and onto the ground.

The courtyard fell very, very quiet.

Miller, sprawled on the ground, his wheelchair on its side with one of the wheels spinning, looked up to Huey and felt his blood begin to boil. He had had enough of these strangers. It was time to deal with them in the fashion that he had suspected was inevitable from the moment they arrived. "Mr. Woodson!" his voice echoed off the stone walls. "Would you come here, please?"

Cook Woodson stood up from a table across the courtyard. He walked towards them and began to remove one of his gloves.

"You're a dead man, stranger," Miller said. Huey's face went white, and Miller could read it like a book. He knew that Huey regretted the terrible decision he had just made, all to defend the honor of a woman.

Huey then did something that Miller was not expecting. Huey did perhaps the very last thing Miller was expecting.

Huey took off his glove and tossed it on the ground, right in front of him.

"I demand satisfaction," Huey said.

CHAPTER 29

Huey slowly walked down the long, dark road back to the dead schoolteacher's house. He, along with Val and Ernie, had been asked to leave The Feast of Roux. Apparently challenging the host of a party to a Showdown is considered a bit of a faux-pas.

He still wasn't exactly sure why he had done it. Perhaps it was the wine. Perhaps it was the adrenaline. Perhaps it was the fear. When he saw Cook Woodson start to remove his glove, it had all come together. Why Cook Woodson's name was on all those graves in the cemetery. Cook Woodson was Miller Roux's heavy. Cook Woodson killed all the people that Miller Roux wanted dead. Cook Woodson was walking across that courtyard to challenge Huey to a Showdown, a gunfight that Huey would certainly lose. So Huey made a decision in a split second, and it seemed like such a rational idea at the time.

Miller had picked up the glove from the ground, asked Huey to bend down, and then slapped him across the face with it pretty hard. Miller didn't seem to consider apologizing for one second. The Showdown was officially initiated and scheduled for three days from now since one was already scheduled both the next day and the day after. Cook Woodson and his men then escorted the three strangers out of the party. On their way out, Huey overheard much gossip from the party guests. Apparently no one had ever challenged Miller Roux to a Showdown. Not once, ever. Huey had made history. He wondered if this was because Miller was in a wheelchair and people felt bad for him. Or perhaps because everyone thought that since Miller was a Roux, he had the power of God on his side. Most likely it was because everyone was just plain scared to death of the man.

"Why the hell did you do that?" Ernie said. He held a towel to his bloody nose as he walked behind Huey.

"What the fuck, Ernie?" Val said. "Why are you mad at Huey and not the man who pistol-whipped you in the face?"

"Look," Huey said. "If I hadn't challenged Miller, then Cook Woodson was going to challenge me." It made sense in his head. At least he thought it did.

"I'm a feminist who can protect myself," Val said. "But I have to admit that was pretty fucking awesome, Huey." She laughed, still drunk. "When he fell out of the wheelchair, I almost lost my shit. I mean I feel bad for handicap people and all, but that was pretty goddamn funny."

"I'm going to get shot defending your honor, and you think it's funny?"

"You're not going to get shot. The Showdown isn't for three days, and Ernie's cavalry will certainly have found us by then."

"My what?" Ernie said. He gave them a look.

"Your people must have noticed we haven't come back by now," Val said. "Military jeeps and tanks and shit will probably be rolling up on this place any minute."

Ernie stopped walking.

"Um…" Ernie said. A dour expression crossed his bloodied face. Huey and Val stopped walking as well.

"What's wrong?" Huey said.

"I don't have any people," Ernie said. "No one knows we're here."

Huey stared at Ernie for a long, long moment. "What do you mean? Didn't you have a whole team working for you looking for this place?"

"Well, yes. And I suppose some of them know the general location of where I was looking," Ernie said, "But they signed non-disclosure agreements just like you. They would know better than to tell anyone about it."

"What about your wife?" Val said

"She thinks I'm in Las Vegas on business."

"But she must know about The Dragoon? About Etienne Roux? About your lifelong dream to acquire a single stupid fucking gun?"

"Of course. But she signed one too."

"You made your wife sign a non-disclosure agreement?" Huey said. Ernie nodded. "She wouldn't tell anyone even if you mysteriously went missing?"

"Are you kidding? No one would secretly love for me to rot out in the desert more than Misty. Plus her NDA is pretty terrifying. If you had read yours, you'd know that—"

Ernie didn't get to finish, because Val punched him in the already-swollen face. He fell to the ground and clutched his nose, screaming in pain. "Look, I'm sorry," he said. "I'm sorry."

"Oh good, he's fucking sorry," Val said.

"All right, let's calm down," Huey said, although he was glad that Val had punched the old man considering he was about to do it himself. "Ernie, why did you not mention this to us already?"

"It hadn't come up."

"It's come up like fifteen fucking times!" Val said. "We sat in the dead schoolteacher's house last night and had a whole conversation about you calling your wife!"

"If you hadn't noticed, I've been on heroin," Ernie said. "I haven't exactly been thinking straight!"

"How did you think we were going to get out of here?"

"I don't know," Ernie said. "I hadn't really thought about it." Ernie had been so focused on obtaining the Dragoon, leaving New Roux City had clearly been on his back burner. Ernie had most probably been assuming that Huey would be the one to figure that small detail out.

"So, what you're saying is that we're not leaving any time soon?" Huey said. He felt the urge to sit down, so he did so right in the middle of the dirt road. He leaned over and put his head in his hands. "But that doesn't really matter, because I'm going to be shot dead at noon on Thursday."

"Wednesday," Val said. "The Showdown is on Wednesday."

Huey gave her a look.

"Just FYI," she said. "Hey, have you thought about who you want to name your second?"

"I haven't."

"I'm totally up for it."

"Sure, Val. You're my second." She actually seemed excited by this. Huey chose not to tell her that the decision was fairly easy, considering Ernie's broken arm would prevent him from being able to drag Huey's dead body out of the street.

CHAPTER 30

Ernie knocked on the door to Dr. Thundercloud's office. The sound caused his own splitting headache to grow even worse. He hadn't slept a wink the night before, and only partly due to the headache and pain in his arm. The other reason was that Huey and Val stayed up all night discussing whether or not it was actually feasible to walk out into the desert to find help. At about 4:00 in the morning, they concluded it wasn't.

Ernie had never been able to sleep well, not since he was a child. He had always been jealous of the other kids at nap time who could close their eyes and be out like a light in seconds, and to this day he despised anyone who could catch a nap on an airplane. He often found it ironic that he was worth enough money to buy and sell whole countries if he wanted to, but he would never be able to possess the one thing he really wanted: a good night's sleep.

There was no answer, so Ernie knocked again, this time much louder. The headache was piercing now. A moment later the door opened, and there stood Dr. Thundercloud looking half-awake himself. "What?" Dr. Thundercloud said. "What do you want? It's seven o'clock in the morning." Dr. Thundercloud got a better look at Ernie and his expression changed. Ernie's nose was swollen from Miller, and his eye black from Val. "What happened to you?"

"I had a rough night," Ernie said. Dr. Thundercloud laughed and gestured for Ernie to come inside. Ernie stepped in and closed the door behind him. He sniffed the air and caught an unusual scent. "Are you smoking marijuana?"

"Yes. It's settles my stomach. My wife and I had a little too much Roux 81 at the feast last night." Dr. Thundercloud grabbed a lit marijuana cigarette out of an ash tray and took a puff.

"You were there? I didn't spot you."

"We sure spotted you. You and your friends really know how to make a first impression." He laughed and pointed to the sling around Ernie's shoulder. "How is the arm?"

"It hurts. It really goddamn hurts."

Dr. Thundercloud held out the marijuana cigarette. "Want a puff?"

"No, I need something stronger than that. I need more Tears of the Moon."

Dr. Thundercloud eyed him for a moment, then extinguished the joint and stood up. "Follow me," Dr. Thundercloud said. This clearly wasn't the first time someone had walked into his office requesting more of the drug. Dr. Thundercloud walked to the door at the back of the office and he followed. They stepped out into the muddy, trash-filled alley that ran behind Main Street. Dr. Thundercloud crossed the alley and started walking into the woods.

"Where are you going?" Ernie said.

"You'll find out when you follow me, won't you?" Dr. Thundercloud disappeared into the trees. Ernie shrugged and followed into the dense forest. They walked down a path for a few minutes, then came upon a log cabin with a large stone chimney sticking out of the back. Smoke emanated from the chimney and Ernie immediately caught a whiff of an unusual smell. Far more unusual than marijuana smoke. Dr. Thundercloud headed to the front door and pushed it open, stepping inside. Ernie held back a second, not sure if he was being lured into some weird trap. "Come on," Dr. Thundercloud said from inside the cabin.

All the windows had been blacked out, so the cabin was fairly dark. The only light came from dozens of strange-looking oil lamps that had been placed around the room, each next to a cot. There were people lying on the cots, most seeming to be asleep. Those who weren't asleep were huddled over the lamps and smoking from long pipes.

"All right," Dr. Thundercloud said. "A cot is 50,000 roux an hour with a minimum of four hours." He pointed to a vacant cot in the corner. "Lamp use and product are included. If you want to stay overnight, it's an additional fee."

Ernie, his head fairly foggy, had finally put together where he was standing. "Is this an opium den?" he said. He had a vague knowledge of the concept, primarily coming from a scene in the 1984 film *Once Upon a Time in America*. He had once screened an actual 35mm print of the film in the Swords Ranch private theater, along with the rest of Sergio Leone's oeuvre. His personal favorite had been the mostly now-forgotten *Duck, You Sucker*.

"Yes," Dr. Thundercloud said. "Of course it is."

"Why would you bring me to an opium den?"

"So that you can smoke opium."

"I just need something for the pain."

"Just like everyone else." Dr. Thundercloud gestured around the room. Bandages were wrapped around various body parts, and many limbs were missing. Gordon Lee, the Asian man whom Ernie had seen lose The Showdown the day before, was passed out in the corner with a bandage around the spot on his left leg where his fiancée had shot him. "Like I said, the beds are 50,000 roux an hour. I need payment up front."

Ernie thought for a moment, eying the other inhabitants. They seemed lethargic and out-of-sorts, and that honestly looked incredibly desirable to him at the moment. "I still don't have any money," he said.

"Then why did you walk into my office?"

"Because you're a doctor, and you should care about the well-being of your patients."

Dr. Thundercloud just stared at Ernie. Something then seemed to occur to him. "If you don't have money, then how did you afford these new clothes?"

"Val, one of my fellow strangers, paid for them. She made some roux playing piano at the saloon."

"Oh yeah, I heard about that. My wife saw her. Said she's very talented. Why don't you ask her for the money?"

"I did. She told me to go fuck myself. She's upset with me."

"Well, then. I guess I could take that holster off your hands." Dr. Thundercloud gestured down to the holster around Ernie's waist.

"My holster?" Ernie looked down at it. It was a nice leather belt with a shiny metal buckle. "Don't I need it? The Showdown conditions and everything? Won't I get shot down in the street if I'm not wearing it?"

"The conditions state you need to carry a gun. Not a holster."

"If I don't have a holster, then where do I carry the gun?"

"In your waistband. Just be careful, though, or you'll shoot your pecker right off." Dr. Thundercloud let out a laugh. "Which I have seen happen, trust me."

Ernie weighed his options for a moment, then took out his revolver and placed it down on an empty cot. He undid the belt buckle and removed the holster, handing it over. "All right," Dr. Thundercloud said as he slung the holster over his shoulder. "Let's get you set up."

Dr. Thundercloud had Ernie recline on the cot, a pillow under Ernie's head, and then gave him a lesson on how to use the lamp. Dr. Thundercloud placed a small amount of opium on a long needle, which he called a "yen hanck," then held it over the burning oil. He rolled the needle and Ernie watched the opium swell and bubble to about ten times its original size, turning from black to brown. Ernie began to notice a creamy odor, and the other smokers seemed to enjoy this. Dr. Thundercloud then quickly twirled the opium on the broad surface of a bowl, occasionally putting it in the flame of the lamp in order to cook it more thoroughly. He explained that this was called "chying the mass." Dr. Thundercloud then rolled it again in the bowl until it formed into a ball the size of a pea. He used the long needle to force the opium into a small hole in the bowl and then leveled it off. He had Ernie grasp the stem of the pipe in his hand and hold it across the flame to heat both it and the opium at the same time. Dr. Thundercloud then poked the needle into the center of the bowl and withdrew it with a twisting motion which left a hole in the center of the opium. He had Ernie hold the pipe over the lamp, tip it above the flame, and inhale. Ernie's lungs were filled with the thick black smoke.

Ernie took a few hits, then sat back to get comfortable. Dr. Thundercloud checked on a few of the other smokers to make sure they were all right, and then he excused himself to head back to his office. Ernie lay back on the cot, staring at the ceiling, and let the effects of the drug waft over him.

"Who got you?" a gruff voice said. Ernie slowly turned his head to see that it was an old man lying on the next cot. The old man was missing his right leg and wore an eye patch over his left eye.

"Huh?" Ernie said.

"Your arm," the old man said. "Who shot you?"

"I wasn't shot. I was in a helicopter crash."

"Oh, all right." The old man didn't seem to question this statement.

"What about you?" Ernie said. "What happened to your leg?"

"Lost a Showdown a while back. Cocksucker shot me once in the arm and once in the leg. Doc told me I only had enough roux to save one or the other. I opted for the arm."

"Oh. That's unfortunate."

"Yeah," the old man said as he went back to his lamp. "Unfortunate indeed."

Ernie returned his gaze to the ceiling. He closed his eyes and let himself drift away. He began to slip into a state of euphoria, and the pain in his arm soon disappeared.

CHAPTER 31

Huey sat at the bar at The Prospector and stared up at the stuffed buffalo head on the wall that seemed to be staring right back at him. He didn't really give a shit how much it was worth.

The place seemed pretty full for a Monday morning. Just about everyone's attention was on Val, who sat at the piano and made her way through Carly Simon's songbook. She was currently singing "You're So Vain" and the crowd was eating it up, her tip jar overflowing with roux. She kept asking the patrons for requests, but they didn't know any songs other than old Civil War hymns that she was unfortunately unfamiliar with.

"Can I buy you a drink?" a voice said. Huey looked over to see Pearl, once again clad in a red duster and hat, leaning against the bar.

"No thanks," he said. "I'm good."

"Come on," Pearl said as she sat down onto the stool next to him. "I must buy a drink for the man of the hour. The man who made the incredibly asinine decision to challenge Miller Roux to a Showdown."

"So you heard about that?" The night before, Huey had actually noticed that neither Josephine Jackson nor any of her Crimson Guard were in attendance at The Feast of Roux. He figured not everyone in town enjoyed celebrating the man's legacy.

"Heard about it?" Pearl said. "You're the talk of the whore-house, Huey. If you want to come on by later today, you could probably get a freebie from any of the girls."

"I think I'll pass."

"Then at least let me buy you a drink."

"Like I said, I'm good." He gestured to a tray on the bar beside him with seven shots of whiskey sitting on top. "Because you're a bit late for that."

"It appears so." She laughed.

"These four are from the women playing Mahjong over there." He gestured to a group of older Chinese women sitting at a table with wooden tiles spread across it. They smiled at him and he nodded back. "I told them they didn't need to buy me one *each*, but they didn't listen."

"Maybe *you* should be offering *me* a drink?" Pearl said. He got the hint and slid one down to her. "Much obliged," she said. She took a sip.

"I don't get it," he said. "If people hate Miller Roux so much why doesn't someone just do something about it?"

"Do what exactly?"

"I don't know. Shoot him."

Pearl laughed again. "Shoot a Roux? That's sacrilege for someone from this town."

"But it's okay for me to try?"

"You're not from this town." She gave him a smile. "Besides, Miller is surrounded by highly-paid and highly-skilled gunmen at all times, and he's always holed up in either Castle Roux, the gunsmith shop, or that goddamn litter of his. Any move on him is a suicide mission. And trust me, the Crimson Guard and I have looked into it."

Huey shook his head and finished the shot. He glanced up to the chalkboard Showdown calendar to notice that Roux/Palmer had been written for Wednesday. "How are my odds looking?" he said. He found this question surreal, since he had spent so many hours of his life studying the odds of others. The hunter had become the hunted.

"Last time I checked you were 25-to-1."

"25-to-1? Jesus Christ. Is Miller that good?"

"No one knows. Never seen him shoot before."

"So he's like the Bears?"

"Sorry?"

"The Chicago Bears. They're a sports team. At Las Vegas sports books we call them a 'public team,' because no matter what their record is people just bet on them anyway. Because they're the Bears and they're supposed to be good, even if they're not." Huey immediately decided he was going to bet all the roux he could muster up on himself. He figured if he won, then he'd be rich, and if he died, then he didn't need the money anyway.

"How about you?" Pearl said. "You any good with a gun?"

"No, not at all." He had never even really been in a fight before. Once, in high school, a douchebag named Kevin Crater had knocked his lunch tray out of his hand, so Huey tackled him to the ground. Kevin Crater then broke Huey's jaw, but Huey had always thought of it as a moral victory for himself.

Val finished the song she was playing and the crowd applauded. "Thanks, everyone," Val said. "Thank you. That was one of my favorites. This next one goes out to a new, but dear friend of mine. A pilot by the name of Huey." Val gave Huey a wink, and he couldn't help but let out a little smile. Val began to sing "Nobody Does It Better."

Huey listened to the song for a moment, then gave Pearl a look. "Let me ask you something, Pearl," he said. "Has anyone ever been a no-show?"

"A no-show?"

"Has anyone ever just not shown up to The Showdown when they were supposed to?"

"Sure, it happens occasionally. Folks get too yellow or too drunk. Sometimes people just forget. The calendar gets so backed up that your Showdown is scheduled for a few weeks away and you just kind of get caught up doing other things."

Huey laughed at this. He was pretty forgetful sometimes, but he knew he could never let a duel to the death slip his mind. "And what happens to them?" he said. "The people who don't show up?"

"They get shot."

"So no one has ever gotten away with it?"

Pearl's demeanor changed, and Huey could tell that he had

struck a chord in her. She set down her shot glass and took a moment, thinking. She leaned in a little closer, as if she was about to reveal a secret. "Maybe," she said in a whisper. "You see, there was a woman. 'Bout ten years ago. Name was Winnie Crider. She was challenged to a Showdown, and come noon on the day, she hadn't shown up to Main Street, so a posse went to her house searching for her. It looked like she had packed up and just left."

"Into the desert?"

"Nobody knows for sure. Some say she went to go hide out in the East Woods." Pearl gestured out the window. Huey looked out at a dark patch of green in the distance. Thick, dark woods. "Hunters claim to see her from time to time. Say she's gone all primal. Like a tribal woman or something."

The clock tower outside began to chime. The entire room immediately reacted. Patrons began to finish up their drinks and head out the door. The women playing Mahjong abandoned their game without a second thought. Shaky put a "Closed" sign on the swinging doors.

"It's eleven o'clock," Pearl said as she finished her shot and stood up. "Time to get a good spot. Thanks for the drink, stranger."

"Any time," Huey said.

Pearl walked out through the swinging doors with everyone else. Val stopped playing the song she was in the middle of, since her audience had just made a mass exodus out the door and only she and Huey were left in the large room.

"Man," Val said. "People are really starved for entertainment around here." She collected her tips and shoved them into her pocket, then headed over to Huey. "You wanna go get a spot?"

"Nah," he said. "I think I'll stay here." He gestured to the tray of shots that the Chinese women had bought him. "I've got some work to do."

"I was thinking. As your second, I should go over to Miller Roux's later and see if I can broker a peace with him."

"I doubt it would do any good."

"Can't hurt to try, right?" She gave him a smile.

"I guess not."

"Well, I'm gonna go get a spot."

"Enjoy the show." He nodded to her, and she headed out through the swinging doors.

Huey sat there alone for a few minutes, lost in thought. He reached down and took his gun out of its holster, gripping it in his right hand. It was surprisingly heavy. He pointed the gun at the buffalo head on the wall, aiming the sight right between the beast's eyes.

"Bang," he said.

CHAPTER 32

Having attended scores of rock shows as not the tallest girl in the world, Val had mastered the art of finding a good view. She utilized this skill to climb atop a stack of barrels in an alley off of Main Street and peer over the already large crowd that had assembled to watch today's Showdown. She held her hand up to shield her eyes from the bright sun, and this caused her to wonder why they always do these things at noon. It was damn hot at noon, and in this arid climate it was a bit brutal to stand out in direct sunlight sweating through wool coats. A Showdown at dawn or dusk would be much more of a pleasant experience for both the participants and spectators, but she assumed the logic of that argument would only fall on the deaf ears of those obsessed with tradition.

"Morning, beautiful," a voice said. Her fifteen-year-old admirer, Walt, climbed up to sit next to her. "Fine day for a Showdown, ain't it? I like your new clothes, by the way."

"Thanks, Walt," Val said.

"I saw you at the feast last night and was planning to come over and say hello, but you got kicked out before I had the chance."

"Shit happens."

"That is does."

Val let out a laugh and looked out to the crowd. There were thousands of people flooding onto every nook and cranny of Main Street. Something occurred to her. A question that been on her mind since they had first arrived. "How are there still so many of you?" she said.

"Sorry?"

"The population. How is there still such a huge population in this town after over a hundred years?"

"Do I need to explain how babies are made, Val? Or maybe show you?"

"Don't be gross."

"The founders stressed that it was our duty to be fruitful. Me, I got six brothers and four sisters. Hope to have me at least a dozen little ones myself one day."

"But still. You people seem to be killing each other in the street every day."

"We don't have Showdowns *every* day, but when it rains it pours. We'll have none for weeks, and then a bunch all at once. If you ask me, it's got something to do with the moon. And a lot of Showdowns don't end with someone getting killed. Just maimed or something less exciting. Today's, though? Today's should definitely end in a fatality."

"Why is that?"

"'Cause Cook Woodson is up." Walt gestured across the street, and she looked over to see Cook Woodson sitting in a chair getting his boots shined. "He never fails to disappoint."

"Who is he fighting?"

"Claude Bienvenu." He pointed to a distinguished-looking man wearing a suit and top hat. The man leaned against a wall, a pipe sticking out of his mouth, and seemed to be rehearsing a speech he had scribbled on a piece of paper. "He runs the print shop," Walt said.

"Why did Cook Woodson challenge him?"

"He was trying to start up a newspaper. A weekly. *The Weekly New Rouxian.*"

"What's wrong with that?"

"The Roux family isn't such a big fan of newspapers. There was a popular one about ten years ago called *The New Roux Observer* that published a letter to the editor about the Roux family and about how maybe they weren't the nicest bunch. Cook Woodson ended up

Showdowning the entire editorial staff, one after the next. Took him a whole week."

"And so what did Claude Bienvenu write that got Cook Woodson so angry?"

"Nothing. Like I said, Claude was trying to start the paper up. Mentioned it to few folks around town."

"So his newspaper doesn't even exist yet? Cook Woodson is Showdowning him just for talking about it?"

Walt nodded, matter-of-factly. "Anyone can Showdown anyone for anything." Val looked back out to Claude Bienvenu, who seemed calm and collected as he studied the piece of paper in his hands. Claude didn't seem scared one bit considering the fact that he was about to face the fastest gun in New Roux City.

A few minutes later, Val watched as Claude and Cook Woodson walked into the street and faced one another. Cook faced north, and Claude faced south. The clock struck 11:55, and Claude Bienvenu took the piece of paper out of his pocket and unraveled it. He had prepared a speech.

"Good People of New Roux City," Claude said in a steadfast tone. "I stand here before you today a victim. Victim, coming from the Latin word 'victima', which meant a creature killed as a part of a religious sacrifice. And that is what I am. I am sacrificial lamb to the gods of corruption and oppression. I am an offering, being placed on a pyre of wickedness, that has infested this town like a plague." The spectators were listening with their full attention. Cook Woodson merely stared at Claude from twenty paces away, emotionless.

Claude gestured down to his gun. "The gun that I carry, the one that I was forced to buy from the very man who has brought me here today, is loaded with blanks." Val's eyes widened. It was just like Clementine Darling had told her at the haberdashery the day before. She noticed that some people in the crowd began to murmur. "I have never carried real bullets," Claude said. "And I never would have in the future. I say 'would' and not 'will,' because I do not expect to walk away from this Showdown alive. I fully expect that Cook Woodson, the errand boy for Miller Roux, will shoot me dead.

I accept this, because I know my place in this town. I know that I am a victim."

Claude nodded to the crowd, then slipped the paper back into his pocket. His speech was complete. The crowd was now on the edge of their seats.

The clock struck 11:57.

Cook Woodson stood there, facing Claude, and said absolutely nothing. He just stared Claude down. Claude stared at him right back, unblinking.

Val leaned over to Walt. "He's not going to say anything?" she said in a whisper, paranoid about being shooshed.

"Nope," Walt said. "Never does." She was a bit surprised by this. She would have expected Cook Woodson to mock or torment his prey. Perhaps his silence was even worse.

Two minutes passed without Cook saying a single word, and the clock struck 11:59. Both men placed their hands over their holsters and waited. The seconds ticked by very, very slowly.

The clock struck 12:00. Claude removed his gun from its holster and pointed it up in the air. Cook removed his gun and pointed it at Claude.

Bang.

Claude fired a shot into the air.

Cook didn't pull the trigger. He just kept the gun aimed square on Claude's head. Claude stared Cook down, putting his own gun back into its holster.

Cook slowly walked towards Claude, all twenty paces, his gun trained on Claude's head the entire time. Val, and everyone else in the crowd, waited with baited breath. He finally reached Claude, then put his gun right up to the young printer's forehead. The tip of the barrel pressed against Claude's temple.

"Just fucking do it," Claude said.

"All right," Cook said.

Bang.

Cook fired, shooting Claude at point blank range. Claude's body slumped to the ground.

Val had to cover her mouth to stop from screaming. No one said a word.

Cook put his gun away, then reached down and grabbed Claude's gun out of the dead man's holster. He opened up the chamber and dumped the bullet shells, all blanks, onto Claude's body. He then held the gun up high so that every single spectator could see it. "This is what you get, folks," he said. "This is what you get." He tucked the gun into his waistband and walked off. Claude's second, a young woman who Val assumed was his wife, rushed to the dead man's side. The woman wept as she cradled Claude's lifeless body in her arms. The crowd began to disperse. They didn't seem that phased or surprised by The Showdown's outcome.

Val just sat there on the barrels, not sure of how to feel. She had been around death all of her life in one way or another, but never saw someone murdered in cold blood right before her eyes. She took out her gun and held it in her right hand, feeling the cold steel against her palm. It amazed her that such a small object could create such a big mess. "That's what you get for being a Blank, huh?" she said. "Shot in the head."

Walt gave her a look. "What did you just say?"

"You hope for mercy, but you sure as shit don't get it."

"You know about the Blanks?" he said in a whisper. "Who told you about the Blanks?"

She gave Walt a look, not sure how to respond. She didn't know the teenager's feelings on the matter, and didn't want to rat out Clementine Darling in case it resulted in the seamstress standing on Main Street getting her brains blown out. "It doesn't matter," she said.

"Are you carrying blanks right now?" Walt said. She again wasn't sure what to say, but didn't know the point in hiding the truth.

"Yeah," she said. "Yeah, I am."

"Let me see."

Val eyed her gun and quickly realized she didn't even know how to open it. She handed the gun over to Walt instead, and he opened the chamber to inspect the bullets. He closed the chamber and handed it back.

Walt then took out his own gun and opened its chamber. He took out a bullet and held it up to show it off.

It was a blank.

"You're a Blank?" Val said. Walt gave her a wink. He put the bullet back and reholstered his gun. He jumped down from the barrels and held his hand out in order to help her down.

"Come on," Walt said. "I need to show you something."

CHAPTER 33

Huey searched the dead school teacher's house on a mission. He looked in every nook and cranny, finally coming upon exactly what he was looking for in a cabinet by the back door. Glassware. He had noticed a lot of glass around New Roux City, not only bottles and windows, but even eyeglasses, and it turned out there was not one but three different glassblowers in town. All you needed to make glass was sand and heat, and the Nevada desert had an abundance of both.

He gathered up six water glasses and took them to a fence behind the house. He neatly lined the glasses in a row, each about a foot apart, and then walked twenty paces away.

He held his hand over his holster, closed his eyes, and took a breath. "Okay," he said to himself. "Here we go."

Huey drew his gun and fired.

Bang.

The bullet pierced a tree, a good five feet away from any of the water glasses. "Shit." He put the gun back in the holster and took a moment. He then pulled the gun right back out and fired again.

Bang.

The bullet hit the bottom of the fence, a good two feet below any of the water glasses. He didn't bother to put the gun back, but fired again. Bang. And again. Bang. And again and again. Bang. Bang.

Click. The chamber was empty. Every single bullet had wildly missed the glasses. He eyed the gun and let out a sigh.

"Man," Ernie said. "You're terrible."

Huey turned to see that Ernie stood in the back doorway to the house. Ernie appeared pale and disheveled, as if he had been bitten by a zombie and was now slowly turning into one. "Jesus Christ," Huey said. "You look terrible."

"Well, I feel like a million roux," Ernie said with a smile. "Although I'm not sure what the exchange rate is on that."

"What happened to your holster?"

"Long story." Ernie gestured to the row of water glasses. "How long you been at it?"

"Just a couple of minutes."

Ernie sat down on the back steps, wincing in pain a bit as he did. "Remember to breathe. It's all about the breathing."

"You a good shot?"

"Shit, you kidding me? I grew up in Texas, Huey. Took marksmanship classes starting when I was seven. When I was nine, I won the 'Lil' Shooter Award' from the San Antonio Gun Club." Ernie eyed the cast on his arm and shook his head. "Of course that was using my right hand."

Huey thought about Ernie's advice, then reached into his pocket and pulled out the box of ammunition that Miller had sold him along with his Roux Snapdragon. He opened up the chamber, dumped the empty shells onto the ground, and reloaded. "When you're ready to fire," Ernie said, "take a deep breath and exhale about halfway. Then hold your breath when you squeeze the trigger. But remember that if you hold your breath too long, your heart starts beating faster which then raises your pulse and makes your hand all twitchy."

Huey closed the chamber, then pointed the gun back at the water glasses. He took a breath according to Ernie's instructions, and fired six more times.

Bang. Bang. Bang. Bang. Bang. Bang.

He missed six more times.

"Wow," Huey said. "I am terrible."

Ernie couldn't help but let out a laugh. "Yeah, you are. You're like Jimmy Stewart in *The Man Who Shot Liberty Valance*."

"Don't think I ever saw that one," Huey said. He actually hadn't seen that many Westerns at all. His father hated the genre and was more of a war movie guy. As a child Huey once begged his father to take him to see the *The Muppet Movie*, but upon their arrival to the theater his father pulled an audible and the plan was changed to see *Apocalypse Now* instead. Twice in a row. And the movie was three hours long. In the eighties, his father had bought an early model VHS player just so he could watch *The Deer Hunter* over and over, a fact that Huey later on realized was a little disturbing.

"It's pretty great," Ernie said. "Jimmy Stewart plays this pansy lawyer who comes to this small Western town where this guy Liberty Valance, played by Lee Marvin, is being a total prick to everyone all the time. One night, Liberty Valance challenges Jimmy Stewart to a duel, and of course Jimmy Stewart doesn't believe in guns because he's a pansy lawyer so at first he refuses. Finally, Jimmy Stewart has had enough and accepts the duel, so they draw their guns and Jimmy Stewart shoots and kills Liberty Valance right in front of the whole town. Everyone now sees Jimmy Stewart as a badass who stood up for the people and he becomes this hero. He uses the fame to become a US Senator."

"And I remind you of him?" Huey said.

"Well, there's a twist. You see, there's this tough rancher played by John Wayne who lives outside of town and he was the only guy to ever really stand up to Liberty Valance, but he just so happens to be out of town the night that Jimmy Stewart wins the duel. But in the end of the movie…" Ernie stopped and gave Huey a look. "Do you mind if I ruin it for you?"

"Go ahead," Huey said. Spoilers were the last of his problems right now.

"In the end of the movie, it turns out that John Wayne was in fact in town the night of the duel and was hiding in the shadows. When Liberty Valance and Jimmy Stewart drew their guns, John Wayne secretly pulled out a rifle and shot Liberty Valance. But everyone thought it was Jimmy Stewart. So Jimmy Stewart gets all the credit, and John Wayne decides to keep his mouth shut out of honor and goes on to become a drunk who burns his house down. That part was actually kind of sad."

Huey thought about this story for a moment, then eyed the water glasses sitting on the fence. All six still remained, glimmering in the sun. He then eyed the bullet holes in the fence caused by his poor shooting ability.

He then had a monumental realization.

"Ernie," he said. "You're a genius."

"I am?"

Huey eyed the gun in his right hand and let out a little smile. "I need to find a John Wayne."

CHAPTER 34

Val heard thunder in the distance and looked over to see storm clouds approaching over the mountains. "How often does it rain here?" she said.

Walt, who was leading her on a path through the woods, looked up to the sky and thought for a moment. "Every couple of weeks or so I guess," he said. "Sometimes more, sometimes less. Basically just enough to keep the farms going."

They continued up the path, and a few minutes later Val began to feel raindrops sprinkling down. "I hope we get to where we're going soon."

"We're here," Walt said. They stood before a run-down old church. She hadn't even noticed them approaching it, because the wooden structure was overgrown with vines and weeds, reclaimed by the forest. The church appeared to have been abandoned for quite some time. A row of stained glass windows across the front were all broken, and the steeple was cracked and leaned to one side.

"What happened here?" Val said.

"Pastor died. No one really stepped up to take over the place."

"You all lost your faith?"

Walt shot her a look as he knocked exactly five times on the door. Five slow, evenly spaced knocks. A few seconds later, the door opened and a young bearded man sporting an eye patch peered out. He nodded to Walt, then noticed Val and his expression changed. "What is this?" the man with the eye patch said.

"She's one of the strangers," Walt said. "Her name's Valerie, but she prefers Val. Val, this is Chango."

"Hi, Chango," Val said.

"I know who she is," Chango said. "Everybody knows who she is. Why did you bring her here?"

"Because she's a sympathizer," Walt said. "She was carrying blanks in her gun."

Chango eyed Val up and down. "Let me see," he said. She took out her gun and handed it over. Chango checked the chamber and saw the blanks, then handed the gun back and nodded. "All right," he said. "Come in." He opened the door and gestured for them to step inside. Walt, being a gentleman, allowed Val to go first.

She stepped in and surveyed the church interior. The place was incredibly dusty and riddled with cobwebs. There were rows and rows of pews before an altar above which hung a large crucifix.

Two dozen young New Rouxians sat in the pews, all staring at her. They said nothing, just stared.

"Hey," she said. "What's up?"

"Val!" a young woman's voice said. Val looked over to see Clementine Darling stand up from one of the pews and wave at her. "So good to see you here!" Clementine headed over and gave Val a big hug.

"You two know each other?" Walt said.

"Of course," Clementine said. "Who do you think dressed her so nice?" Clementine gave Val a wink. "How are the boots feeling, by the way?"

"Pretty good," Val said. "Still need to break them in a bit, but pretty good considering." She then gestured to all the young people sitting in the pews awkwardly staring at her. "So, what exactly is going on in here?"

"Val," Walt said. "I'd like to introduce you to the No Weapon Alliance. The NWA."

Val couldn't help but let out a huge laugh.

"You think that's funny?" Chango said. "You think people wanting to fight for change is funny?"

"No," she said. "It's just that where I come from, NWA stands for something different."

"What does it stand for?" Clementine said.

"Uh…" Val eyed a handful of young black New Rouxians

sitting in the pews staring at her. "It's a musical group." She wasn't against having to say the n-word if need be, but at that moment she didn't feel like trying to explain the racially satiric intricacies of a hip-hop group's name to a bunch of strangers who didn't even know what hip-hop was. "Anyway," she said to change the subject. "You guys are all anti-gun then? Because I'm so anti-gun."

"We are much more than just that," Chango said. "We are a resistance." The other Blanks all nodded in agreement, then sat her down and gave her the full story.

The NWA had been formed years before as a group of like-minded individuals who believed that law and order needed to be brought to the town. That men should not be left to rule themselves, because men cannot be trusted. The group's objective was to secretly protest the town's beliefs by giving the citizens exactly what it thinks they did not want, but in actuality desperately needed. Public services. The NWA did things for New Roux City that a government would do if there was one. They removed trash from the sidewalks. Smoothed out the forest paths to create trails. Provided clean drinking water and food to those in need, especially the orphaned children. Some of them had basic medical training and offered it to those who could not afford Dr. Thundercloud. And they did it all in the dead of night, for otherwise they would be Showdowned for subversion.

"Someone would Showdown you just for helping other people?" Val said. Chango exchanged a look with the other NWA members. She immediately understood that she had asked an obvious question. "So are you guys also behind the Silk Specter, then?"

"No," Clementine said. "You think I'd rob my own store? No one knows who that pain in the ass is."

"The NWA only helps people," Walt said. "And we would never do anything to hurt anyone. And until now we've always done it under a shroud of secrecy. But we've decided to change that. All inspired by your friend."

"My friend?" Val said.

"Huey Palmer," Chango said. "His challenging of Miller Roux to a Showdown was an incredible act of defiance. The mark of a brave, brave man."

"I'm not sure if Huey would agree with you." The night before she had heard Huey refer to his challenge as "idiotic" and "fucking stupid," but not "brave."

"We have decided to follow in Huey Palmer's footsteps," Chango said. "The NWA will publicly protest for the first time. We're going to do something that will cause the whole community to open their eyes and think twice about the way they've been living."

"What exactly are you going to do?"

The NWA members eyed one another. Their demeanors changed and they didn't seem so cocksure. "We haven't really figured that out yet," Clementine said. "That's why we're meeting now."

"Maybe you've got some ideas, Val?" Walt said.

"Me?"

"Yeah."

"Um…" The NWA members all stared at her. "I mean I don't really have anything off the top of my head."

"Whatever it is," Chango said. "We plan to do it during tomorrow's Showdown. Or maybe the day after."

"The day after could be better," Walt said. "Since that's when Miller Roux and Huey Palmer will be facing off."

"Actually," Val said. "I hate to burst your bubble, but there's not going to be a Showdown between Miller Roux and Huey."

The NWA members eyed one another, confused. "What do you mean?" Chango said. "Does Mr. Palmer plan to run? He must be aware that he'll never make it out of the desert alive."

"Yeah, he's well aware. Huey's not going to run. As his second, I'm going to go meet with Miller Roux this afternoon and convince him to call off The Showdown."

The NWA members immediately burst into laughter, finding Val's plan hilarious. Walt then noticed that she looked annoyed by their response. "Wait a minute," Walt said. "Are you serious?"

"Yeah. Of course I am."

"Oh, okay," Chango said in a condescending tone. "And how exactly do you plan on pulling that off?

"I don't know," she said. "I haven't really figured that out yet."

CHAPTER 35

Huey sprinted down Main Street, trying his best to stay out of the rain. Val had offered to buy him a raincoat when they were at Darling's clothes shop the day before, but he had declined, assuming it never rains in the middle of the desert.

He reached the entrance to Madame Jackson's House of Pleasures and was greeted by one of the Crimson Guard acting as bouncer. She looked him up and down as he stood there in the rain, taking her sweet time before she stepped aside and allowed him through the door. He entered into the large, ornate foyer and was greeted by a scantily-clad hostess holding a clipboard. The hostess recognized Huey and flashed him a smile. "Afternoon there, stranger," the hostess said. "Aren't you all wet?"

"Yeah," he said. "It's raining."

"So I've heard. My name is Goldie and I'll be your hostess today. Now, I know you're new, but have you visited any of the brothels in town yet?"

"No, I'm actually here to—"

"Okay then, let me just explain some things that you might not be used to. All the whores in New Roux City are unionized, which means all prices are fixed and non-negotiable." Goldie handed over the clipboard to Huey, and he looked down to see that it was a menu. "This menu details the services that the ladies provide, and next to each service you'll see listed a price per twenty-minute increment."

"Okay," he said. He was actually impressed by this document for some reason. "But I'm actually not here to see one of the ladies."

"Ah, more into the gentlemen are we? I suspected that might be the case. There are several establishments here in town that can cater to your needs, I personally can recommend Peter's Peters on the east side of town." Huey momentarily wondered why she suspected that might be the case.

"No, that's not what I mean," he said. "I'm here to see Madame Jackson."

"Sorry," Goldie said. "Madame Jackson isn't available for fucking."

"I just need to talk to her."

"She's not available for talking either. But any of the other girls are. You'll see it listed third on the menu." Huey looked down, and sure enough "talking" was listed as costing 140,000 roux for twenty minutes. "You're of course allowed to touch yourself in the talking session," Goldie said. "And the talking doesn't necessarily need to be dirty. Some gentlemen like to just come in and chat about whatever's on their mind."

"I need to talk to Madame Jackson about a non-whore related matter."

Goldie thought about this for a moment, confused. "I don't understand."

"It's all right," a woman's voice said. Huey looked over to see Pearl leaning against the wall, lighting up a cigarillo with a match. She blew a puff of smoke into the air and gave him a look. "Come with me."

Pearl deposited the match into a nearby ash tray, then turned and walked down a dimly-lit hallway. Huey gave Goldie a polite nod and then followed. The hallway was lined with numbered doors, and he could hear moaning coming from some of the rooms. He observed that some of the girls who worked at the House of Pleasures were better at faking it than others. Pearl held up a pack of cigarillos in her hand and held it out to him. "You want a smoke?" she said.

"No thanks. I quit a while ago. It's actually been pretty well-researched that smoking is terrible for you."

"Why am I not surprised?" She reached a door at the end of the hall and knocked twice.

"Come in," Josephine said from within the room. Pearl opened the door and gestured for Huey to step inside.

Josephine's large office was much more modestly decorated than the rest of the establishment. She sat behind a wooden desk, eyeglasses perched atop her nose, and appeared to be in the middle of building a ship-in-a-bottle. He was surprised by this, not expecting a madame to be into a hobby he associated with eighty-year-old sea captains. He noticed that there were dozens of ships-in-a-bottle scattered on shelves around the office and also taking up most of the mantle above a lit fireplace.

"Hello, Huey," Josephine said. He wondered how she knew it was him, considering she had never looked up. "You've made quite the splash in our little community in only a few days time. I'd say that I was impressed, if I didn't know this splash was going to result in your untimely death."

"My untimely death is exactly what I'm here to talk to you about," he said. He glanced back at Pearl, who was leaning against the wall. "Could we talk alone?"

"No," Josephine said. "Please, have a seat." She gestured to a chair across from her desk without ever looking up from the ship. Huey stepped over and sat down. He noticed that the rain was now pounding on the windows. "I'm listening," she said.

"I challenged Miller Roux to a Showdown which is to take place in two days."

"Yes, I've heard."

"I'm a terrible shot."

"How unfortunate."

"The clock tower in the middle of Main Street. It's three stories tall, and it has a perfect vantage point of the entire Showdown area. If a sharpshooter was to hide within the clock tower with a rifle, then he or she could take out either one of the duelers with ease."

For the first time, Josephine stopped working on the ship and looked up at him. She glanced over to Pearl, who seemed intrigued by this conversation, then looked back to Huey. "And why on earth would he or she do something like that?" Josephine said.

"To make it appear that someone who didn't win The Showdown had actually won The Showdown."

"Oh no, I very much understand what you're implying, Huey. I'm not an idiot. My question was why on earth would he or she do something like that?"

"Because you, more than anyone, want Miller Roux dead."

"Well, I don't know about that," she said. She took off her eyeglasses and set them on the desk. "A lot of people want Miller Roux dead pretty badly."

"But you have the most to gain. I may be a stranger, but I can already see how things work around here. You and Miller Roux run this town, but you don't do it amicably."

"What makes you say that? Milly and I might very well be the best of friends."

"Then why were you and your girls the only people in town who didn't show up to The Feast of Roux?"

"Don't call us 'girls,'" Pearl said.

"There's clearly an animosity between the women of Madame Jackson and the douchebags of Miller Roux," Huey said. He thought for a moment. "A douchebag is slang for someone who—"

"I can infer what the term 'douchebag' implies," Josephine said. She then slowly leaned back and folded her arms. "So let me get this straight, Huey. You'd like me to send one of my Crimson Guard up into the clock tower on Wednesday morning."

"Whoever your best shooter is."

"That'd be me," Pearl said.

"You want me to send Pearl here up to the clock tower on Wednesday morning," Josephine said. "Lie in wait for a few hours. Then come Showdown time, you and Miller Roux will take to the street and say your bullshit statement and then stare each other down the way manly men do. When the clock strikes noon, Pearl is to shoot Miller Roux with a rifle before Miller Roux can draw on you, thus killing the man and putting the entire town under the impression that it was you who pulled the trigger."

"It could work," Huey said.

"It could also *not* work. And if it didn't, do you know what would happen? Cook Woodson and all of Miller Roux's douchebags would blow the clock tower to bits with Pearl still inside of it. They would then march in here, claim I conspired to manipulate the sacred Showdown conditions, and shoot me on the spot along with my entire Crimson Guard and probably all my employees." Josephine leaned back up and looked Huey in the eyes. "And I should take that risk, all to save the life of a stranger that I just met and honestly don't like very much?"

"And also to take control of this town," Huey said.

"Maybe I don't want control of this town. Maybe I like the piece of the pie I've carved out for myself and think putting up with a self-entitled monster like Miller Roux is a small price to pay."

"You don't really believe that."

"You don't know me one iota, Huey, so don't sit here and lecture me on what I do and do not believe. And if I may dispense some free advice, I would suggest you not mention this brilliant clock tower plan of yours to anyone else. If Miller Roux gets wind of it, he'll make sure he shoots you in the gut come Wednesday morning and let you bleed out nice and slow."

There was a loud crash of thunder and flash of lighting at that exact moment that Huey thought couldn't have been more ominously timed. Josephine merely sat there, staring him down. He could tell that she wasn't going to budge.

"I was hoping this conversation would have gone differently," he said.

"Tough shit," she said.

CHAPTER 36

Miller sat by the fireplace in his private library, a glass of Roux 62 Pinot Noir in his hand, and read a worn copy of *Murders in the Rue Morgue* by Edgar Allan Poe. He had read it a dozen times before and was aware of the book's twist ending, but it was one of his favorites and he could never resist the urge to dive back in. There were only about a hundred books in his collection, and he had read them all at least twice by now. His favorites were the thick Russian epics that his father had called "doorstops": *War and Peace*, *Crime and Punishment*, and *The Idiot*. He also had a soft spot for *Little Women*, but this was a well-kept secret. Only two novels had actually ever been written in New Roux City, printed on the press that the founders brought with them. 13's *Hail to the King* and 52's *Lawless*. Both were satires of the Roux family, and both authors had gotten themselves Showdowned for the works. All copies were subsequently burned.

"Dear Husband?" a voice said. Miller looked up to see Number 5 standing in the doorway. She was wearing an apron over her dress. "Sorry to intrude, but you have a visitor."

"Who is it?"

"The woman."

He sighed. The new levels of stupidity from his wives never ceased to surprise him. "The woman? Can you be more specific?"

"The stranger. The one that you slapped."

He shot Number 5 a look. He didn't care for that description, even if it was true. "Send her in," he said. He set the book down and poured an additional glass of wine.

Number 5 disappeared, and moment later Val stepped in. She

got a good look at the place, paying attention to Miller's many books lining the shelves. "Nice collection," she said.

"Thank you. Please, have a seat by the fire to warm up." He gestured to a seat next to his wheelchair, and Val headed over and took it. He then held out the additional glass of wine that he had just poured. "Here. A Roux 62."

Val thought for a moment, then took the glass and tried a sip. "Oh wow," she said. "That's really good."

Miller gave her a smile and then took a sip himself. "I was expecting Mr. Palmer's second to visit me today. Thought it might happen before five o'clock, though." Miller gestured to an old cuckoo clock on the wall. "And didn't think it was going to be you."

Val flashed him a forced smile, and he could tell she was holding back what she really wanted to say. Miller wasn't stupid. He knew this girl despised him because she was ignorant and didn't understand him or the ways things were in this town. He also knew she would hold back expressing her ignorance in order to try and save Huey Palmer's life through diplomacy. "I'm just happy to have the job," she said.

"So, let me guess. You're here to try to negotiate a peace."

"Yes, I am. First off, I want to apologize to you. What I said about your daughter was out of line and I had a few too many drinks. I understand that this is no excuse, but I was wrong and I see that now. I'm realizing that this town has its own customs, and I need to learn to understand and appreciate those things. I understand why you slapped me. To be honest, I would have slapped me too."

Miller knew Val meant absolutely none of this. "And Mr. Palmer feels the same way?" he said.

"He does. We both understand that upon further thought, perhaps polyamorous relationships could actually be quite beneficial to all involved. I mean lord knows I would appreciate having another woman around the house if I ever got married."

Miller just eyed her for a moment. He then turned his chair a little bit to better face her. "I appreciate you coming here, Valerie. I really do. But... well, there's a problem."

"A problem?"

"I know you're new to all this Showdown business and don't quite understand the etiquette. Yes, one of the duties of a second is to attempt to negotiate a peace, which you are indeed doing at this very moment. But you're not supposed to do it with me directly. You actually really shouldn't even be talking to me at all."

"Oh," she said. "I'm sorry, I didn't realize that. Who should I talk to then?"

"*My* second."

"I see. Well, who is your second?"

Miller gestured behind her. Val hadn't noticed, but Cook Woodson appeared behind her minutes before and had been watching the conversation unfold. Val turned to see Cook, and Miller saw her immediately tense up. She was afraid of his right-hand man. "Evening, Mr. Woodson," Miller said.

"Evening, boss," Cook said.

"Still raining out there?"

"Nah, it finally let up. Should be dry enough in a few hours to do that thing I need to do. What's going on here?"

Miller pointed to Val. "Valerie here, acting as Mr. Palmer's second, has come to try and negotiate a peace."

"Is that so?" Cook said. He took a few steps into the room, eyeing her up and down. "You tell her the etiquette?"

"I did."

"Yes, I'm sorry," Val said. Miller detected a slight tremble in her voice. "I guess I should be speaking with you."

"Here I am," Cook said. "Speak away."

"Huey is very sorry about what he did."

"You mean pushing a man out of his wheelchair?"

"Yes, that. He's very sorry. It was an accident, and his Showdown challenge was an impulsive decision that he regrets. He's new here, we're all new here, and we're still learning the ways."

Miller watched as Cook seemed to think about this for a moment. "She's pretty convincing, boss," Cook said.

"She is indeed," Miller said.

"I'm obliged to believe her."

"As am I."

Cook took a few more steps into the room to face Val, standing over her as she remained seated. "Tell you what," he said. "I think we can probably all come to an agreement to call this Showdown off. You make a lot of good points, and it's the right thing to do."

Miller saw Val let out a smile. "Great," she said.

"Thing is, though." Cook scratched his beard. "Thing is, well, I'm going to need something from you."

"What?"

Cook reached down and unzipped his fly. "I'm going to need you to suck my cock."

Miller took the greatest pleasure in watching Val's face instantly turn white. He could almost feel the chill run down the girl's spine.

"Come on now," Cook said. He gestured down to his open fly. "We'll call this whole thing off and you can spare your friend Huey's life. Just put your sweet little mouth on my pecker here."

Val looked to Miller, as he if it was up to him to step in and help her. He took a sip of his wine. "Sounds like a good deal," he said. "Actually, I'd like in on this. When you're done with Mr. Woodson, I'll take a go too."

"Good thinking, boss," Cook said.

Val turned and looked into the fireplace, as if the crackling embers would provide a solution to the sticky situation she suddenly found herself in. Miller wondered if she was actually considering the offer.

Val chugged the rest of her wine, stood up, and looked down to Cook's manhood before her. "You know what," she said. "I forgot to bring my glasses with me to New Roux City." She then looked Cook right in the eyes. "So I can't suck something so small I can't find it."

Miller couldn't help but let out a laugh. This girl had wit, he'd give her that much. Val turned and headed for the door.

"Valerie," Miller said. "One more thing before you go." She

stopped in the doorway and turned to look back at him. "I want you to give Mr. Palmer a message for me."

She stared at him, saying nothing.

"Pick a number one through twelve," Miller said. Val still said nothing. It was clear she didn't feel like humoring him. "All right, then. Mr. Woodson, would you pick a number one through twelve, please?"

"Four," Cook said.

Miller drew the Dragoon from its holster, aimed it at the cuckoo clock on the wall, and fired.

Bang.

Val jumped, startled. Miller spun the gun around and placed it back into its holster in a smooth, swift move. Val looked over to see that he had shot a hole right in the middle of the "4" on the cuckoo clock's face. The shot was perfect, and he had done it in a flash.

"Way to fuck up your clock," Val said. She turned around and walked out of the room.

CHAPTER 37

When Val was sixteen, she went on a date with a boy in her class named Hector. They were supposed to go to the movies, but instead Hector drove them out to an industrial neighborhood and put the moves on her in his car. She hadn't been ready to go all the way, but Hector was inclined to take her whether she wanted to or not and he started to get rough. She punched Hector and fled the situation, flagging down a delivery truck. The experience was the most afraid Val had ever been, and it didn't hold a candle to what she had just been through.

She stumbled down the stairs in the main hall of Castle Roux, dazed. Her heart was racing. She started to breathe faster and faster, and wondered if she was having a panic attack. She had never had one before, but suspected that this is what it must feel like.

She reached the bottom of the stairs and leaned against the stone wall, unable to keep going. Her breathing was even faster now, and there didn't seem to be anything she could do about it. For a moment, she left her body. For a moment, none of this was real.

She heard a noise behind her and tensed up. For the first time, she regretted having put blanks in her gun.

"Are you all right?" a young woman's voice said. Val turned to see that it was Number 5, the wife who had escorted her up to the library.

Val wanted to tell her yes. That she'd be fine and would like to be left alone. But she couldn't. She was breathing so fast now she found herself unable to speak. "Come with me," Number 5 said. "You need to sit down." Number 5 stepped over to Val and put an arm around her for support.

Number 5 escorted her down a series of hallways until they were met with a row of doors, each marked with a number. When they reached the one marked "5", Number 5 opened it and led Val inside. Val assumed this was the girl's bedroom, but to her it looked more like a prison cell. The stone walls were bare, and the one small window barely let in any light. A small cot sat against the wall, facing a wooden dresser with nothing on it but a white candle.

Number 5 gestured for Val to take a seat on the bed and she did so. Number 5 left the room, and a moment later returned with a glass of water, handing it to Val before closing the door. Val took a sip and felt her breathing start to slow. Her heart had stopped racing. Whatever this was that was happening to her seemed to be winding down.

"Thank you," Val said. Number 5 said nothing in response and Val looked up to see that she was just standing there, facing the wall. "You can look at me."

"He says we are not allowed to—"

"He's not here."

Number 5 considered this, then slowly looked up to Val. Val studied her face. She looked like someone whose spirit had been broken. There was sadness in her eyes. "What's your name?" Val said.

"Number 5."

"Your real name. Not what he calls you."

"That is my name. It was changed."

"What did your parents call you?"

Number 5 hesitated for a moment. "Annie," she said. "Annie Coleman."

"Nice to meet you, Annie. I'm Valerie. You can call me Val." She saw Number 5 let out a little smile. A very, very pretty smile.

"Nice to meet you, Val." Number 5's smile quickly faded, as if she realized she was doing it in the first place and knew such show of emotion was unacceptable. Number 5 turned and headed over to the dresser, opening the top drawer. She pulled out a box of matches, struck one, and lit the white candle. Soon a soft light spread over the bare stone walls.

"This place could really use some sprucing up," Val said. "Maybe a poster or two. Or some flowers."

"My husband does not like the wives to decorate their rooms," Number 5 said. "He says it is a distraction."

"Is that so?" Val said. She couldn't even imagine this girl's life. What it must be like for her here. Val herself had always been opposed to the idea of marriage in general. She thought it was an archaic institution created thousands of years ago to settle contracts between families which had been corrupted into a billion-dollar wedding industrial complex that brainwashed the minds of little girls. This was how she felt about basic marriage, between just two people. Number 5's situation was one she didn't even know how to comprehend. She had a million questions for the girl.

The questions would have to wait, however, because at that moment Val heard the sound of a bell ringing in the distance. A deep bell, like a gong. The sound caused Number 5 to stand to attention and take a step to the door. "I must go," Number 5 said. "It is time to prepare supper."

"I'll get out of your hair." Val stood up, setting the water glass down.

"Can you find your way out?"

"Yeah, I think I got it." Val nodded to her, then stuck out her hand. "Thanks again, Annie."

Number 5 eyed Val's hand for a moment, then shook it. "You're welcome, Val."

CHAPTER 38

Ernie wasn't sure if he had ever actually experienced a rocking chair before. He had always just thought they were for old ladies, and it never even occurred to him to take one out for a test drive. But now, as he slowly rocked back and forth in the schoolteacher's house while listening to the stories of Huey and Val's afternoons, he instantly understood their appeal. When he got back to San Antonio, he planned to buy one, if not several.

"Well," he said. "I'd have to say Val's meeting went way worse."

"I'm going to have to agree," Huey said.

"You need to kill that son of a bitch, Huey," Val said. "No peace agreement. No calling it off. Shoot the motherfucker in his motherfucking face."

"I'd love to, Val," Huey said. "But the odds are looking slim." Ernie knew that the actual odds were indeed looking slim. He had checked at Kooper's Card Room earlier that day to see that Huey had fallen to a 33-to-1 underdog. "And I can't exactly post up fliers on Main Street looking to hire a sharpshooter."

"What about these NWA folks?" Ernie said. Val had filled him and Huey in on her meeting with the rag-tag organization. "Maybe one of them can shoot? They must want Miller Roux gone, right?"

"They're peaceful, Ernie," Val said. "They're literally called the No Weapons Alliance. And even if they weren't, not a single one of them looks like they even know how to hold a gun let alone snipe someone from fifty yards away."

The three sat there for a few minutes in total silence. Ernie could almost hear Huey and Val racking their brains as all of the viable options seemed to be running out. Val eventually stood up and began pacing back and forth. "We have to do it," she said. "We have to run."

"We can't," Huey said. "We've been over this. We won't make it five miles. I grew up in the desert, Val. I know how brutal it can be."

"We can try."

"Yeah, but if we try and fail then we all die. If we stay and I fight this asshole, then it'll just be me."

"I appreciate your noble gesture," she said with what Ernie picked up as a hint of sarcasm. "But how long do you think before Cook Woodson or some other psycho throws a glove down on the ground in front of me or Ernie? I'm honestly surprised it hasn't happened already."

"Yeah, me too," Ernie said. For a brief moment he wondered if no one had challenged him to a Showdown yet because they felt bad for him, his arm in a sling in all.

"Who knows?" Huey said. "Maybe I'll win. Maybe God will hook me up and give me the power to draw quick and shoot straight."

Val shot him a look. "Huey, this isn't funny. You're going to die."

"I'm well aware of that," Huey said. "But we're out of ideas here. Unless a sharpshooter comes knocking at our door, then I don't know what the hell else to do."

At that exact moment, there was a knock on the door. A loud, booming knock. Ernie eyed the other two, surprised. No one moved or said a word. Whoever it was knocked again, harder this time. Huey finally walked over and opened the door.

A woman stood on the doorstep. She was wearing a red duster and hat. Her face was smudged with something black and hair disheveled. "Pearl?" Huey said. "What are you—?"

"Come with me," she said. "Right now." She then turned and walked off into the darkness.

"She a friend of yours, Huey?" Ernie said.

"I'm not sure," Huey said. He shrugged and walked out. Ernie and Val soon followed.

Pearl headed up a dirt path towards a hill and they hurried to catch up with her. "What's going on?" Ernie said.

"You'll see," Pearl said. "You'll smell it first, though."

Ernie took her cue and sniffed the air. Smoke. Something was burning. He looked ahead to see that a plume of black smoke was coming up into the dark sky.

They made it over the hill to see a large farmhouse and chicken coop engulfed in flames. A crowd had gathered and were standing a safe distance away, watching the blaze.

"Holy shit," Val said. "I guess I won't even ask if you guys have a fire department."

Pearl shot Val a look and led them over to the crowd. Ernie noticed that most of the spectators were Crimson Guard members or girls he had seen in the windows at Madame Jackson's House of Pleasures, and just about all of them were covered with ash and dirt. It looked as if they had tried to put out the fire to no avail.

Josephine stood in the middle of them all, her arms around a young woman who was crying. "It's all right, Suzanne," Josephine said. "It's all right."

"What happened here?" Ernie said.

Josephine looked up to see the three strangers. She gestured to one of her girls to take over consolation duties, then stepped away from the crowd. "Walk with me," Josephine said. She led them back up the path a bit so that they could speak privately, but still have a clear view of the fire. "This farm belonged to one of my girls, Suzanne. She took it over after the prior owner passed, even though Miller Roux disapproved. Even after Miller Roux's men had slaughtered all the chickens. Suzanne thought she could maybe raise some more chickens one day, or some other livestock if she saved up enough money. She could have set herself up a nice life here." Josephine looked to the flames, which were growing bigger and brighter. "But not anymore, because tonight Miller Roux's men came by and did this."

"What?" Val said. "Why?"

"Because Miller Roux is a man who doesn't like to be defied."

"Are you sure it was Miller Roux's men?" Ernie said.

"Yeah, I'm sure," Josephine said. "Because they're still here watching their handiwork." Josephine gestured over, and Ernie looked to see that sure enough Cook Woodson and a dozen or so of Miller Roux's men were sitting on haystacks watching the farm burn to the ground. The men were sipping on bottles of whiskey and laughing.

"Well, fuck," Val said. "Go do something about it for Christ's sake."

"I am doing something about it," Josephine said. "I'm doing something about it right now by telling you what I'm about to tell you." She looked away from them and towards the fire, the reflection of the flames casting an ominous glow in her eyes that Ernie thought made her look otherworldly. "You can have the best sharpshooter in New Roux City for your gambit," she said. "But it's not Pearl. She's good, but she's not the best. And you're going to need the best to shoot down Miller Roux in the street like the dog that he is."

"So, then, who is the best?" Ernie said.

Josephine finally looked back to them. She then gestured out to the dark, ominous East Forest in the distance, "A woman by the name of Winnie Crider."

CHAPTER 39

Winnie Crider squatted beside some bushes near the river and quietly relieved herself. She hated going when she was out on a hunt, because she knew the animals could smell it and it kept them away, but she had stupidly drank way too much tea that morning and couldn't hold it in any longer. She thought about just getting into the river and going there, but that would involve taking her boots and pants off, and she wasn't in the mood. She finished up and re-cinched her homemade leather belt, then checked out her reflection in the river water. She thought her long blonde hair was starting to look pretty ragged, so she'd have to wash it soon. It'd been quite a while since she last bothered, not exactly anyone up here that she was trying to impress.

She grabbed the bow that she had left leaning against a tree and made her way out deeper into the woods. She had laid seven traps the night before, and if she was lucky then one of them hit and she'd be able to cook up a nice meal. Her average breakfast was squirrel or rabbit, but occasionally a pig would wander up from one of the farms and she'd be able to fry up some bacon. When this happened for Winnie it was like goddamn Christmas morning.

She checked the first two traps to find that they hadn't been triggered, which wasn't much of a surprise. The third had been triggered but nothing had been caught in the rope, so it just dangled from the tree like a hangman's noose without a victim. Most likely the trap had been set off by an animal that was too quick for it, but every now and then one of the fur trappers would wander up from town and accidentally get caught up. Winnie used to be worried that they'd figure out it was her setting the traps, but luckily they always just seemed to blame it on one of the other fur trappers since none of them seemed to get along with one another.

She reset the trap and moved on. She checked the next three to come up empty handed again, none of them had even been set off. She made her way through the brush to the final trap, knowing that if it too came up empty then she'd be staying mighty hungry this morning.

As she approached the final trap, she heard a noise and immediately froze. Winnie had been out here long enough doing what she does to know that the first thing you need to do upon hearing a strange noise is stop and listen to pinpoint exactly where it's coming from. The mountains sometimes created an echo, and the last thing you wanted to do was run away from trouble just to find out that you ran right into it. She listened closely, and could tell the noise was coming from the west, from down the mountain. She crouched and slid between some bushes, pulling an arrow out of the quiver slung over her shoulder and placing it into the bow. She took a breath and listened closer. It was definitely a man's footsteps, and not an animal. She knew right away that whoever this man was didn't know the first thing about trying to hide one's approach, and he might has well have played a trumpet to announce his arrival. The steps got closer and she crouched down further. She leaned in to peer through the bushes and was finally able to see her visitor.

It was one of the strangers who had arrived to town a few days before. The younger of the two men. He looked lost, and he seemed to be studying a crudely drawn map in his hands. He stopped walking and just stood there for a moment, then held the map up to align it with some large rocks. He nodded, as if he was in the right place. Why on earth he would have a map leading him to this spot was beyond Winnie. There was nothing up here. Nothing except her. She thought it best to sit quietly and wait for him to leave. She had spent eight years avoiding detection, and she sure as hell wasn't going to break her streak by showing herself to one of the strangers.

"Hello?" Huey said. "Ms. Crider, are you here?"

Winnie's pulse quickened. That's the last thing she expected him to say. She clutched the bow in her hands tighter, unsure of his intentions.

"Ms. Crider, my name is Huey Palmer and I've been sent up here on the recommendation of Josephine Jackson. I need to speak with you."

Winnie stood up, drew back the bow, and aimed it at the back of Huey's head as she stepped out of the bushes. "Drop your weapon," she said.

Huey seemed to perk up at hearing Winnie's voice. He started to turn around to face her. "I didn't say turn around," she said. "I said drop your weapon."

"Sorry." He reached down, took his gun out of its holster, and set it on the ground.

"Put your hands up," she said. The stranger did as he was told. "Now you can turn around to face me."

He turned around, seeing her face for the first time. She could see surprise in his eyes. He probably thought she looked remarkably composed for someone who had supposedly gone tribal. Lord only knew what stories he had been told.

"What did you do to her?" Winnie said.

"To who?"

"To Josephine? How did you get her to tell you where I was? Did you torture her?" Madame Josephine Jackson was one of the only friends Winnie had left in New Roux City, and she had also helped Winnie escape in the first place. Josephine had vowed to never give away Winnie's precise location in the East Forest, a promise she had impressively kept until this moment.

"What?" Huey said. "No, I didn't torture her."

Winnie brought back the bow a bit, tightening it. "Don't lie to me."

"No, I swear. I've never tortured anyone in my life. Although, my daughter says when I play CCR too loud in the car it's torture."

"Bullshit," she said. "Josephine wouldn't just tell you where I was."

"She did. She even drew me a map." Huey held up the map so that Winnie could inspect it. It did appear to be Josephine's handwriting.

"Let's say I believe you," Winnie said. "Why the hell would she tell you where I was?"

"Can I put my hands down?"

She nodded. "All right, but if you try anything I'll split your skull open."

"That sounds fair." He lowered his hands. "Josephine sent me here to talk to you because you're the only one who can help me with a problem."

"I assure you there's no problem that I can help you with."

"But there is. I've challenged another man to a Showdown, but I couldn't hit the broadside of a barn with a cannon. So I need to fix the gunfight in my favor."

"Fix it? What do you mean fix it?"

"I need to get someone who knows their way around a rifle to hide in the clock tower on Main Street, and at exactly noon I need them to take the shot for me."

"That's the dumbest fucking thing I ever heard."

"I know. But it could still work."

"And Josephine suggested me for it?"

"She said you're the best. Said you could shoot the flea off of dog's back at a thousand yards."

That was an exaggeration, but Winnie was pretty damn good with a rifle in her hands. Still, none of this made any sense to her. Why would Josephine care so much about whether this stranger lived or died? What had he done in two days to impress her so much? That's when something occurred to Winnie, and it all started to fall into place.

"Who are you supposed to fight?" she said. "In your Showdown?"

"Miller Roux," Huey said.

Winnie lowered the bow, loosening the string. "Is that a fact? Miller Roux."

"So you know him?"

"Yeah, I know him. Who do you think put him in the wheelchair?"

CHAPTER 40

Letter sent to The New Roux Observer
Dated April 5th, 77
Published April 7th, 77

To Whom It May Concern,

My name is Winnie Crider, and by the time you read this I will have already done what I plan to do. I will have murdered Miller Roux.

This letter is not to act as a confession, for I plan to murder Miller Roux before dozens of people in broad daylight, so the identity of his killer will not be mystery. No, this letter is to act as an explanation for why I did what I did. A motive for my crime. I fully expect to be shot down myself soon after the murder by Cook Woodson or one of Miller Roux's other lap dogs, so this letter is to be my voice from beyond the grave. In a way, I suppose it also serves as my suicide note.

I come from a large family, or at least a family that was large at one time. My father and mother, Marcus and Jolene Crider, had six children, including me. Clifton, Hannah, Gaye, Barton, and Bruce. My father was an honest, hard-working man. Farmed corn and attended church every Sunday.

When I was ten years old, one night my father accidentally bumped into Miller Roux at the saloon, and by that I mean he literally bumped into Miller Roux. My father wasn't paying attention to where he was walking, probably because he had been drinking, and bumped into Miller Roux causing Miller to spill a whiskey all over his brand new coat. My father apologized profusely and even offered to clean the coat, as was witnessed by many who were in the saloon that night, but Miller Roux did not accept the apology and instead had Cook Woodson throw down the gauntlet. Cook Woodson shot my father dead in the street three days later as you all watched. For getting a coat dirty.

As a child, growing up in this community with what I now realize holds a warped sense of values, I saw nothing wrong with this. I was sad that my father had passed, but did not question why. This is how life worked in New Roux City.

My mother was next. She encountered Miller Roux on Main Street a few weeks later, still mourning the loss of her beloved husband. I was with her, as were my two sisters, and witnessed the encounter first hand. Miller Roux commented on the fact that my mother was wearing all black, mocking her by saying, "You're never going to find a new husband if you look so damn sad all the time." My mother slapped Miller Roux, and rightfully so. Miller Roux had Cook Woodson throw down the gauntlet, and my mother immediately apologized saying she wasn't thinking clearly. Miller Roux did not accept her apology, and Cook Woodson shot her in the gut a few days later. My brother Clifton acted as her second, holding her in the dirt as she laid in agony and you all watched. It was not a quick death. From then on, I was an orphan.

Clifton got drunk one night and walked right up to Castle Roux, banging on the front door and demanding to see Miller Roux. Cook Woodson eventually appeared and ordered my brother away. Clifton threw down the gauntlet, and for the first time Cook Woodson showed a tinge of mercy. He handed the gauntlet back saying, "I've killed enough Criders this month." This made Clifton even angrier, so he threw down the gauntlet again immediately and called Cook Woodson a "Yellow Cunt." Cook Woodson accepted The Showdown this second time, and shot Clifton in the throat a few days later as you all watched.

Many years went by without incident. Hannah, the eldest

remaining, did her best to look after the rest of us. It was a constant struggle, and we went to bed many nights dirty and hungry. When Hannah was seventeen, she ended up going to Madame Josephine Jackson and becoming one of her whores in order to help make ends meet. Hannah was paid well and taken care of. Ms. Jackson was always kind to us, one of the few people in this town who ever was. Hannah was required to live at the House of Pleasures however, so Gaye took over as head of household. Barton, Bruce, and I had to drop out of school to look after the farm.

One night, Miller Roux and his men went by the House of Pleasures, and Miller Roux selected Hannah to be his whore. Hannah refused, saying she wanted nothing to do with the man and that he could "rot in hell." Miller Roux struck Hannah in the face, and before he and his men were ejected from the establishment by Madame Jackson's Crimson Guard, Cook Woodson had the chance to throw down the gauntlet before Hannah. Hannah refused to apologize, and Cook Woodson shot her three times in the chest a few days later as you all watched. Miller Roux's men were banned from the House of Pleasures after that.

I have now learned that it was at this point that Miller Roux decided the Crider family could begin to pose a problem. Miller Roux figured that the last thing he needed was four bitter teenagers growing up to one day seek revenge on him. So he took a preemptive step.

Four nights ago, there was a knock on our door. Gaye answered it to see Cook Woodson standing there with a crooked smile on his face. Cook Woodson threw down the gauntlet and challenged Gaye to a Showdown. For no reason. Absolutely no reason whatsoever. Gaye demanded a reason, and Cook Woodson remarked that it was because, "We no longer care for the Criders very much." Gaye apologized, not even sure why, but Cook Woodson did not care to listen. Cook Woodson picked up his glove and then threw it before Barton, challenging him to a Showdown the day after Gaye. Then he threw it before Bruce. Then he threw it before me. We all apologized, and he refused each time.

On Miller Roux's orders, Cook Woodson planned to kill us all. Four days in a row. For no goddamn reason. We were innocent teenagers, and there was nothing we could do to stop him.

This past Tuesday at noon, I stood on Main Street and watched Gaye get shot down as you all stood by and did nothing.

This past Wednesday at noon, I stood on Main Street and watched Barton get shot down as you all stood by and did nothing.

This morning, I stood on Main Street and watched Bruce get shot down as you all stood by and did nothing.

As I held Bruce in my arms, feeling him take his last breaths, he looked up to me with a hollow look in his eyes. His final words were, "You have to do something about this, Winnie. This isn't right." As I write this letter, my hands are still stained with his blood.

I have now lost my entire family. Because my father once bumped into a man in a saloon causing him to spill his whiskey. My brother Bruce spoke the truth that you are all too blind to see. This isn't right. And I do plan on doing something about it.

I will not be showing up to The Showdown tomorrow. I plan on finding Miller Roux first thing in the morning, most likely at the Prospector where I know he likes to have breakfast, and killing him. I plan to shoot him in the back. I do not want to give him the chance to draw his gun or the satisfaction of knowing who his murderer was.

Once Miller Roux is dead, perhaps things can begin to change around here. Perhaps it will be the spark to ignite a revolution.

- WINNIE CRIDER

CHAPTER 41

Ernie stood in Kooper's Card Room and stared up at the odds board on the wall, one of about thirty people doing so at that moment. The Showdown was going to start soon, and people needed to get their bets in. There were a lot of options, way more than Ernie was expecting.

MacKenzie to wound Chambers on first shot—2-to-1

MacKenzie to fire into the air—15-to-1

MacKenzie to kill Chambers on first shot —50-to-1

MacKenzie to fire and miss on first shot—1-to-1

MacKenzie to fire at Chambers and miss on first shot
then fire again and wound on second shot—1-to-2

MacKenzie to fire at Chambers and miss on first shot
then fire again and kill on second shot—25-to-1

MacKenzie to wound Chambers then end Showdown—1-to-1

MacKenzie to win Showdown—1-to-2

Chambers to wound MacKenzie on first shot—12-to-1

Chambers to fire into the air—7-to-1

Chambers to kill MacKenzie on first shot—200-to-1

Chambers to fire and miss on first shot—1-to-5

Chambers to fire at MacKenzie and miss on first shot
then fire again and wound on second shot—8-to-1

Chambers to fire at MacKenzie and miss on first shot
then fire again and kill on second shot—40-to-1

Chambers to wound MacKenzie then end Showdown—8-to-1

Chambers to win Showdown—12-to-1

"A bit overwhelming, aye?" Rawlings said. Ernie looked over to see the bearded old man standing beside him, also eyeing the board. He had a bottle of whiskey tucked underneath his left arm.

"I'll say," Ernie said. "I don't even know who these MacKenzie and Chambers fellas are."

"Only one of them's a fella. Chambers. MacKenzie is a lady."

"And she's favored to win?" Ernie was surprised by this. He wasn't sexist or anything, he knew very well a woman could shoot just as well as a man. But better than a man head-to-head?

"Oh yeah, she's pretty good."

"What are they Showdowning about?"

"Standard collections dispute. Ida MacKenzie works for Bank of Roux, which lent Warren Chambers a big chunk of change to help buy him some grain seed. But Warren of course blew it at that table right over there." Rawlings gestured to a craps table in the corner of the card room. It was empty at the moment, as were the half dozen blackjack and poker tables, since everyone was focused on The Showdown betting board. "Now he's past due and bank policy is to Showdown you."

"That's harsh," Ernie said.

"Yep. That's why I don't deal with banks."

Ernie gestured to the board. "So what do you think is going to happen?"

"Well, MacKenzie is gonna win. She always does. And the size of the debt usually dictates whether she intends to maim or kill."

"What was the size of this debt?"

"Not sure, but I heard it was two or three million roux. That's right on the border between maim-worthy and kill-worthy."

Ernie reached into his pocket and pulled out the 100,000 roux that he had snagged from Val's jacket while she was asleep. He knew he needed to at least double it in order to buy another four-hour session at Dr. Thundercloud's, although a six-hour session would be ideal. "How about MacKenzie wounding Chambers on the first shot?" Ernie said. "You think that's a smart bet? 2-to-1?"

"No bet is smart, but it certainly ain't dumb."

Ernie pondered for a moment and finally decided to go for

it. He stepped to the betting window and told the employee which wager he wanted. He then handed over the 100,000 roux and received a bet slip in return.

He headed out to Main Street to find a good spot for the show. He had walked into town alone that morning, Huey having gone off into the East Forest to find the mysterious jungle woman, and Val deciding she'd seen enough Showdowns for a while and instead was going to "work on a Plan B," whatever the hell that meant.

The sidewalks began to fill up quickly, and by 11:30, Main Street was packed. At 11:54, Ida MacKenzie and Warren Chambers took to the street to face one another, MacKenzie facing north and Chambers facing south. MacKenzie was an older woman, probably in her early sixties, and not at all what Ernie would have imagined a top gunslinger to look like. Chambers was a bearded younger man who looked like he had been up drinking all night and might have trouble finding his holster let alone pulling a gun from it. Ernie was beginning to feel better about his bet, as long as Ida MacKenzie didn't kill the poor son of a bitch.

The clock struck 11:55, and it was Chambers's time to speak.

"Look," Chambers said. Ernie thought he sounded a little drunk. "When I went to—"

Chambers didn't get to finish. Without warning, two dozen young people stepped out of the crowd and walked right into the middle of Main Street. They stopped before the clock tower, then turned to stand in straight a line. Their bodies formed a wall, blocking MacKenzie and Chambers from seeing one another. Ernie thought the young people looked like they were about to play the schoolyard game "Red Rover." He recognized one of them as Clementine Darling, the girl from the clothing store whom he was tied to for three hours. Another was Walt, that kid with the massive crush on Val.

The crowd started to murmur. This was apparently very unusual. "What the fuck is this?" Ida MacKenzie said. She seemed incredulous.

"This is a protest," the young man in the middle of the line said.

"My name is Chango Quinn, and I along with these fine citizens represent the NWA. The No Weapon Alliance. Some of you already know who we are, for we have helped you in the night. Some of you may not be familiar with us, but I guarantee that you know our work. We're the ones that keep your streets clean and—"

Bang.

A shot rang out and a bullet hit the dirt at Chango's feet, kicking up dust. Ernie, along with everyone else, looked over to see that Cook Woodson stood on the roof of the gunsmith shop along with five other of Miller Roux's men. Cook held a rifle in his hands, aimed right at Chango.

"You're probably wondering if I missed on purpose," Cook said. "I did. Now get the fuck off of Main Street."

"We will do no such thing," Chango said. "We stand here today as an act of defiance. We stand here as a symbol."

"You stand there as a pain in my ass. You also stand there in violation of The Showdown Conditions, which gives me, and anyone else here today who feels up for it, permission to kill you right now."

"Permission?" Chango said. "Permission granted by who, Mr. Woodson? By you? By Miller Roux? By God? By God's only son, Etienne Roux?" Ernie noticed that this caused some snickering amongst the crowd.

"I'm gonna give you ten seconds," Cook said. "Then me and my boys here are going to fire." Cook eyed the men standing behind him. "I'm gonna take aim at Chango there. Each of you pick a favorite of the bunch. Try not to go for any of the ladies, though. We ain't savages." The men laughed and eyed the NWA members, shifting their rifles upon making a choice of which member they were in the mood to shoot.

"You have no right," Chango said.

Cook began to count, very slowly. "Ten… Nine… Eight…"

"People will not stand for this. People will not stand for unwarranted violence against peaceful dissent."

"Seven… Six… Five…"

Ernie scanned the faces of the NWA members. Some of them looked defiant. Some scared. "Anyone who wishes to walk away can walk away," Chango said to them. No one moved.

"Four... Three... Two..."

Chango looked out to the crowd. "Do not stand for this. You do not have to stand for this."

"One."

Bang.

A bullet ripped through Chango's chest and he dropped to the ground, dead. Clementine screamed.

Cook Woodson nodded to his men, and they opened fire.

Bang. Bang. Bang. Bang. Bang.

Five more shots rang out. One went through a tall NWA member who seemed like an easy target. Another went through an older Native American member. Three went through Walt. They all dropped dead.

No one in the crowd spoke or moved a muscle, just stared at the pile of bodies. Ernie felt the need to lean back against a post to keep himself from collapsing.

Cook sighed and glanced at his men. "Really? Three of you picked the same goddamn one?" He gestured to Walt's body, and his men only shrugged. He then looked back out to the remaining NWA Members still standing in the street, some of whom were now splattered with the blood of their fallen compatriots. "Now we can do this all day if you want me to count to ten again. Or you can pick up your friends there, give 'em a proper burial, and never speak a word of this NWA bullshit ever again."

The remaining NWA members eyed one another. Ernie noticed most looked to Clementine Darling. She must have been the second-in-command. Clementine seemed to think for a moment and finally nodded to the rest, as if she was ready to wave the white flag. She bent down, grabbed Walt by his legs, and began to drag him off of Main Street. The others NWA members quietly followed suit.

"Good choice," Cook said. He slung his rifle over his shoulder and looked out to the crowd. "Well folks, I guess today's Showdown is postponed."

"Really?" MacKenzie said. Ernie realized she was annoyed. "Can't we just move the bodies and get on with it?"

"Yeah, I'd really like to get this over with," Chambers said.

"It's already past noon," Cook said. He gestured to the clock on the clock tower, which Ernie saw read 12:03. "And The Showdown happens at noon, that's how it is. We'll reschedule you both for Thursday. Now everyone disperse."

The crowd did as they were told. MacKenzie and Chambers both begrudgingly left Main Street.

Ernie leaned against the post, still processing what had just happened. He watched as The NWA members laid out the four bodies on the sidewalk nearby, side-by-side. He noticed that Walt's eyes were open and the kid seemed to be looking right at him. Ernie started to feel sick. He needed to get to Dr. Thundercloud's as soon as possible so he could forget about this.

He eyed the bet slip in his hand. He wondered if it was refundable.

CHAPTER 42

Huey quickly discovered that unlike everyone else in New Roux City, Winnie Crider had a lot of questions about the outside world. A lot. She had led him back to her cabin, a one-room shack deep in the woods that she built herself, and offered him a glass of moonshine. They had been sitting on hand-carved wooden chairs for hours now, Winnie asking him anything and everything. He quickly realized trying to explain 135 years of human civilization is quite complicated. He had tried to do it linearly, but found himself jumping around in a nonlinear fashion quite a bit, which provoked him to remark that he "felt like he was in a Quentin Tarantino movie." This in turn forced him to explain Quentin Tarantino, and upon mentioning his love for the film *Inglourious Basterds,* he was forced into explaining World War II. This in turn forced him into explaining the Holocaust, which made Winnie rather upset. He quickly tried to segue off of the topic and onto the fact that Jonas Salk found a cure for polio.

The stories that seemed to fascinate Winnie more than anything else were the advancements in travel. How people could go see any part of the world and experience strange new cultures with relative ease.

"Is it common to visit Africa?" Winnie asked. "I've always wanted to go to Africa."

"Sure," Huey said. "Although some parts of Africa are a bit more *unstable* than others. But The World Cup was in South Africa a few years back." This led him into a twenty-minute tangent explaining both soccer and apartheid. Soccer of course had been around for hundreds of years and in theory Winnie could have known what it was, but just like most Americans she was blissfully unaware.

"What about Egypt?" she said. "Can you go see the pyramids?"

"Egypt is also a bit unstable at the moment. But it's getting better."

"And China?"

"Parts of it."

"Cuba?"

Winnie somehow had a supernatural gift for picking countries with complicated US relations. He wondered why she couldn't ask about Spain or Hawaii.

"And people use flying machines to go to far off places?" Winnie said.

"Yeah. Those who can afford to, at least."

"Like the one you came here in? The one that was shot down?"

"A helicopter. Sometimes, but usually people travel on airplanes."

"What about balloons? Hot air balloons?"

"Not really so popular. Sometimes people—" Huey stopped in the middle of his thought as something occurred to him. Something Winnie had just said finally registered in his brain. "Winnie, how did you know we were shot down?"

"Sorry?" She gave him a confused look.

"You just said 'a flying machine like the one you came here in, the one that was shot down.' I never mentioned that we were shot down." He thought it over again to make sure. He definitely hadn't mentioned it. In fact, he hadn't mentioned it to Josephine Jackson or anyone else since the crash.

Winnie stared at him for a moment. A long moment. He had seen the look currently on Winnie's face on his daughter's dozens of times when he caught her sneaking out of the house in the middle of the night. Winnie looked very, very guilty.

"You're the one who shot us down, aren't you?" he said.

"Yeah," Winnie said. "I sort of am."

Huey found himself growing angry, but knew he needed to keep his cool. Just like when he dealt with Jenny in the middle of the night. "Why?" he said.

"I panicked. I was out hunting with my rifle." She gestured to a rifle leaning against the wall in the corner. "I heard a noise and looked up. Saw this giant metal flying… thing coming right at me."

"And your first inclination was to shoot at it?"

"Well, yeah."

He couldn't believe this, but he actually wasn't that surprised. He thought back to the newspaper article on the wall of the Aviatrix, the one about the uncontacted Amazonian tribe throwing spears up at the helicopter taking their photograph. Perhaps there's an innate human emotion inside us all that when we are presented with something we don't understand, we immediately want to kill it.

"Look, I'm sorry," she said. "Once I realized what I had shot down, I felt really bad about it."

"Well, at least I know you're a good shot," he said. He gestured to the rifle. "Hitting a moving helicopter from the ground with that thing? Josephine was right about you."

Winnie took a sip from her glass of moonshine and appeared to think for a moment. "About that," she said. "I don't want you to get the wrong idea here. I'm not going to help you. Shoot Miller Roux, I mean."

Huey gave her a look, confused. She had kept him here for hours, making him explain everything from penicillin to the Sony Playstation, and he had just assumed she was on board. "Why not?" he said.

"Because." Winnie said.

"Because? He's a monster, Winnie. You said so yourself."

"And while paralyzing the man may have not been my intended objective all those years ago, I've made peace with it being a satisfying punishment."

"Now he's just a monster in a wheelchair."

"I've kept to my own up here for eight years for a reason, Mr. Palmer. And it's not just because I'm hiding from Miller Roux." Winnie gave him a look, seeming to be on the fence about revealing something to him. "I've been working on a way out of here," she said. "I'm leaving, and I'm leaving soon. Helping you is a risk, and it's just one that's too big for me to take when I'm this close to being finished."

"Finished with that?"

She thought for another long moment, eying him. He could tell she had a secret that she was dying to tell someone. She stood up and set down her glass. "Come with me," she said. "I'll show you."

They walked through the woods for a few minutes and reached the base of a stone cliff on the side of the mountain. Winnie looked around, making sure they weren't being watched, then approached a dead bush leaning against the cliff wall.

She pushed the dead bush aside to reveal the entrance to a cave. She stepped inside and he stayed right behind her. Near the entrance were several torches affixed to the wall that Winnie lit to cast a dim glow over the place. Huey looked around to see that the cave was massive and seemed to go on forever.

Several objects hanging off of hooks on the wall caught Huey's attention. He stepped closer to get a better look, and his eyes widened as he recognized the objects instantly.

The Silk Specter's mask, coat, and two guns.

"You're the Silk Specter." Huey said.

"I don't really call myself that," Winnie said. "Other people call me that, I guess. I don't mind it though, it's rather spooky."

"You tied us up? In the clothing store?"

"Yeah, sorry about that. Cost of doing business. That's how I recognized you in the woods this morning."

Huey took the Silk Specter mask off of the hook and eyed it. It menacingly stared back at him. "Why? Why do you go around stealing people's linens?"

Winnie let out a smile and pointed behind him. "For that." He turned around and almost dropped his torch when he saw what was spread out over the cave floor.

A deflated hot air balloon.

It looked like it had been stitched together with hundreds and hundreds of pieces of cloth. Dresses, sheets, napkins, curtains, scarves, handkerchiefs, and so on. A large, crudely made wicker basket sat next to it, a metal bucket attached to the top that he assumed was for making a fire to provide the hot air.

"She's my baby," Winnie said. "My pride-and-joy. And she's finally ready to go." She stepped over to the wicker basket and ran her fingers along it as if it were a new hot rod. She then turned to Huey and let out another big smile. "And she seats two."

CHAPTER 43

Val stood in the market and looked over the wide selection of apples. The variety was impressive, and she assumed they were all organic and pesticide-free considering the circumstances. She picked one up and inspected it closely, looking for bruises. She found none.

This was all a ruse, of course. She could have cared less about buying an apple. She didn't even like apples. Her attention was really focused on Number 5, who stood in the back aisle collecting jars of honey.

Val had spent the morning hiding in the bushes outside of Castle Roux, trying to concoct a plan to sneak inside. The castle was heavily fortified and even more heavily guarded, but she knew that if she thought long and hard enough, she'd figure out a way. She always figured out a way. She ended up not needing to, however, when the large front door opened and three of Miller Roux's wives walked right out. She had no idea which number two of them were, but she recognized Number 5 the moment the girl stepped into the sunlight. Number 5 held what appeared to be a list in one hand and empty bags in the other. Val, staying hidden, followed the three women down the trail and here into town. One of wives went off to the butcher shop and one to the gunsmith. Number 5, the target of Val's stalking, came here to Kinney's market.

Val glanced around to see if the coast was clear. The only other inhabitant was Old Man Kinney, the owner, who appeared to be trying to fix the sole of a cowboy boot. He paid neither she nor Number 5 any attention.

Val slipped over to the back aisle, right next to Number 5. Number 5 still hadn't noticed her, lost in thought, looking over the jars of honey. "Afternoon, Annie," Val said. Number 5 gave her a surprised look, clearly caught off guard by the use of her real name.

"Valerie," Number 5 said. "I mean Val. Good afternoon." Number 5 looked around to make sure they weren't being watched and was relieved they were not. "Please, do not call me that here."

"Sorry," Val smiled and gestured to the jars. "Doing a little shopping?"

"Yes. I am in charge of the grocery list. It is one of my responsibilities."

"I'm surprised your husband lets you out of the house."

"Some of the wives are allowed to leave Castle Roux, if it is required as part of our responsibilities. But not until after one o'clock. My husband does not approve of us attending the Showdown. He says it is not for the eyes of a lady."

"He might be right about that." Val eyed Number 5 for a moment. She knew it was time to end the small talk and get down to brass tacks. "Can I ask you a question? Maybe in private?" Val gestured to Old Man Kinney across the store.

"You don't need to worry about him," Number 5 said. "He's as deaf as they come."

Val considered this and eyed the old man again. He was still sitting behind the counter, fixated on the sole of the cowboy boot. "Hey! Grandpa!" she said in a very, very loud voice. The man didn't even flinch.

"What did you want to ask me?" Number 5 said.

"How old are you?"

"Twenty-seven."

"How old were you when you married Miller Roux?"

"Fifteen."

"And is the life you're living the one you imagined when you were a little girl?" Number 5 gave her a look and did not respond to this question. Val already knew the answer anyway. "Annie, do you realize how much power you have?"

"I asked you not to call me that."

"I don't care. It's your name."

Number 5 looked down to the ground. "Power?" she said. "How do you figure that?"

"Because you can very easily kill Miller Roux," Val said. Number 5 looked back up to Val and her eyes widened. Val could tell that Number 5 was beginning to grow quite uncomfortable with this conversation. "Don't tell me you've never thought about it."

"Of course not. He is my husband. I love him."

"Bullshit. You can tell me the truth. You and me, we're just two girls talking at the grocery store. Val gestured to the gun that Number 5 was carrying in a holster around her waist. "Don't tell me you've never thought about taking that thing and ending him with it."

"My gun holds no bullets," Number 5 said. "None of the wives' do. He has forbidden it."

"Because he's smart," Val said. "But there are other ways. I know you've thought about it."

Number 5 took a deep breath and closed her eyes. Val knew that she wanted to talk about this. That she had been probably been wanting to talk about this for years with someone, and now was her time. Right here, with this stranger.

"On the night he married Number 15," Number 5 said. "A few years back. We had eaten a big meal, like we always do when he takes a new bride. I was in the kitchen helping wash dishes after. I heard screaming coming from upstairs. A few minutes later, she came in. Number 15, I mean. She was covered with blood. It was all over her wedding dress. She had a deep cut across her cheek. He had gotten rough with her in the bedroom. Got upset, screaming that she was 'just lying there like a dead fish' and all sorts of awful things. She was only thirteen years old. She didn't know any better." Val clenched her teeth, angry.

"There was a frying pan hanging on the wall of the kitchen," Number 5 said. "I grabbed it. I started walking up the stairs. Planned on hitting him over the head with it. Just hitting and hitting until he was dead. But I stopped halfway up. I couldn't do it. I was too scared. I didn't have it in me."

"Maybe now you do?" Val said.

"That's easy for you to say. You don't know how things work here."

"I'm getting real fucking tired of people telling me that."

"He's a complicated man. He loves us. He apologized to Number 15 for what he did. He admitted that he made an error in judgment."

"An error in judgment? An error in judgment is when you order the chicken at a seafood restaurant, not beat a thirteen-year-old girl."

Number 5 shook her head. "I know what you're doing here, Valerie. You want me to ruin my own life just to help you save your friend."

"This isn't about my friend. This is about everyone else. This is about all the people your loving husband has ordered to be killed, including four of them in the street today."

Number 5 gave Val a look. "What?"

"That's right. Four of them at once. And they did nothing wrong. Their crime was that they helped people. One of them… one of them was just a dumb sweet kid who I should have been nicer to." Val felt a tear running down her cheek. She wiped it away. "You think if you kill Miller Roux you'll ruin your life? Annie, if you kill Miller Roux then you'll be seen as a goddamn hero."

"You talk like killing a man is easy."

"It is."

"Have you ever done it?!" Number 5 slammed her fist against the shelf, causing some of the jars of honey to wobble. She glared at Val. She was angry.

In that moment, Val had a massive realization. That she herself had become everything she hated. She was being an imperialist. A cultural tourist. She had come into a situation that she didn't understand and told the locals what was right for them. She was asking a young woman to commit an act that she herself would never have the balls to do.

"No," Val said. "I haven't. I'm sorry"

The door to the general store opened and Val looked over to

see a woman head in with three small children. The children were singing a song that Val didn't recognize. She assumed they had made it up.

She looked back to Number 5, who still held anger in her eyes. "I'll let you get back to your shopping," Val said. She nodded and walked out of the store.

CHAPTER 44

Ernie laid on a cot at Dr. Thundercloud's and started to come back into the real world. The opium had brought on a long, lucid dream involving he and Ylianna Guerra, Miss Texas 2015, attending the Houston rodeo. It was pretty amazing. He had thankfully been able to refund his bet slip after the MacKenzie/Chambers postponement, and the 100,000 roux, in combination with his hat and vest, were able to buy him a cot for a few hours. Dr. Thundercloud agreed to cut the minimum stay down from four hours to three, and Ernie was very grateful for this concession.

He sat up in his cot, the memories of he and Ylianna eating corn dogs quickly fading, and looked around the room to see that pretty much all the other patients were conked out. Everyone except for the one-legged man, who was staring right at him from the next bed.

"Afternoon," the one-legged man said. "You must have had a nice dream. Had a big old shit-eating grin on your face."

"It was pretty nice. It involved Miss Texas."

"Miss Texas? She like the queen or something?"

"Not exactly."

"Huh. Say, is it true your friend challenged Miller Roux to a Showdown?" Apparently word of Huey's idiocy had spread to every dark corner of this town.

"It is."

"Oh, swell," the one-legged man said. "I had heard chatter about it, but didn't know if I had made it up or not. Things are a little foggy in my head sometimes. You know how it is. I might have to pull myself out of here and go see that one. Haven't watched a

Showdown in years, not since my son Jack's, but this one sounds like it can't be missed."

"How did he do?" Ernie said.

"Pardon?"

"Your son. Jack. How did he do in his Showdown?"

"He got killed. Never was quick on the draw, that one. In more ways than one."

"Sorry to hear that."

"Them's the breaks. You got any kids?"

"No. My guns are my children." Ernie had said this expression many times before when asked that question, and he genuinely felt it. He put an intense amount of love and care into each firearm that he acquired, because he knew that his collection would be his legacy. That's why people have children, after all. Legacy. To leave something of themselves for future generations. It was written into Ernie's will that upon his death, a considerable portion of his fortune would be used to set up the Swords Center in downtown San Antonio. The massive complex, which would be built on land that he had purchased years before but not yet developed, would contain both the entirety of his firearm collection and a museum dedicated to his life. Right in the center of the museum would be a tree-lined atrium centering around a life-size bronze statue of Ernest Paxton Swords. Sitting in the statue's hand, for all of eternity, would be the Special Edition Colt Third Model Dragoon Percussion Revolver.

"Let me ask you," Ernie said. "What do you think would happen to this town if Miller Roux got killed tomorrow?"

The one-legged man leaned back and seemed to really think about this question for a moment. "Probably chaos," he said.

"Chaos? Really?"

"Well, somebody would have to step up and take his place. Most obviously Cook Woodson. Of course Cook Woodson ain't Miller's kin, his wives are, which means they'd inherit the gunsmith and Castle Roux and the whole shebang." Ernie was surprised to hear the term "shebang" come from the one-legged man's mouth. He was beginning to realize a lot of slang was much older than he thought. Since he had been in New Roux City, Ernie had heard people say "dude," "funky," "puke," and "booze," all of which surprised him. Ernie had also heard a handful of terms that must be unique only to this place. Everyone called an outhouse a "Debbie Maguire" for some reason.

"And Miller's children," the one-legged man said. "They're all pretty small, even though he's got quite a few of them, so they ain't stepping up to try and take over. If I had to guess, I'd think Cook Woodson would challenge the wives to Showdowns one by one for whatever bullshit reason, until they were all dead, then he'd just march into Castle Roux and take it over. Probably wait until the kids are old enough and then Showdown them too."

"So, basically killing Miller Roux might be pointless unless you kill Cook Woodson and all of his men as well?"

"Might be," the one-legged man said. "But then who am I to say? I'm just a one-legged opium addict." He gave Ernie a smile, then lied back down on his cot and pressed an opium pipe to his lips.

Ernie sat there for a few minutes, thinking about what the one-legged man had said about chaos. This town may very well be beyond repair. He eyed a clock on the wall to see it was almost 5:00. He should probably get going, go see how Huey's meeting with the jungle woman went. He probably had time for one more hit, though.

CHAPTER 45

Huey sat at the desk in the schoolteacher's house and finished writing a note. He had to use a 19th century fountain pen, the only writing instrument that he could find in the place, and it was a bit messy and kept needing refilling. He was surprised that a schoolteacher wouldn't have any pencils around, but then maybe pencils didn't exist at all in New Roux City. Maybe they used all the lead for bullets.

When the note was finished, he read it back over.

> *Val and Ernie,*
>
> *I've been given a chance to get out of here, and I'm going to take it. I can't really explain in great detail, but if all goes according to plan then I should be able to find help by tomorrow and will come back for you first thing. I promise. Lay low.*
>
> *Huey*

He nodded to himself in approval. The note was solid. Short and sweet. Vague, but not ominously so as if to imply that he was going off to kill himself. He had decided to leave a note rather than waiting to tell Val and Ernie in person because it just seemed easier on everyone. He knew they would have a million questions about Winnie Crider and *how* exactly Huey was leaving that he either couldn't or shouldn't answer, and so it was probably best to avoid them all together. He also didn't want to have to explain why he felt that *he* should be the one to ride in the hot air balloon over them, even though it of course made the most sense considering he was going to be shot dead the next day.

He read over the note again. When he finished, something

began to occur to him. He read over it one more time. His suspicions were confirmed.

"Shit," Huey said to himself. The note was almost identical to the one he had left Jenny when she was nine years old. Same sentence structure. Same underlying message.

Archie Gomez, an old friend of Huey's father, had called Huey up and offered him an opportunity in Los Angeles. Archie was helping to produce a movie called *Blood & Lettuce,* and they needed some helicopter shots, but the movie was low budget so they needed to shoot them without permits. No pilot in L.A. would touch the job, not wanting to piss off the film unions, but Archie had heard all about Huey and his reputation for doing things under the table. Archie sold Huey on the fact that if Huey did a good job, then many of his producer buddies would come calling for more work and Huey could even set up shop in Hollywood. Huey had always dreamed of working in the movies, and couldn't wait to jump at the chance. The only problem was that *Blood & Lettuce*'s shooting days were the same exact weekend as Jenny's ninth birthday party, which was going to be held at Circus Circus Casino on the upper floor dedicated to children, filled with video games and a midway instead of slot machines. Huey and Terry had just recently decided to spend some time apart, and Jenny stressed how much she wanted both parents to be at the party, most likely in some sort of attempt to get them back together. Huey rationalized that going to Hollywood, and potentially setting up shop there, was in the best interest of Jenny in the long run, so he made the decision on the morning of the party to leave her a note.

Jenny,

I've been given a chance for an amazing job and I'm going to take it. I can't really explain in great detail, but if all goes according to plan then I should be able to introduce you to some famous movie stars soon. I promise. Have fun.

Dad

Huey had left the note on Jenny's dresser as she slept, assuming it was the best way to explain his actions, then quietly snuck out of the house and flew to Hollywood. His assumption was very incorrect. Jenny was so upset that she wouldn't leave her room and the entire party at Circus Circus was canceled. Terry called Huey's act "the straw that broke the camel's back" and filed for divorce a few weeks later, referring to him as a "selfish jerk" in official court documents. On top of all of that, when he arrived to Los Angeles he learned that *Blood & Lettuce*'s financing had fallen through and there was no job.

Huey thought about all of this as he stared at the note currently before him on the desk. He wondered if he was once again being a selfish jerk. He wondered if he shouldn't have to wonder at this point in his life, and should just already inherently know.

There was a knock at the door. He wasn't exactly expecting company and wasn't even sure who in town knew he was staying there. He put the note down and slid over to the window, pulling aside the curtain and glancing out. No one appeared to be standing there. He drew his gun, because he felt like that's what someone with a gun would do in this situation.

There was another knock. "Hello?" a little girl's voice said.

He leaned over to peer down, and could now see that a little girl was standing there, staring right up at him. "Hey, stranger," the little girl said. She waved. The little girl looked familiar to Huey, and he soon recognized her as one of the children hiding under the table from the Silk Specter on the night that he arrived. He put away the gun and opened the door.

"Sorry if I'm bothering you," she said.

"No, it's okay," Huey said.

"My name's Sally. And your name's Huey. Huey Palmer."

"It is."

"My brothers and I, we made you something." She held an object up and put it in Huey's left hand. It was a five-pointed star made out of papier-mâché that had been painted gold. The word "Sheriff" was written across the front in black letters. "It's a badge," she said. "Our pa, he always tells us these stories. Stories that his pa had told him about how there used to be lawmen who would look after the good people and shoot down the villains. He and my ma, they talk about how sometimes they wish a lawman would come to our town. They only talk about this at home, 'cause they know they can't talk about it up in town."

"I'm not a lawman," Huey said.

"But you've come to town to shoot down the villain. My brothers and I, we thought maybe that after you win The Showdown tomorrow, you'd consider becoming the Sheriff. Maybe help to shoot down some of the other villains too." She smiled at Huey, and he could see the hope in her eyes. It wasn't something that he had seen in most of the people here in New Roux City, people who had been beaten down by this way of life. But he knew Sally hadn't been beaten down. Not yet, anyway. She still thought the future could be sunny and bright.

"What makes you think I'm going to win The Showdown tomorrow?" Huey said.

"Because God is on your side," Sally said with a smile. "I know he is. Now you have a good day." She nodded to Huey, then turned to walk back towards her farm. He looked down to the badge in his hand. He turned it over to see that the children had attached a pin to the back so that he could fasten it to his jacket. He thought for a moment, then placed the badge in his pocket.

He stepped back into the house and closed the door. He walked over to the desk and read over the note one more time.

CHAPTER 46

Winnie's father had been quite the reader, and when she was a kid the family had a shelf overflowing with books. They had been passed down through generations of Criders, and each and every book was a highly prized treasure since new ones were impossible to come by in New Roux City. When she was eight years old, Winnie read Jules Verne's *Around the World in Eighty Days* and immediately became infatuated with it. She too one day wished to venture to far-off India, China, and Japan just like Phileas Fogg.

Another book from her father's collection that caught her attention was one that was a bit more obscure. Written by a man named André Jacques Garnerin in 1802, the book was titled *Aeronautica*, although the actual full title was *Aeronautica, or, Voyages in the Air; Containing the Principles of Aerostation and of Flying Machines, Description of the Montgolfiers' Balloon; Aerial Voyage of M. Pilatre de Rozier, and the Marquis de Arlandes; Together with All Those Performed in England, from Lunardi's, Including Those Lately Performed by M. Garnerin; to Which Are Added, the Uses Air Balloons May Be Applied To*. It was the longest book title Winnie had ever seen.

While *Aeronautica* highly peaked her interest, she was unable to read it due to the fact that it was written entirely in French. And since no one in New Roux City spoke French anymore, there was no way to translate it. A handful of the founders spoke French, including Etienne Roux himself and Winnie's own great-great-great-grandfather, hence his ownership of *Aeronautica* in the first place, but the language had been phased out over the last hundred years because no one really had a need for it. *Aeronautica* was still filled with diagrams and pictures of 19th century aircraft, however, so Winnie was able to look at those.

The morning that she shot Miller Roux in the back as he was eating breakfast at The Prospector, she unexpectedly managed to dodge the gunfire from his men and rush out the back door. She ran to her house and packed up a sack with a handful of essentials before heading into the East Forest, where she planned to hide out until things had calmed down following Miller's death. She was in such a rush while packing that when she went to grab *Around the World in Eighty Days* in order to have something to read, she accidentally threw *Aeronautica* into the sack instead. It was the greatest mistake she ever made. That night, Winnie's books, along with the rest of her house, were burned by Miller Roux's men. Days later, Winnie would learn that she unfortunately hadn't killed Miller, but on the bright side he would never walk again.

She spent the next few years without a single book to read except for a guide to ballooning in a language she didn't understand. Upon staring at the diagrams and pictures of aircraft day in and day out, however, she realized that an entire chapter was dedicated to teaching the reader how to build their very own hot air balloon. A few years later, she had done just that.

That morning, when Winnie had asked Huey to go with her on her inaugural balloon trip out of New Roux City, he seemed quite surprised. As he should, she had just met the man a few hours before after all. What the stranger didn't realize was that flying the thing was really a two-person job, so Winnie was going to have to recruit a copilot to go with her sooner or later anyway, and there wasn't anyone in town she particular trusted, or liked. She was thrilled when Huey agreed to go along, although she did her best to hide it.

Now, as Winnie stood outside of the cave, moving pieces of the balloon into a large clearing that would be the launch site, she was furious that Huey had gone and changed his mind.

"What do you mean now you're not going?" she said.

"I don't really believe in spirituality and all that," Huey said.

"But a little girl showing up at your door at the exact right moment to hand you a Sheriff's badge has to be some kind of sign."

"Look, once we fly out of here to safety, we can call in the cavalry to come back and liberate the people from the tyranny of Miller Roux. We don't have to do it ourselves."

"And what if we don't make it to safety?"

"Why wouldn't we?"

"Because I've never flown a hot air balloon before, and our hot air balloon is made out of lingerie and living room curtains. If we crash halfway out into the desert, which is *very* likely, we're done for."

"I didn't build this thing just to stare at it," she said. "Crashing in the desert is a chance I'm willing to take. "

"And so am I." Huey took a step closer and gestured to his gun. "*After* I kill Miller Roux. But not before. I'm not going to abandon these people when I could possibly help them."

"These people?" Winnie said. "You don't even know these people, Mr. Palmer. I do. And trust me, they're worth abandoning."

"I know that these people are people. That deep down, most of them are good, but they need a little help dealing with the few that are bad."

"I'd rather go to a place where no one is bad in the first place."

"I hate to break it to you, Winnie, but that place doesn't exist on planet Earth. The outside world is not much better than New Roux City, and we've got our own fair share of evil men doing evil things."

Winnie looked at the balloon pieces on the ground, her mind racing. She felt so close to freedom. All this time working so hard, and she was so close. But damn it, he was making a lot of sense and she hated him for it.

"I didn't come back up here to convince you to help me," Huey said. "I just wanted to let you know that I'm going to go to The Showdown tomorrow."

"You're going to face Miller alone?" Winnie said. "You won't stand a chance."

"Maybe you could give me some pointers."

She eyed Huey for a moment, then took a good look at his gun.

She gestured to an apple tree in the distance, far on the other side of the clearing. "Shoot that apple tree," she said.

"What?" Huey said.

"Shoot that apple tree over there. So I can see your form and give you some goddamn pointers."

Huey drew his gun, aimed it at the apple tree, and fired.

Bang.

Huey missed wildly, the bullet hitting a large rock a good five feet to the right of the tree.

"Jesus, you're awful," Winnie said.

"I know. I never said otherwise. What do you suggest I do?"

"Nothing. You're beyond help." She grabbed her rifle, aimed it at the apple tree, and fired.

Bang.

The bullet ripped through a dangling apple, dead center, causing it to explode. Bullseye. She lowered the rifle and gave Huey a look. "Guess I'll just have to shoot him for you," she said.

CHAPTER 47

Val looked up to the clock tower. It was midnight, exactly twelve hours until what the bookies at Kooper's Card Room had dubbed "The Showdown of the Year." Main Street was empty, the only sounds coming from a group of rowdy preteens playing a drinking game inside The Prospector, and they didn't notice her sneaking through the shadows and entering into the structure.

She had learned from Shaky that the tower had been one of the first buildings built by the founders when they settled New Roux City, every citizen pitching in to help as a symbol of their new community. Etienne Roux had purchased the clock at an auction in New Orleans in 1873, salvaged from a bank that had burned to the ground, and planned for it to one day be erected in the original Roux City in Louisiana. When the founders headed west, they took the clock with them. It had been maintained ever since by the community, the only thing in town treated as such. Shaky told her that this fact was never openly discussed, but quietly understood.

She climbed up the rickety tower stairs to the third floor, where she found herself standing in a large room. The giant wrought-iron clock face took up a whole wall before her, the gears and weights hard at work behind it. The giant minute hand moved to 12:01, although to her it was literally counter-clockwise.

"Pretty cool, huh?" Huey said. Huey, Ernie, and a woman she assumed to be Winnie Crider stood in the corner, watching her from the shadows. Winnie, who held a rifle in her hands, was more beautiful than Val had expected. If Val was ever stuck out in the woods for eight years, she could only pray to look half that good.

"This is Winnie Crider," Huey said. "Winnie, this is Valerie Trujillo."

"Nice to meet you," Val said.

"We've actually already met," Winnie said.

"She's the Silk Specter," Ernie said. Winnie raised her hands up in the air, as if to say "you got me."

"Of course," Val said. She then thought about this reveal for another moment. "Wait, why? Why do you steal people's—?"

"I'd rather not get into it." Winnie shot Huey a glance.

"So you really think you can do this, Ms. Crider?" Ernie said. "Shoot Miller Roux from up all the way up here?"

Winnie stepped to the wrought-iron clock face, the large numbers appearing backwards, and looked down to the street below. Val could see that it was indeed a perfect vantage point of exactly where Miller Roux would be positioned in twelve hours' time. Winnie lifted up her rifle, stuck it through the iron number six, and aimed. "Yeah, this should work just fine," Winnie said.

"And you'll know exactly when to shoot?" Val said.

"I'll know when to shoot. Don't you worry about me." Winnie slid the rifle back out from the clock and slung it over her shoulder. She then gestured to Huey's gun in its holster. "Now listen up. It's very important that you have blanks in your gun when your draw tomorrow," she said.

"Blanks?" Huey said. "Why?"

"Because if you fire a real bullet and it hits some window or wall or innocent bystander, then people are going to question how exactly you both killed Miller Roux and fired a second shot at the same exact time."

"You'd be a regular Lee Harvey Oswald," Val said. She laughed, and Winnie gave her a confused look. "It's a long story."

Deep down, Val hoped all this secret plotting was going to be for nothing. She had a good feeling that she had gotten Number 5 to come to her senses earlier, and perhaps Miller Roux was even already dead at that moment. Val hadn't mentioned the specifics of her "Plan B" to the others, because if it worked then she'd be able to surprise them, and if it didn't then they'd never know it had failed. Plus, it didn't involve Ernie ending up with the Dragoon, so he never would have been on board anyway.

She noticed that Huey had taken his gun out of its holster and was eying it. It had clearly never occurred to him that he wouldn't be able to carry real bullets, and this prospect must have made him even more nervous about The Showdown than he already was. He gave Winnie a look. "You better not miss," he said.

"I won't," Winnie said. She took her rifle and leaned it against the wall, then looked to Val and Ernie. "And you two, you need to act normal tomorrow like nothing is up. Don't glance up here at the clock tower every ten seconds. Miller's men will wonder why you're suddenly so fascinated with this structure and start looking themselves. You'll give me away."

"Why would we be looking at the clock tower every ten seconds?" Val said.

"Nerves," Winnie said. "You'll want to look at the exact thing you shouldn't be looking at without even realizing it."

"I think we're a little smarter than that."

"Oh yeah? Don't look at the rifle I just leaned against the wall."

Without any hesitation, Val instinctively looked right at the rifle. "Shit," she said.

"But also don't not look at the clock tower at all tomorrow," Winnie said. "That'll look equally as strange. It is how people tell time around here, after all."

"So we need to find the sweet spot between looking at the clock tower too much and too little," Ernie said. "Got it."

"Good," Winnie said. She then gestured to the floor behind her. "Now, if you don't mind, I need to get some sleep. You should probably all get some too."

"You're going to sleep here?" Val said.

"I am. Can't risk someone seeing me come up here in the morning. I'm a wanted woman, remember?"

"Right. That makes sense. Do you need anything? A blanket? A nightlight?"

"No, I'll make do. Already got a clock." Winnie gestured to the gigantic backwards clock face behind her. "Besides, I've lived in the wilderness for the last eight years, so this place is a luxury fucking hotel in my book."

"Well then," Huey said. "Good luck." He stuck out his hand, and Winnie shook it.

"You too," Winnie said.

CHAPTER 48

Miller Roux sat at the dining room table with his wives and enjoyed a nice breakfast of ham and eggs. It was a tradition around Castle Roux that he and all of the wives eat their meals together, and as Miller took on more and more brides over the years, the table got longer and longer. Miller always sat at the head, and the seating arrangement was such that the more recent wives sat closer to him. Number 1 and Number 2, who were also the oldest of the bunch, were seated as far away from Miller as possible. This was for the best, because at this point he had heard everything the two women had to say.

Despite The Showdown today being Miller's first, there wasn't a nervous bone in his body. He had always used his man Cook Woodson to Showdown for him out of convenience, not ability. Miller had spent countless hours in his private firing range both testing out new guns and practicing with his own Dragoon, so he was well aware that he himself was the fastest draw in town. And more importantly, he was a Roux. It was in his blood. He had God on his side. He was going to win today. He was 100% confident in that fact. Which is why he had decided to make the announcement that he was about to make.

"Listen up, all of you," Miller said. Every single one of his wives immediately gave him her full attention. "I've been thinking, and I want you all to attend The Showdown today." A collective gasp fell over the room. His wives clearly couldn't believe it. This was unheard of. He hadn't allowed some of these women to leave Castle Roux in fifteen years. "I know it may seem unusual," he said. "But I want you to see what's going to happen today. I want you to understand that when your husband needs to take matters into his own hands, he does so. I have already arranged a viewing area in front of the gunsmith shop. You will be able to see everything from there. In addition, I want you all to wear your finest dresses. And I of course will need my finest suit pressed and laid out for me."

He looked to a wife at random. "Number 13, please handle that."

"Yes, dear husband." Number 13 stood up, cleared her unfinished plate, and headed out of the dining room.

He then looked around to another wife at random. "Number 8, also see to it that my boots are shined."

"Which boots, dear husband?" Number 8 said.

"The snakeskin. Obviously."

"Yes, dear husband." She stood and headed out of the room.

He looked around again, and his eyes settled on Number 5. "Number 5," he said. He reached down, took The Dragoon out of its holster, and held it up in the air. "Polish my gun."

Number 5 just sat there, not saying a word, her eyes transfixed on the gun. "Number 5?" Miller said. "Are you fucking deaf?"

"Sorry, dear husband," she said. She stood up and walked over to him. She grabbed the gun in her right hand and eyed it.

He looked back to his ham and eggs and continued to eat. After a few seconds, he realized that Number 5 hadn't moved. She was still just standing there, staring at The Dragoon in her hand. It annoyed him to no end when the wives took their goddamn time to do as he had requested. "Something wrong, sloth?" he said. "Go. Now." He gestured to the door.

"Yes, dear husband," Number 5 said. She turned and left the room. As she was walking out, Cook Woodson walked in.

"Hey boss," Cook said. "There's someone here to see you."

"I'm in the middle of breakfast."

"It's one of the strangers. The one you smashed in the face in the elevator."

Miller thought for a moment, wondering what on earth that liar wanted with him now. He looked to the wives who still remained at the table. "Everyone out," he said. "Now." The wives all stood up without a moment's hesitation. Each grabbed her plate and shuffled out the door. Miller nodded to Cook, who stepped out and reappeared a moment later with Ernie Swords.

"Morning, Mr. Roux," Ernie said. Miller sized Ernie up, thinking the stranger's physical conditional was in a fairly pathetic state. The man looked like he hadn't slept or eaten in days.

"If you're here to try and talk me out of The Showdown," Miller said, "I'm afraid it's too late for that."

"No, that's not why I'm here. I'm here because you're going to give me your Special Edition Colt Third Model Dragoon Percussion Revolver." Ernie stared at Miller, unblinking. He was being serious.

"Am I?" Miller said.

"May I sit?"

Miller took another bite of ham, then gestured to one of the empty chairs at the table. This would be entertaining.

Ernie took a seat. "Are you familiar with a long con?" he said.

"Con as in a confidence trick?" Miller was familiar with term because one of the books in his private library was *The Confidence Man* by Herman Melville, which he had read half a dozen times. Melville's final work, the novel told the story of a mysterious stranger who sneaks aboard a riverboat heading down the Mississippi and proceeds to try and swindle the passengers. The Roux family had always looked to this book as being fairly prescient, for they knew that one day a stranger might come into New Roux City and try to swindle them all.

"Yes," Ernie said. "But it's a specific kind of confidence trick. It's one where you plant a seed in someone's head, then wait for them to give you the idea that will end up biting them in the ass. I've always thought that it's the most successful way to get ahead in business."

"And you've played a long con on me?" Miller said.

"No, not *on* you." Ernie said. "*For* you."

Miller gave Ernie a look. This was getting very interesting. He set down his fork and wiped his mouth with his napkin. "How so?"

"I told Huey Palmer a story about a man named Jimmy Stewart

who once needed a man named John Wayne to secretly fight a duel for him. Huey then came up with the idea, all on his own, to go out and find the best sharpshooter in New Roux City to secretly shoot you at today's Showdown instead of him."

"That would never work," Miller said.

"Not even if it was Winnie Crider?"

Miller's heart nearly stopped. He had not heard that name in a very, very long time. It was not allowed to be spoken with the walls of Castle Roux. It was sacrilege.

"And I can tell you exactly where she is," Ernie said. He leaned back and put his feet up on the table. "If you just promise to hand over the Dragoon after you've killed Huey with it."

CHAPTER 49

Huey sat at the bar at The Prospector and sipped on a glass of water. He hadn't been in the mood for whiskey, especially because he figured it best to have his faculties about him during his first gunfight. He had walked down to Main Street with Val a few hours before, Ernie was already gone when they woke up, and Val now sat on the piano playing away. She had opted for classical pieces this morning in lieu of pop songs; Huey recognized Chopin and Schubert, and it was really starting to bum him and everyone else in the establishment out.

He refilled the fountain pen that he had taken from the schoolteacher's house and returned to writing the letter in front of him.

Jenny,

If you're reading this, it means things didn't go according to plan and I lost The Showdown. I'm sure by now the whole world knows about New Roux City and what went on here. It's probably all over the news and Matt Lauer has already done an episode of The Today Show standing on Main Street. As a final wish, do me a favor and please don't read this letter on television. Please don't go on some news show and cry a lot and read this letter to weepy piano music. I know I'm dead, but it's still embarrassing. This letter is for you. Just for you.

First of all, I'm very sorry that I missed your graduation. At this point you understand why. I guess I should say you know why, but maybe don't understand why. Maybe you'll never understand why and neither will I. I realize I'm not making much sense. You know the thing about writing on parchment with a fountain pen is you can't really go back and delete the earlier parts of the note very easily. You have to just crumple up the whole sheet of paper and start over or leave it.

I'm sorry for a lot of things. I'm sorry for never being there for you when you needed it. I'm sorry for always putting myself before you. I was a bad husband to your mother and a bad father to you. I know that. I'm not blind. I had tried to make it up to you these last few years, but I realize it was too little too late now. Maybe if I had had more time, I could have caught back up to where I should have been. Guess we'll never know.

My father was kind of an asshole. It took me a while to realize it, but I know it now. He never pushed me to do what I wanted to do. He made it clear that my path in life was set and I'd be a helicopter pilot just like him. I'm not sure what else I would have done with my life if he'd been supportive of me exploring, hell I may have been a helicopter pilot anyway, but the option would have been nice. I'm not blaming him for my behavior. I'm just saying I want you to go out and find yourself and do what you really want to do. My parting words to you, I guess. If you want to be a marine biologist or ballet dancer or food critic, then go out and try it.

I don't really have anything inspirational to end this letter on. Hopefully you'll never read it anyway and this is all a moot point. Just know that I love you, Jenny. I love you more than anything.

- DAD

He folded up the letter and sealed it in an envelope, writing "Jenny Palmer" on the outside. He handed the letter to Shaky, who had agreed he'd hide it in the event of Huey's death and give it to no one but Jenny herself, no matter how long it took. Huey had thought about giving the letter to Val or Ernie to hold, but he honestly wasn't too confident in their longevity in this town if he lost to Miller Roux today. A grim thought, but unfortunately true.

The clock tower began to chime. Val stopped playing. Eleven chimes, signaling it was 11:00. Huey didn't have to turn around. He already knew that all eyes in The Prospector were on him. People slowly got up and started to head for the door to claim a good spot. He didn't feel the need. His spot was going to be the best in the house after all. A handful wished him good luck on their way out. Rawlings stopped and slapped him on the back. "You better win today," Rawlings said. "I got a lot of roux riding on you. You're at—"

"Never tell me the odds," Huey said. It was a line that Han Solo spoke in *The Empire Strikes Back*, and he had been waiting his whole life to work it into conversation.

"All right," Rawlings said. "I won't."

"Actually, tell me the odds. I'm curious."

"75-to-1."

Huey shook his head. He was momentarily annoyed, not at the outrageous odds against him but because he had forgotten to go by Kooper's Card Room and bet on himself. He wondered if it was illegal to bet on yourself, then remembered nothing was illegal here.

"Anyway," Rawlings said. "Good luck." He nodded to Huey and headed out with all the others. Shaky flipped the "Open" sign to "Closed" and gave Huey a look.

"You need anything before I go find a spot?" Shaky said.

Huey shook his head, and Shaky nodded before heading out through the swinging doors. It was now once again just Huey and Val in the large saloon. Val still sat at the piano and gestured down to the keys. "Anything you want to hear before we go?" she said.

"Like a last request?"

"If that's how you want to put it."

Huey thought about this for a moment. What is the last piece of piano music he'd ever want to hear? The answer, which then seemed so obvious, came to him and he smiled. "You know the end of 'Layla'?"

"No. Sure don't."

He sighed.

CHAPTER 50

11:50

Val stood on the corner of Main Street and shielded her eyes from the bright sun. She did everything in her power not to look at the clock tower, except for when it was natural for someone like her to look at the clock tower. Instead, she scanned the crowd to see that everyone was out today for The Showdown, even those who didn't normally attend the event. Josephine Jackson, Pearl, and the Crimson Guard watched from outside the House of Pleasures. Clementine Darling and the remaining members of the now-defunct NWA stood in the back of the crowd, dour expressions across their collective faces. Dr. Thundercloud and a collection of opium heads were perched in front of the doctor's office. Miller Roux's men stood on the roof of the gunsmith shop, rifles in hand.

She realized that someone was missing. She turned to Huey, who was standing next to her, and leaned in to whisper. "Have you seen Ernie?" she said.

"No," Huey said.

"Don't you think that's a little strange?"

"Yeah. Let's hope nobody else does." She looked back up to Miller Roux's men on the roof of the gunsmith shop. They were all watching Huey. "I haven't seen Cook Woodson either," Huey said. "Or Miller Roux for that matter." Val wondered if perhaps her "Plan B" had worked. She imagined Miller Roux's wives popping open bottles of champagne at Roux Castle at this very moment as they kicked their husband's lifeless corpse. She wasn't sure if there was even champagne in New Roux City, but the fantasy was nice nonetheless.

A few seconds later, Val learned the fantasy was indeed only a fantasy. She, and everyone else on Main Street, heard a noise and looked over to see Miller wheeling himself down the path from Castle Roux. He wore a dapper black suit, a top hat, and the Dragoon around his waist. He was flanked by his wives, all seventeen of them, all dressed in their Sunday best. Val heard a gasp fall over the crowd. This was unusual. Seeing a Roux wife at The Showdown was like seeing a vampire out in broad daylight.

Val made eye contact with Number 5 as the group passed her. Number 5 carried only a blank expression on her face, and she quickly looked away. "Shit," Val said.

"What's wrong?" Huey said. He gave her a look, confused.

"Nothing."

Miller stopped before the gunsmith shop and gestured to a viewing area on the sidewalk out front that had been roped off. The wives nodded and stepped within the rope. Val thought they looked like farm animals being shoved into a pen. Miller then wheeled himself right into the middle of Main Street, taking his position facing south. He glanced at the clock tower, and then to Huey. He said nothing.

11:54

Winnie clutched her rifle and eyed Miller sitting in his chair in the middle of the street. Her positioning was perfect, and as long as Huey did what he was supposed to do then this trick shot would be a piece of cake. She was tempted to slide the rifle through the giant backwards six and blow the bastard away now, but she knew patience was a virtue.

She watched as Huey stepped out into the street and took his position, facing north. The two duelers stared each other down. It was quiet. Very quiet.

That's when she felt the barrel of a gun press to the back of her head.

"Drop the rifle," a voice said. She recognized it immediately. She turned around to see Cook Woodson standing behind her, his revolver in his right hand. "Now," Cook said.

She realized that someone else was in the room too, and looked over to see Ernie Swords standing in the corner holding a long length of rope, as if he was about to lasso a calf at a rodeo. She began to turn red with anger, knowing she had been sold out. "Sorry," Ernie said. "It's just business."

"Put the rifle down, Winnie," Cook said. He cocked his gun. "I ain't gonna ask again." She thought for a moment, unsure of what to do. She was stuck.

She put the rifle down. Cook gestured to her holster. "That one too." She removed her revolver and dropped it to the floor. Cook kicked both guns away, then looked to Ernie. "Tie her hands," Cook said. Ernie began to do as he was told, although his tying was rather awkward considering one of his arms was in a sling.

"You're a fucking idiot, Mr. Swords," Winnie said. "If I kill Miller Roux, Huey will win The Dragoon as a spoil. It would be yours."

"*If* you kill him," Ernie said. "But what if you don't? Why take a chance when you can go with a sure thing?"

"What makes you think Miller won't just Showdown you tomorrow and take his gun back?"

"Because The Dragoon means nothing to him," Ernie said. "And he understands that it means everything to me." Winnie could do nothing but shake her head.

"Would you two shut the fuck up?" Cook said. Cook stepped over and peered out through the clock face to the street below. Winnie could see that Huey and Miller were still staring each other down. Miller glanced up at the clock tower, pretending to check the time, and he and Cook made eye contact. Cook nodded to him.

"Nice view," Cook said to Winnie with a smile. "Let's watch what happens, shall we?"

11:55

Miller glanced back down from the clock tower and put his gaze right back on Huey. "You don't seem very scared, Mr. Palmer?"

"Maybe because—"

"Shut up," Miller said. "You'll get your turn to speak. For the next two minutes, you have to stand there and listen to me." Huey went quiet, as Miller suspected he would. The stranger knew what was good for him.

Miller turned his head and looked out to the thousands of faces staring back at him from the crowd. His subjects. "The Roux family has been called many nasty things over the years," he said. "Tyrants. Thugs. Despots. But there's one thing that even we have never been accused of being. Cheaters. Mr. Palmer here, however?" He pointed right at Huey. "Well, he's a cheater plain and simple. His first ever Showdown, and he isn't even standing here like a man ready to face his fate, his fate being a cripple in a wheelchair." Miller saw that the citizens were beginning to eye one another one, just as confused as Huey appeared to be.

Miller then shook his head, lifted his hand, and slowly pointed up to the clock tower. "No, Mr. Palmer had to pay someone to hide in the clock tower to shoot me on his behalf."

Huey's face went white. Miller, along with everyone else, looked to the clock tower to see Cook Woodson pull open the clock face and step out of with a tied-up Winnie Crider. Cook held up Winnie's rifle and showed it off to the whole town.

"Oh fuck me," Val said.

The crowd gasped. Some were shocked at Huey's cheating. Others were shocked to see Winnie Crider after eight years. Miller looked to Josephine Jackson, who could only close her eyes and shake her head. She knew that her conspiracy with the strangers had failed. Miller's men atop the gunsmith shop laughed. Miller's wives appeared to have no idea what the hell was going on.

"Ernie!" Val said. She pointed up to him on the clock tower, having realized that her supposed compatriot had betrayed her. "You're a piece of shit!"

"Quiet!" Miller said. "You say one more word during my speech time, and I'll have one of my men shoot you dead." Val shut up, smart enough to know she should live to fight another day. He suspected that once The Showdown was over, no matter what happened, she wouldn't be able to take off her glove and toss it before Ernie fast enough.

"Now," Miller said. "It is in my right, according to The Showdown Conditions, to have one of my men shoot down Mr. Palmer right now due to his violation. But I have decided against that. I will proceed with the duel as planned, because I am a man of honor, as the Rouxs always have been and always will be." He gestured to Huey's gun sitting in its holster and smiled. "Let's see what you're made of, Mr. Palmer."

11:57

The whole town shifted its attention to Huey. It was his turn to speak. The murmur of the crowd faded away, and Huey thought Main Street must have now been the quietest place on earth.

He wanted nothing more than to draw his gun and wipe the smile right off of Miller's face with a bullet. He knew that this was impossible, however, because his gun in fact held no bullets. He had replaced them all with blanks that morning, and by the look on Miller's face, it appeared that Miller knew this crucial piece of information. Ernie must have told him.

Huey had no idea what to say. He had gone over his speech several times that morning, but it was irrelevant now. The crowd didn't want to hear about how he was virtuous and Miller Roux was the devil or whatever nonsense Huey had planned to spout. There was no way out of this. He had fucked up, and he had fucked up bad. Even if he hadn't listened to Winnie and left real bullets in his gun, he knew he didn't have a chance in hell of winning this Showdown anyway, with or without God on his side.

A good thirty seconds went by. He said nothing. "Jesus Christ, Huey," Val said. She was growing impatient. "Say something." Huey looked over to the faces in the crowd, they too seemed to be growing impatient.

"You're right, Miller," Huey said. "I did try to cheat at The Showdown today. But you got one detail wrong. I didn't have to pay Winnie Crider a dime, or a roux or whatever you all call it. Winnie Crider was up for the task of killing you merely because you deserve it. You murdered her family and you destroyed her life." Huey glanced up to Winnie, who was still being held by Cook Woodson with her hands tied.

"He's right," Winnie said. "It would have been my pleasure."

"Quiet!" Miller said.

"Fuck you, Miller."

"Ms. Crider, if you say one more word I'll—"

"Actually, Miller," Huey said. "If *you* say one more word during my speech time then I'll have *my* second here shoot you where you stand." This was an empty threat, Val not having real bullets in her gun either, but Miller backed off anyway realizing that he had violated his own rules. "Now everybody but me shut up," Huey said. Everybody did.

He composed himself and took a deep breath. "In two minutes, that clock is going to strike twelve. When that happens, Miller is going to pull out his gun and kill me. I literally don't stand a chance, because I don't have real bullets in my gun." He gestured to his gun. The crowd was confused. "It's complicated. But the point is that Miller Roux is going to win. Miller Roux is always going to win, as long as you all keep playing this stupid game." Huey stared right at Josephine. "Which is all The Showdown is. It's not a system of justice. It's a game." Josephine appeared to think about this for a moment, then she looked away from him.

Huey glanced up to the clock tower to see the time. He made eye contact with Winnie, and she gave him a little smile. "My time is up," he said. "Thanks for listening."

11:59

Ernie wished that researchers from NASA could have somehow studied the minute that went by before the clock struck noon. There must have been some disruption in the space time continuum, because every second felt like an hour. He, along with everyone else on Main Street, held his breath the entire time.

Ernie knew that Huey only had one minute left to live, and for a brief moment he wondered if he had made the right decision in selling the pilot out. Maybe Winnie Crider was right, and she could have pulled the shot off. But then what? Ernie had to remember what the one-legged man said to him about the town turning to chaos. He had to remember that thwarting Huey's plan and allowing Miller Roux to win the Showdown was actually the best thing for the sake of the entire community. Sure the town might be insane, but at least Miller Roux kept order. At least the trains ran on time. Were there trains here, that is.

The clock, which Ernie was standing right next to, struck twelve. The minute which felt like an eternity ended.

12:00

Huey watched as Miller Roux drew the Special Edition Colt Third Model Dragoon Percussion Revolver out of its holster, aimed it at him, and fired before he even had the chance to touch his own gun.

Bang.

The shot loudly echoed through the town like thunder. No one in the crowd made the slightest move.

Huey looked down to see that he had not been shot. He was fine. Not a scratch on him. He looked up to Miller, who seemed incredibly confused.

Miller fired again.

Bang.

Again, nothing happened. The crowd was also growing

confused. Miller eyed the Dragoon in his hand. "What the fuck?" he said. Miller put the gun on his lap, wheeled himself a few paces closer to Huey, then picked the gun up and fired again.

Bang.

Again, nothing. At this point Huey drew his own gun, merely because he thought that's probably what everyone would expect him to do. He thought about firing it, but then he didn't really see what good that would do, so he just stood there holding it instead.

Something then seemed to occur to Miller. He opened the Dragoon's chamber and looked inside. His face slowly grew beet red. "Blanks," Miller said.

Miller, along with Val, looked right at one of Miller's wives standing in the viewing area before the gunsmith shop. If Huey remembered correctly, she was Number 5. She wore a mighty satisfied look on her face.

"Whoops," Number 5 said. "Guess I made an error in judgment."

Miller threw the Dragoon to the ground in anger. Huey quickly considered his options. He wanted to end this, and he wanted to end it as soon as possible. He raised his gun into the air and fired.

Bang.

"Satisfaction has been brought!" Huey said in a loud, clear voice. He then lowered his gun and put it back into its holster.

"Fuck you," Miller said. Miller looked up to Cook Woodson on the clock tower. "Mr. Woodson, please shoot Mr. Palmer."

Cook raised the rifle and aimed it at Huey.

Josephine Jackson then drew her gun and aimed it at Cook. "You interfere with this Showdown and I'll shoot you where you stand," Josephine said.

This action prompted Miller Roux's men to aim their guns at Josephine, which in turn prompted Pearl and the Crimson Guard to aim their guns at Miller Roux's men. The two groups lined up on opposite sides of the street like soldiers ready for battle. Huey realized that he was now smack dab in the middle of a Mexican standoff.

"Mr. Woodson," Miller said. "Shoot him."

"Don't do it," Josephine said. She cocked her gun.

"You can't hit me from there, Josephine," Cook said.

"You want to find out?"

Time once again slowed down. No one seemed to be sure who was going to make the first move. Huey looked up to Cook's rifle aimed down at him. He was pretty sure that Cook could hit him with ease. He looked to Winnie, who had an expression on her face that told him everything he needed to know. She nodded, and he nodded back. It was time to end all of this once and for all.

Huey gripped his gun, which was still in its holster. He had five blanks left, and all they could do was make noise. But that's all he needed right now. He just needed to ignite a spark.

Huey fired.

Bang.

The shot rang out, and it was just the motivation that the plethora of itchy trigger fingers needed.

Everyone started shooting.

Cook fired first, but Winnie threw her body into him as he did so, sending them both falling off of the clock tower and hurtling three stories towards the ground below. Cook's shot missed Huey by inches, the bullet hitting the dirt near his left foot. Winnie and Cook fell into an awning above The Prospector and rolled off onto the sidewalk with a thud, Winnie using Cook's body to break her fall.

People began to scream and duck for cover as Miller's men and the Crimson Guard opened fire on one another from opposite sides of the street. Pearl was able to take out three men in quick succession before being shot in the chest and falling to the ground, dead. Josephine and the rest of the Crimson Guard riddled the gunsmith shop with bullets, shattering the glass windows.

Huey grabbed Val and pulled her behind a barrel as a hail of bullets rained around them. He saw that most citizens were running for the hills, but many had decided to pick a side and join in the fray. Scores were being settled. Aggressions were finally set free. When people ran out of bullets, they tackled one another and duked it out with their fists right there in the dirt.

Winnie rolled off of Cook Woodson and got her bearings, her hands still tied behind her back with rope. Cook started to stand up, and she quickly jumped over her tied hands so that they were now in front of her. She lunged at Cook from behind, wrapped the rope around his neck, and pulled as hard as she could. Cook struggled, grabbing for the rope as he gasped for air. Huey saw that Clementine Darling and the former NWA members were standing there, watching this happen. Cook's eyes pleaded for someone to step in and help. But no one moved a muscle, they just stood there and watched Winnie Crider pull on the rope as hard as she could until all the life had left Cook Woodson's body and he slumped to the ground, dead.

"What happened to Miller?" Val said. Huey looked over to see that Miller's wheelchair still sat in the middle of the street, but it was empty. He and Val crawled a few feet closer to get a better look, and they finally spotted Miller dragging himself down a muddy alley, searching for a place to hide. The search was short-lived, however, because Number 5 stepped in front of him to block his path. Miller looked up to see her, the other wives by her side. "That's my girl," Val said. "That's my girl."

"Where you going, dear husband?" Number 5 said. "Showdown's not over yet." She kicked Miller in the face, sending him falling onto his back. She and the other wives exchanged a look.

And then they were upon him.

CHAPTER 51

Article from The Palmerville Free Press, *Volume 1, Issue 1,*
"Battle Brings Revolution" by Shelley Walker

Many of you were there, but for those who fled to their homes when
the shooting started or chose not to attend Wednesday's Showdown
in the first place, it was an event that this town will never forget.
At approximately 12:03, the duel between Miller Roux and Huey
Palmer, one of the three strangers who had recently arrived in town
when his "helicopter" crashed, erupted into a townwide gunfight
that most are now calling "The Battle of Main Street." The battle
itself lasted a little under forty-five minutes, a ceasefire finally agreed
upon when Miller Roux's wives dragged his nearly unrecognizable
corpse down Main Street. With Miller Roux and his man Friday,
Cook Woodson, both killed, Roux's men and supporters quickly
gave up the fight and put down their weapons. The total death toll
was thirty-seven.

The town in disarray, brothel-owner Josephine Jackson climbed
to the top of the clock tower on Main Street and called all citizens
of New Roux City together for an emergency town meeting. Word
was spread, and soon a large crowd had gathered. Ms. Jackson asked
the crowd how to proceed with a show of hands.

First, Ms. Jackson asked if the citizens wanted there to be law
in New Roux City. An overwhelming majority raised their hands.

Second, Ms. Jackson asked if the citizens wanted government
in New Roux City. An overwhelming majority raised their hands.

Someone in the crowd suggested Ms. Jackson to be interim mayor while elections are arranged. An overwhelming majority approved this and Ms. Jackson accepted. It was agreed that a group of soon-to-be elected officials would gather in the upcoming weeks to write laws which would be approved by a vote.

Third, Ms. Jackson asked if citizens wanted to change the name of New Roux City to something other than New Roux City. An overwhelming majority raised their hands. Someone in the crowd suggested Palmerville, in honor of Huey Palmer. Mr. Palmer himself tried to dissuade the citizens from making this decision, but his objections fell on deaf ears and an overwhelming majority agreed.

Ernie Swords, one of the three strangers who had arrived with Mr. Palmer last week, disappeared during the battle and has not been seen since. Several witnesses claim to have seen Mr. Swords heading into the forest south of town a few hours after the battle, and a posse has been formed to look for him as he is wanted for further questioning.

Five days have now passed since the Roux/Palmer Showdown and its fallout, and already many citizens agree that there has been an improvement in the quality of life here in town. The fact that you are reading this story now, in this brand new newspaper's very first edition, is proof of that. We at the *Palmerville Free Press* look forward to bringing you further positive stories on a weekly basis about the rebirth of this community.

CHAPTER 52

Huey, along with almost three thousand others, stood by in awe and watched as the hot air balloon slowly expanded into a gigantic round dirigible. Just about every resident of the former New Roux City had come out to see the launch, and many recognized their own sheets, curtains, and clothing stolen by the Silk Specter stitched into the balloon. Some seemed annoyed by this, but most were glad that the linens had been dedicated to a good cause.

Once the balloon was completely inflated, Winnie inspected her creation one last time to make sure all the parts were in working order. "Okay," she said. "She should fly." She looked to Huey, who was finishing up loading firewood into the wicker basket.

"Not *should*," Huey said. "She *will*. She will fly."

"Let's hope so," she said. She smiled and gave a look to Val, who was in the middle of packing up a bag with supplies for the journey. "You remember what you're supposed to do?"

"Yeah I remember," Val said. "You've told me a million times. It's flying a balloon, it's not rocket science." Huey laughed at this, because it sort of was. "Are you sure that you really want to do this, Winnie?" Val said.

"Do what?"

"Give me your seat. It's your balloon after all."

"I'm sure," Winnie said. "You two have a life back there. But this is my home." Winnie smiled and gave a look to Josephine, who stood nearby and observed. One of Josephine's first acts as interim mayor had been to grant full asylum to Winnie Crider and subsequently abolish The Showdown Conditions. "I'm ready to help this place grow into a real town," Winnie said.

"Speaking of which," Huey said. "Maybe you should have this?" He reached into his coat pocket and pulled out the papier mache Sheriff's badge that Sally had given him. Winnie eyed it and let out a laugh.

"Are you kidding me?" Winnie said.

"Why not?" Huey said. He then gave a look to Josephine. "Seriously, why not?"

"I can't think of any good reason," Josephine said. She looked out to the crowd. "What do you all think? Does Sheriff Crider have a nice ring to it?" The crowd nodded and cheered in approval. Josephine stepped over, took the badge, and pinned it onto Winnie's jacket. "Congratulations, Sheriff Crider. You're the law in these parts."

Huey could tell that it was all Winnie could do to keep from breaking down into tears. He assumed she didn't, however, because she knew it would make a terrible first impression for the new top law enforcement official to cry in front of the whole town. "Thanks," Winnie said. "Sounds like a fine job."

Josephine smiled to her, then looked to Huey and Val. "There's one other thing we need to discuss," she said. "We've all been talking, the citizens I mean, and we took a vote. If you two make it back to your home alive—"

"*When* we make it back to our home alive," Val said.

"*If* you make it back to your home alive, then we don't want you to tell anybody about us."

Huey and Val exchanged a look. She looked just as surprised as he was. "Really?" he said.

"Yes," Josephine said. "We don't want to become some carnival sideshow. We don't need teams of scientists and journalists descending upon us, disrupting the new life we're trying to get started here."

"That's crazy," Val said. "The world out there is awesome. You have to check it out."

"Maybe eventually, but not just yet. We're not ready. We'd much prefer to get our act together first." Josephine looked back to the crowd, who all seemed to agree with her.

"All right," Huey said. "If that's what you want, then mum's the word."

"Although don't be surprised if one day someone comes looking for that dipshit Ernie Swords," Val said. "Or that stupid gun."

"We'll cross that bridge when we come to it," Winnie said.

"Actually," a voice said. They all looked over to see that Number 5 was standing in the crowd with some of the other wives. She stepped forward and held up the Special Edition Colt Third Model Dragoon Percussion Revolver. "You can have the stupid gun." She handed the gun over to Huey, and for the first time he got a good look at it. The plating. The etchings. It truly was a work of art.

Huey thought about it for a moment, and then shook his head. "No," he said. "No, you all should keep it. You should keep it as a symbol of the—"

"Huey," Val said. "Shut up and take the fucking gun. You can sell it to pay for your daughter's college education for Christ's sake."

"Yeah, Huey," Winnie said. "Take the gun."

"I agree," Josephine said. "We don't even want it."

Huey laughed, then tucked the Dragoon into his belt. "Well, thank you all then," he said. He smiled and looked out to the crowd. "You sure know how to make a stranger feel welcome."

CHAPTER 53

When Ernie Swords was a boy, every year he begged his father to take him to the Texas State Fair. Held in Dallas, the event featured carnival rides, incredibly unhealthy food, a 55-foot cowboy statue named Big Tex, and the annual "Red River Shootout" football game between The University of Texas and Oklahoma University.

Ernie always had a blast, and his favorite part of the whole fair was by far the midway. There one could knock over bottles to take home a stuffed bear or toss a ping pong ball into a goldfish bowl to win the goldfish within. The game he excelled at the most, though? That would have been Bullseye Bonanza, which involved the player aiming a BB gun pistol at a moving target covered with balloons. You had three shots, and if you were able to pop a balloon then you won a prize. Pop three balloons, and you took home a brand new bike. Ernie won so many bikes, that when he was fourteen the fair decided to ban him from playing Bullseye Bonanza anymore. This was one of his proudest moments.

Fifty years later, as Ernie sat on a rock in the forest south of New Roux City and stared up the sky, Bullseye Bonanza was all he could think about.

Maybe it was because he hadn't really eaten or slept much in the last five days, but when he first spotted the hot air balloon flying overhead he thought it was a hallucination. After staring long enough and blinking about a hundred times, however, he was convinced it was real.

He took the gun out of his waistband and thought about how it resembled the BB gun pistol that he had used all those times to win those bikes. He looked up to the hot air balloon in the sky and thought about how it resembled one of the balloons on that moving target.

He wondered if he could hit it from here.